Mission to Sonora

D1557606

Rebecca Cramer

Mission to Sonora
A Book World, Inc. Publication
February 1998

This is a work of fiction. The characters, names, incidents,
dialogue and plot are a product of the author's imagination, or are
used fictitiously.

ISBN 1-881542-50-5
Copyright © 1998 by Rebecca Cramer
Cover: Glen Johnson
Author Photo: Luke Cramer
An Original Trade Paperback

Published by:
Book World, Inc.
9666 E Riggs Rd #194, Sun Lakes, AZ 85248

Be sure to visit our web site at:
www.bkworld.com

For Luke Cramer Ryan
whose life and work
inspire my own

and for the Students
of San Xavier Mission School
Children of the Sonora

A portion of the proceeds
of this book
will be devoted
to their education

Prologue

Desert Sonora provides shelter for predators. The cactus wren builds its nest amid boughs of thorns to protect its young from pack rats and king snakes. The poisonous centipede wraps its soft tentacles around an unfortunate insect and fondles its victim in lethal foreplay. Even the ubiquitous roadrunner, famous of stage and screen, earns its supper by plundering the burrows of sand squirrels and by using its sharp beak to slash the throats of baby cottontails.

Benton Brody had amassed his fortune against this arid backdrop, squirreling away millions of dollars in offshore banks. From where he stood, moments before his death, he could see his magnificent villa high in the foothills of the Santa Catalina Mountains north of Tucson. There, he wrapped his women in winter mink and summer silk, and from his offices downtown he wielded the financial and political power to control people and events in this corner of the Southwest.

He had achieved these advantages by raping, system-atically and without mercy, the social and physical landscape around him. His construction crews had bulldozed saguaro groves to make way for luxury residential developments. His grounds keepers had poisoned fox, bobcat, coyote, and mountain lion to keep his clients content. His building contractors had squandered precious groundwater to fill enormous fountains and to create vast areas of bluegrass. His supervisors had exploited the talent and skill of his workers while keeping them at the bottom of the wage scale, using their ethnic differences to turn them against each other when they asked for better. Benton Brody was a master of predation.

Now he stood at the other end of the spectrum. As his assailant pushed him down the path toward a fate he could never have foreseen, he began to understand the terror felt by the victim, the blind frightened eyes of the quail as it was snatched into the jaws of death, the scream of the javelina as it was dragged down in the night.

In a desert broom bush, a brown recluse spider swaddled a fly which had floundered into its funeral shroud. The sight froze him. He looked down with sudden nausea, in such a state of desperation and disbelief that he thought he might soil his hand-tailored suit. The single bullet, fired from behind him the next moment, penetrated his heart and prevented it. Benton Brody, the prey, turned and fell. With hopeless eyes, he looked up into the barrel of the gun. The yellow glare of a Western sun threw a dazzling light into his face. He tried to speak, but choked from the blood making its way into his throat, and his last confused thoughts were about impending contracts and whether or not his killer was a carnivore.

<>>>> One <<<<>

Finders, Keepers

Matty Bluenight planted his long sixteen-year-old legs astride the trail head to Ventana Canyon. At seven o'clock in the morning of a clear November day, the fragrance of the Sonora wafted across his senses. Peering down the trail ahead of him, a ribbon of sand winding back into the front range of the Santa Catalina Mountains, he prepared to enter his favorite place, often described as the most scenic wilderness in southern Arizona. The boy, who lived near the Tohono O'odham reservation to the south, had hiked these trails many times. This day he regretted having only a couple of hours for a brief excursion to the maiden pools two miles ahead.

Before heading into the canyon's quiet, this man-child turned his slender six-foot frame to look back at the city of Tucson below him. He had fallen in love with the "Old Pueblo" and its people — Hispanic, Yaqui, Apache, and his

adopted Tohono O'odham — from the moment his mother
had brought him as an eight-year-old to live and attend school
at San Xavier Mission. Likewise, he had grown to hate the
increasing development and the brown cloud of car exhaust
that often hung over the Tucson Valley. When the two
Bluenights emigrated to the Southwest, the odious crown of
dirt and noxious fumes was visible only for about two weeks
a year. Now it was apt to rear its toxic head at any time. This
morning recent showers and the fall breezes from Baja had
blown it north toward Phoenix. Matty scratched his long neck
and worried that Tucson might go the way of its sister in the
Valley of the Sun, a tangled mess of freeway and suburb,
emasculated by tourism and land speculation.   Uttering a
famous teenage epithet, he swigged water from his canteen to
wash down the fry bread he had consumed during the drive
north from the "Res."

     Earlier, Tommy Orozco's mother had fed Matty a
breakfast of popovers and honey when neither he nor Rita
Orozco had been able to pry his friend out of a sound sleep.
Matty had just missed Tommy's father, the high school
basketball coach, who was driving to the much larger
O'odham reservation west of San Xavier district. There,
Tom, Sr. would check on a field of century plants which his
own father had planted twenty-five years ago near
Baboquivari Mountain. Now the fruit of the enormous and
slow-growing agave was ready to be harvested, and he would
prepare the field for cutting.

     Matty had maneuvered his beloved ancient pickup truck in
another direction, north across town and the affluent foothills
to this parking lot at the entrance to the canyon. In its infinite
wisdom, the city had granted building permits to a construction company called Eastman Enterprises for a luxury

apartment complex beside the trail head. Now it hindered access to the canyon and the trail was seldom used, especially since hikers were warned by a sign saying, "Resident parking only, by order of Eastman Inc. and the Tucson Police Dept. Violators will be towed at own expense." Matty had displayed his contempt for it by parking the battered blue Chevy just to its left.

The architecture of Paradise Hill Apartments aped the traditional adobe. Surrounded by flower and cactus gardens and overlooking the skyline, tenants enjoyed majestic, expansive views of valley floor and mountain peak. Most were immigrants from states with names that began with "I," and most were unaware that their lifestyle was fouling their scenic refuge with demands for water, gasoline, and fresh air. Non-residents like Matty were discouraged from partaking in the peace and beauty once available to all, without lease.

The boy spat his contempt and turned up the trail. He had covered no more than twenty yards of the narrow track when he spotted a tall blonde figure sporting the khaki uniform of the U.S. Forest Service some distance ahead. His irritation was instantly forgotten. "Yo, Andrea, wait up!"

As he hurried to catch up with Andrea Winser, a graduate student in environmental studies and part-time protector of his sacred place, he noticed that the Sonora came to life in the V-shaped enclosure for which the canyon was named. The saguaros turned a rich shade of green, the birds became numerous and varied, and the lizards and other ground critters grew brave in their hurried journeys through the underbrush.

Andrea turned to greet him with a wide smile, "Hey, kid, you're out of bed early. Not playing hooky, I hope?"

"Nah," panted Matty, catching up with her, "Just out for some fresh air before basketball practice. You making your rounds?"

Andrea nodded, "Going to check on the bighorns at Mt. Kimball. Have time to tag along?"

"I wish," lamented Matty, "I can go as far as the maiden pools with you, though. How's grad school?" The two of them were acquainted from previous hikes, and Matty admired the girl greatly. She reminded him that his own career choices loomed in the not-so-distant future, and she had great eyes.

"I really like it," she answered, her tanned cheeks turning rosy with enthusiasm. "The chance to work with my subject matter as I study it makes the program fascinating. Have you thought any more about an E.S. major in college? You're a junior now, aren't you?"

"Yeah, but it still seems like a long way off," said Matty, as they plunged into the heart of the canyon toward the sound of warblers and rushing water. "E.S. sounds cool, but a degree in forestry might work better for me. Either way, I'd be able to spend time in places like this, maybe keep them out of the clutches of apartment cannibals." He tilted his head back toward the complex behind him for emphasis.

"I know just how you feel," Andrea sighed.

"I've also thought of hiring out to the BIA. My friend, Tom Orozco, and I are always joking about taking the place over and giving it back to the Indians.

"Then again," he continued, talking more to himself now than to her, "an academic job would be fun. I could get into teaching and research. The university faculty seem like laid-back dudes, and the anthropology department is famous everywhere."

"Didn't you tell me your mom was an anthro type?" Andrea inquired diplomatically.

"Yeah, but she gave it up a long time ago." Matty had

never understood why his mother had once chosen the claustrophobic goriness of forensic anthropology over the freedom and adventure of ethnography or archaeology. "In fact, I almost asked her if she wanted to come along this morning after Tommy copped out, but she has in-service today at the grade school."

Truth was that he was also beginning to feel the need for separation, the desire to be his own man. The two of them had been a tiny family since the moment of his birth, and they had shared their years with tolerance and affection. Soon he would have a talk with her. Today, he dropped the cares of adolescence and enjoyed sizing up this arid ecosystem, noting its features and assessing its condition. Something ancient behind his clear dark eyes showed him the fine details of chameleon tracks, how to predict when the cholla would jump, and how to wait patiently for the rattler to cross his path. He was becoming conscious of this ability and believed it had come from that mother, Linda Bluenight, and her albeit distant Cherokee ancestors.

"How's your basketball season going?" asked Andrea, bringing him back to the moment. "Won many games yet?"

"We're doing okay, for a bunch of short guys," he joked good-naturedly. "I got named team co-captain last month and the big homecoming game and dance are next weekend."

Matty saw the dance as both an obligation and an annoyance except for the girl part. He needed to decide which one he would ask, the friend, Peg Grazia, or the babe and principal's daughter, Annette Verasca? Being a non-O'odham kid at the school made him a rare species. He received a lot of attention from females like Annette just for being different, but he did not want it to complicate relationships with his "buds." He also felt more at ease with Peg. Besides, as far as

Matty knew, she did not drink, and that was worth a lot.

As usually happened when they went canyon-walking, conversation soon gave way to the sensuous nature of their surroundings. "I can already hear the water swirling, even though the pools are still a half-mile away," laughed Andrea. Her blue eyes mirrored the brightness of the morning sky.

Matty could hear it, too, cascading down from the peaks after the unusually heavy fall rains, the sound of it noisy and serene. Talking water. They passed a particularly statuesque saguaro beside the trail, fifty feet tall with three arms curved gently toward the sun. "There's my mom's favorite tree cactus," said Matty. "She always remarks on it when she comes here, and it just occurred to me why."

"Tell me," said the girl, as she stopped to examine the abandoned nest of a brown thrasher which had fallen from its perch in a nearby cholla.

"Well, when we moved to Arizona, she sort of gave the world the finger. She quit her job with the police department in Kansas City and took one at the mission school teaching fourth-graders. That saguaro kind of represents her rebellion." Indeed, he saw it as her counterpart as she built a life for them in the desert, its index digit eternally erect, stabbing the dry air in victory.

They crossed the stream created by the overflow of the maiden pools, helping each other over the slick rocks. The cold torrent raced down the canyon crevice to wet the lowlands approaching the valley, and its clearness tempted them to shed their boots and socks. Animal tracks, disturbed brush, and small broken branches lined the creek bank. Such a drinking source was a luxury at this time of year and the canyon's inhabitants were taking full advantage. The two noticed vultures circling nearby, and they came across a trio of coyotes looking for a place to go to bed.

"Those guys are fat," exclaimed Andrea with some surprise. "They must have run onto an unexpected feast. They even seem irritated at the mockingbirds singing along the canyon wall."

"I'll bet there are muledeer on the other side of the creek, just out of sight," said Matty in a low voice, as if he might frighten them. Normally, the herbivores waited for the nocturnal predators, cat or canine, to hand over the day to their kind so that they might drink safely.

The pair of travelers reached the pools just as the sun broke the plane of the eastern ridge, warming the rocky banks and shining full upon their faces. As they stripped off their footwear preparatory to a plunge into the shallow current, Andrea spied a scorpion. Its red body was the length of her forefinger, and its pincers were flexed as its legs danced from under a large rock toward Matty's bare right foot.

"Matt, boy, look out!"

He shuddered and stepped gingerly out of the creature's path. Then he scooped up cold water in his hands and splashed its back, a trick that sent the thing scurrying to its dark home where blindness was no impediment. "Thanks, Andy, that's another reason people say not to go hiking alone." Moving a discrete distance downstream, they sat awhile and let the small animals and birds get used to their presence while Matty prepared his experiment.

"What are you doing with those buttons, gonna mend your shirt?" asked the girl.

Matty laughed and answered, "The last time my mom and I hiked together, she wore hair combs decorated with red Apache beadwork. Actually, we were in Bear Canyon that day. All of a sudden her head was surrounded by hummingbirds, dive-bombing her to see if she was food. I thought I'd see if these red buttons might fool them the same way."

He balanced the shiny plastic pieces on the rocky ledge beside where they sat. After only a few minutes, a rosy-throat about two inches long zoomed down to inspect them, its long needle-like beak glistening. Dubious, it zipped away but returned a moment later for one more look. Piqued by the deception, it careened downstream to hunt the tiny berries left over from last summer's salt bush bloom.

"I'll be damned," exclaimed Andrea. "Excuse me."

"No problema."

They spent awhile counting other birds to see if their numbers had suffered under the summer scorching. Abundant winter rains had ensured the survival of a large number of the year's chicks, and they saw numerous pyrrhuloxia and phainopepla alternately stuffing themselves and singing to their neighbors. These red on silver and white on black cousins of the cardinal had mesmerized Matty since he had first noticed them as a small child. Years later, she had used the three species in their first faltering and comic attempt to discuss the birds and the bees.

Too soon, it was time to leave and reluctantly, they pulled on their boots. "Well, Matthew, I've enjoyed your company. Sure you don't want to come on with me? The sight of big-horn sheep is a rare thing these days, and I have lunch enough for two."

"I'm tempted as hell, Andrea, but duty calls. You be careful up there."

"Believe it, bro. See you next time out, maybe."

Matty looked after the girl a moment, admiring both the view and her persona. He considered another swing by the Orozco place to roll out Tommy. They could go to the gym early for a few extra hoops before practice started, and he could regale his friend with his evolving theory on women. He lingered a moment more in that quiet place first, listening to the Western white-winged doves calling to each other where the canyon disappeared against the peaks that rose north toward Pusch Ridge. Then he began the gradual descent, again passing the famous "V," where the sides of the canyon slanted toward each other like ponderous lovers to intersect and form the perfect letter. Its arch framed the entire Santa Cruz valley and the Santa Rita Mountains fifty miles to the south. As always, the sight took his breath away. He watched as he continued on and was glad for his life.

A few hundred yards further, the wind came up and threw the stench of death into his face. A rare feat for a boy of his age, he understood it and it did not alarm him. A good-sized mammal must have met its fate during the night, or more likely the afternoon before, from the strength of the odor. Maybe that explained the vultures and coyotes they had seen near the stream. Going up canyon earlier, the wind had been behind them, and they had been spared the aroma.

Then he saw the hand, not a paw or a hoof, but a human hand protruding from behind a shed-sized boulder off the trail to his right. Actually, it was the white shirt cuff with the gold cufflink gleaming in the sun that caught his eye. His initial reaction was disbelief, and he entertained a half-frantic notion that the gold piece was just a chunk of iron pyrite, "fool's gold," and that the hand was in his mind, not laying there motionless on the ground. In another second, he knew better. Someone was sprawled behind that huge rock outcrop.

A creeping paralysis threatened to overtake him. His feet were leaden. As if in a nightmare, needing to flee, he found himself glued to the spot, staring wide-eyed, trying to think.

His urge to get away became almost uncontrollable, and he struggled to master himself, to keep his hands from shaking and his knees from buckling. Finally retrieving some control, he looked around quickly to see if anyone else might be lurking in the area. No. Was there a campsite nearby, any sign of human presence? No. He was alone with this lifeless body, Andrea too far away to hear his calls. Concern and curiosity overcame his more primal instincts, and he approached the boulder which had blocked the body from their vision as they had come up the trail from the opposite direction. He was sure the man was dead even before he reached him. A glance confirmed this knowledge and sent him into waves of sickness. He leaned against the boulder for support.

The corpse looked as though it was resting on its side, facing Matty. The back slumped against another even larger boulder so that the torso was partially wedged between the two. The victim was stocky, fair, with a receding blonde hairline, and middle-aged. The expression on his now rigid face turned Matty's stomach inside out. Even with the lower right side of his jaw torn away by some night scavenger, the contortion in the man's countenance spoke silently of a mixture of horror and total surprise carried with him unto the moment of death. His blue-grey eyes were frozen into a look of such utter disbelief that Matty thought shock itself might have been the cause of death. Apparently he had been given no chance to pray or to remember, to surrender to his fate or to hope for better. Mortal panic had been his only companion as he began the journey into forever.

Matty shuddered, bent over, and threw up his fry bread. Then he stood in the numbing aftermath of nausea, wondering if he should search the body for identification. Animals had ravaged it, and the expensive grey business suit, obvious even to Matty's denim-trained eye, had been ripped apart. The hand protruding from behind the giant granite rock and the arm with it were nearly torn from the torso. Pieces of flesh and clothing were scattered about, and coagulated blood covered the ground in a wide circle behind the boulders.

The boy merging into man fought back tears. The poor guy died alone and afraid, suddenly and unprepared, Matty thought wildly. His childhood sense of romance and idealism began to recede in the face of a devastating reality. Looking up he saw the same pair of crimson-capped vultures sitting quietly atop a mesquite tree only a few yards away, waiting for him to leave so they might continue their meal. They had blood on their talons.

The site caused him to turn and run. He stumbled and fell, badly scraping an arm on a catclaw acacia. Unable to stop himself from falling, he called out, then realized that no one would hear him. Tears and sweat clouded his vision, the city before him shrouded by the mist in his eyes. The canyon behind him disappeared in confusion and grief for a stranger. At this moment in his young life, all he wanted was to get clear. All he wanted was his mom.

Linda Bluenight stood on a chair and reached high over her head to hang a dream catcher from the ceiling of her fourth grade classroom at the San Xavier del Bac Mission School on the Tohono O'odham reservation southwest of Tucson. The room occupied a rear corner of the hundred-year-old whitewashed adobe building, and its back wall was lined with windows that faced north toward the Santa Catalina Mountains and Ventana Canyon.

The tall, nutmeg-colored woman in her indeterminate

thirties paused a moment to look toward the sunlit front range and do a bit of daydreaming. This was her favorite time of day. Matty was up there now, she thought fondly, probably romping in the creek and wet from head to toe. Sharing a cup of coffee with him before he left, she had almost volunteered to be his hiking partner. Then she realized that he had made plans with the Orozco boy, so she did her duty and came on over to the school. Since the mountains always tempted her with their quiet and calmed her with their peace, she understood why Matty had chosen to spend his morning among them.

She wiped a layer of the ever-present Sonoran dust from the blades of an aged ceiling fan and fastened the loop connected to the wreath of woven sun-dried reeds to the brass fixture. Then she straightened the whole arrangement before clambering down from the rickety chair and stepping back to survey her work, a tad crooked but serviceable.

The dream catcher was about twelve inches in diameter and finely made, a circle of reeds hand-stripped and tightly bound. The net in the center consisted of a mesh of sturdy fiber threads, a spider-like web with a small opening in the center where a tiny translucent crystal fetish dangled. Its only other decoration consisted of a few orange and white feathers from a painted hawk. A Cherokee form of psychotherapy, the dream catcher was normally placed above the bed. Its purpose was to keep the sleeper from harm, to catch the nightmare in its tangle, and to permit the good vision to pass through the hole in its middle. Often, they were mislabeled as Oneida or Lakota ceremonial objects. In some places, "craftsmen" even constructed them from coat hangers wrapped in buckskin, adorned with plastic beads and little carved animals.

This one, passed from mother to daughter through the generations, was an authentic example of the type made by the Five Civilized Tribes of the Southeast, and it was one of the few remaining heirlooms from her distant connection with them. Her grandmother had found it in an old trunk that had belonged to her own grandmother, and Linda eventually had consulted with the Cherokee Tribal Headquarters in Tahlequah, Oklahoma, for dating and verification. Without papers or genealogical proof of descent, Linda was familiar with her ancestry through the eyes and memory of that grandmother who had held her as a child. She had told Linda of being held in turn by an elderly woman who spoke little English half a century before. That woman had fallen off the Trail of Tears as a young girl and into the arms of the man who became her common-law husband. His family farmed the clay soils of southern Missouri, and their strict Calvinist version of Methodism would countenance no marriage with "the heathen." She stayed with him anyway and proceeded to give her hair, eyes, and name to five generations of Bluenights, including Linda and Matty.

She examined the small square room, her bailiwick and professional home. On a normal Friday, it held twenty nine-year-old Tohono O'odham students. They had asked her to teach them how to make dream catchers to give as Christmas gifts to their families next month. Though she had been educated in physical anthropology, she had taught herself many skills in her career as their homeroom teacher. This morning she would practice braiding yucca and decorate walls with parades of paper turkeys surrounded by cardboard cornucopias laden with native foods, the corn, beans, and squash that so often kept European pilgrims from starving. Scrolls would speak of the greetings given by leaders from

Chief Joseph to Sequoyah, and her children would make their own contributions. That afternoon, she would meet with parents to share her vision for the children's school year and to inquire about their own.

Linda brought tremendous energy to this work, believing that this generation would break the cycle of poverty that had stalked the Tohono people over the centuries. The Apaches had wreaked havoc on their villages, the Spanish had trampled their culture, the Anglos had denied their sovereignty. In recent times, they had simply been ignored to death. The result had been a loss of self-determination which threatened to leave the tribe without an indigenous language or leadership. Now both were making a comeback.

Lost in thought and pushpins, she failed to notice that the principal, Ron Verasca, was standing at her door. Linda and Ron had been close since she and Matty had arrived at San Xavier. He had hired her over the objections of the padres who preferred one of their own, and he had quieted the complaints of tribal members who opposed employing any outsider. Linda now recognized the troubled expression on her friend's weathered face.

"Linda, you need to come to my office right away. You're wanted on the telephone. Adelante."

"Que pasa, Ron? What's up?"

"It's the Tucson policia, Linda. They want to talk to you about Matty."

"My God, Ron, is he all right? Donde es?" She was racing passed him and out the door even as she asked the question.

"The sergeant would only say he needed to speak to you pronto."

Linda Bluenight's biography included long experience

with law enforcement. At one time, she had looked forward to a career in Kansas City as a forensic anthropologist, identifying the bodies of missing persons, homicide victims, and vagrants. She had taken the position with the city's police department to make ends meet during her graduate studies, and later, the money and supposed prestige tempted her away from her doctoral program. After another five years, she threw down her lab coat in disgust and journeyed with her young son to Arizona. The stench of formaldehyde and death, the constant misery of bereaved relatives, and the general level of inhumanity associated with standard police work had taken their toll. This period of her life now flashed through her mind as she hurried down the hall lined with student posters. Her sense of alarm nearly gagged her before she could snatch the telephone in Verasca's tiny office at the front of the building.

"This is Linda Bluenight. Who am I speaking to?"

"Hello, Mrs. Bluenight. This is Sergeant Phil Griffin with the Tucson police. Your son is here in my office. He's fine, but seems he's found a corpse in the canyon he was hiking this morning. We're getting the details from him now, but since he's a minor, we need your permission to question him. Could you give us the okay on that and come down to sign the appropriate form? We'll probably be done talking by the time you get here."

Linda's insides untied and she sank into Ron's worn swivel chair. "Yes, all right, I'll come this minute, but I'd like to speak with my son, please."

"Sure thing. Matty?"

"Hola, Mom, sorry about this. I know cop shops aren't your favorite places, but I didn't know what else to do. The whole scene was pretty horrible." His voice cracked. So did a spot in her heart.

"Everything's going to be fine, sweetheart. I'll be there in just a few, and you can tell me all about it. Are you hurt anywhere?"

"No, but I feel kind of queasy."

"Have the sergeant get you a glass of water. Drink it slowly and take some long breaths afterward. I'm on my way."

Linda's own stomach began to jump again, but she was already headed back to her classroom to fetch her purse and car keys. Ron was waiting for her in the hallway. "Es bien?"

"Yes, he's not hurt or anything, but the cops are questioning him about a corpse he apparently came across up at Ventana. Can you imagine? I have to get down there." Her fear was being rapidly replaced by a nameless irritation.

Ron gave her a knowing look. "Like old times?"

"Not on your life. God, what a terrible saying. I'm sorry."

His laugh heartened her for the trip into town. "Should I go with you? Nothing to keep me here till this afternoon."

"No, amigo, I can handle this one, but if I should get delayed, I may have to call and ask you to reschedule my parent meetings." "No problem. Buena suerte. See you later."

Linda sat for a few moments in the parking lot across from the 18th century mission church, leaning against the wheel of her battered Ranger. A look around at the village, the school, and the historic edifice calmed her. No other sight made her feel so at home.

The village at San Xavier was a rambling series of dirt roads. Set back from them were houses of adobe or cement block half-camouflaged by creosote. In these dwellings lived six hundred Tohono O'odham, the desert people of the northern Sonora. Most worked in nearby Tucson and maintained close ties to their larger reservation just west. They occupied a cultural rocking chair which tilted between two worlds.   Like many other tribes across the Americas, these people had taken back their traditional name, casting off the pejorative "Papago" which had been applied to them by the Spanish. In a complicated cultural accommodation, the "Desert People" had maintained an attachment to Hispanic language and religion even as their participation in Anglo society increased.

The mission church, the "White Dove of the Desert," had been their rock. Reversing the colonial pattern, the O'odham had taken charge of its operation, if not its Franciscan clergy who had served there since the days of the Spanish Empire. The building with its distinctive mismatched domes, its intriguing depiction of the cat chasing the mouse through eternal time, its glistening beauty against sun and sky, had persisted as a symbiosis of cultures, indigenous and imposed.

The elementary and high schools sat just to the west along the one paved road which ran the length of the settlement. They brought the village children into a common family and solidified this small community. Teachers and students celebrated the joys and mourned the sorrows of O'odham life, and buffered the onslaught of modern ways that threatened to tear them from their one source of strength, each other.

As she turned the Ranger toward the interstate which joined the reservation and the city that the O'odham called Schookson, Linda could see the contrast. Centerpiece of the Sonora, Tucson had once existed as an ancient Tohono village and then as a nineteenth century Spanish Presidio. Now it represented one more bastion of Anglo-American urban sprawl. The millennium of Indian habitation had ended after the O'odham were banished by the garrison from Mexico in 1775. Irrigation works dug by them and their predecessors of the prehistoric Hohokam civilization were used even now for runoff from the torrential summer monsoons. After the Gadsden Purchase of 1854, the Presidio and its Hispanic inhabitants had suffered similar exile at the hands of the U.S. Cavalry and the surge of Anglo settlers who came looking for precious minerals and pasture. English-speakers quickly displaced both native and colonial, confining one to the reservation and the other to the barrio. During the twentieth century, tourism and the Air Force substituted one kind of gold for another. In the 1960s, the old Presidio became a parking lot for the new civic buildings of present-day Tucson, to the dismay of the Hispanic community and the Archaeological Society. The crazed Sunbelt exodus of the last two decades had pushed the city to the base of the Catalinas and now butted up against San Xavier. The dry valley was drowning in air conditioners. The Old Pueblo was enclaved by suburbs, and unchecked growth was threatening to snuff out the Sonora.

Linda could see the results, the yellowing sick saguaros, the imported gluttonous grass, the streets of pink stucco houses which seemed to multiply like jackrabbits in springtime. As she approached the small, funky downtown district, the irony of the slick affluence of the urban rim separating the poverty of the inner-city from the impoverishment of the reservation struck her anew.

The municipal buildings surrounded a spacious plaza, complete with fountains, gardens, and moisture-demanding Kentucky blue. She whipped the Ranger into the underground parking lot, jumped out, and ran for the elevator marked

"TCPD," mindful of why she left K.C. She recalled her disillusionment with forensic anthropology, which at the applied level proved to be just another version of grimy police work. Justice had been precluded by political interference, the police chief's political ambitions, the incompetence of the legal system, and the general despair of officers who worked too long for too little.

Linda loved her life now, the people, the place, the work. She and Matty were two happy campers, despite the minor skirmishes of adolescence and the tensions associated with Matty's impending manhood. She feared, in an indefinable way, that this incident would spoil things. As she vowed not to let that happen and marched off to liberate them from "law and order," she found the sights and smells intimidating. All these joints looked alike, she thought with a snort. The victims and perpetrators and lawyers were indistinguishable, while the stenographers wore stony, harried faces and the officers sounded cynical and bitterly humorous.

She entered the bank of offices marked "Homicide," where Sergeant Griffin sat with Matty. She put her hand on Matty's shoulder, and to her mild surprise, he permitted it to rest there.

"Mom! Geez, you made good time. This is Sgt. Phil Griffin. We've been talking police work."

"Glad to meet you, Mrs. Bluenight. Matty's been telling me about your career back in Kansas. We could sure use your help on this one. The pathologist went home sick, and the lab is short on expert analysis to begin with. We have a part-time assistant, but he's green as a freshwater frog. In fact, he turned about that color when he got a look at said corpse. As Matty can tell you, it was pretty beat up. We'd sure appreciate it if you could take a look."

Griffin was a tall, skinny slow-talking southerner with an honest face and an earnest manner which momentarily disarmed her. She recovered quickly and gave Matty an exasperated look. "It's Ms. Bluenight and it was the department in Kansas City, Missouri. I'm awfully sorry, Sergeant, but I have to get back for parent-teacher conferences. Then I need to finish my lesson plans. The academic year is in full-swing with fall programs. I'm sure you understand."

"Of course, I do, but if you could just assist our young intern with a brief examination, a half-hour of your time would be a heap of help to us. Like I told your son, this corpus doesn't appear to have expired of natural causes. I promise we won't tie you up for long. If you need to call the school..."

On one side stood Matty with a look of disappointment on his face. On the other stood her conscience, tapping her on the shoulder. Her exasperation began to mount. Damn!

——•••ᛩ•••——

<>>>> Two <<<<>

The Parent Trap

Before Linda could react, Sergeant Griffin ushered Matty into the canteen and bribed him with a soda and a magazine. Then, turning to Linda, he put on his "Bubba" act while he escorted her to the morgue. "It sure is nice to meet somebody from back home. We're practically neighbors, you from K.C. and me from Little Rock. Of course, I've been out here ten years, a 'near Native,' and all that." He chortled until he realized that his companion was too preoccupied with her dread of the scene a few floors down to pay much attention.

"Matty was apparently hiking with an acquaintance of his, a Forest Service employee by the name of Andrea Winser. They parted company when she went on up to Mt. Kimball to see about that little flock of big-horn sheep people are talking so much about. Your son found the body on his way back.

23

We'll talk to the girl when she surfaces from her little expedition, but I doubt she'll be able to help much."

Linda Bluenight made a mental note to ask Matty about this girl after she extricated them from this place.

The elevator to "cold storage" in the sub-basement cooled noticeably as they descended its depths, and Linda felt the old numbing of mind and heart as, despite the chill, her sides began to sweat. She focused on finishing the task quickly so that she and Matty could make their escape, yet she remembered the excitement, the scientific challenge of forensic work, the sport-like drive to win, to beat the criminal at his own game. She caught herself and stilled an urge to slap her own face. Snap out of it, she nearly said aloud.

The pathologist's assistant, a recent university graduate named Greg Lund, was nowhere to be found when they entered the morgue through a set of squeaky doors. "Never mind," Griffin assured her, "we're just taking an unofficial gander here."

One glance at the body served as a shocking reminder to Linda of the real reason she had abandoned professional forensic anthropology. She had simply grown sick of the sight of death. She was grateful when Griffin deferentially stepped out of the room. Poring over a stranger's lifeless carcass was too intimate a business for chitchat.

The corpse had been savaged by the canyon's many scavengers, and she was horrified to think of Matty stumbling upon it unawares. Pieces of the lower face were missing and a gaping hole showed in the right buttocks where something had gnawed most of the flesh. The torn-away arm had been laid carefully in its place at the man's side by the squad of paramedics that arrived after Matty reached Las Canyones Resort and frantically pleaded with the doorman to call for help.

Since he had mentioned that the victim lay facing him, Linda concluded that Matty had not seen the bullet hole in the man's back. One shot had perforated the rib cage which probably slowed its momentum and caused it to lodge in the heart muscle.

A standard description flashed through her mind: white male, late forties to early fifties, 5'10", 175 lbs., thinning blonde hair, blue-grey eyes which somehow had survived the ravaging of the night creatures. "My God, his eyes!" she exclaimed to no one. He looked as though he could have died of shock. What remained of the damaged face was contorted with bewildered terror, now frozen permanently to his rigid countenance.

Both instinct and experience told Linda that the victim had gone to the canyon voluntarily, accompanied by the murderer. Moments before his death, the killer had revealed his or her intent. That he was to be slain by an assailant known to him had horrified this man almost as much as the act itself.

The situation was all too familiar. Linda had worked on dozens of cases where the victim knew the killer. Over half of all murders in the country were committed by friends, lovers, spouses, co-workers, kinsmen. Still, the look of disbelief on what remained of the deceased's face was absent in the expressions of most such victims.

Linda tore her gaze away and returned to the bullet hole. The small-caliber bullet had sliced the layers of flesh cleanly. She would bet that the weapon which fired it was new and expensive, like the victim's Italian suit. Otherwise the body was 'clean,' with no other wounds or signs of struggle. A quick check of the fingernails and feet revealed that he had probably been a spectator at his own death.

Reminded of her intention never to enter an 'ice box' like this again, Linda prepared to retrieve her son, give Sergeant Griffin the benefit of her observations, and head for the border. Poring over the *Basketball Digest*, he jumped to his feet when he saw the grim look on his mother's face. "What's shakin', lady?"

"Let's get out of here, we'll talk in the car."

They located Griffin at his desk in the crowded, grimy office pool adjacent to the homicide unit. He looked expectant.

In a staccato voice, Linda told him what her cursory examination had indicated. "The man was killed, execution-style, by a single bullet which penetrated his back between the shoulder blades and proceeded downward into the left ventricle of his heart. The gun that killed him was fired from close range. Most likely, the weapon was a well-made and costly small-caliber handgun. The victim probably knew his assailant and he died immediately. Sufficient physical evidence exists to assume premeditation. That's all I can tell from the few minutes I spent with the victim. Thank you for your kindness to Matty. Now, if you'll forgive our hurry, we need to get home." With that, Linda whisked the two of them into the hallway and toward the elevator. The boy, unusually speechless with surprise, tried to slow her down.

Added to that, Griffin was right on their heels. "Aw, Ms. Bluenight. Say, can I call you Linda? Dinkins, that's our pathologist, just called. He's puking with that damn flu, and our regular sub's out of town on a family emergency. Don't you think you might find the time to help little boy Lund with a preliminary examination? We'd sure be beholden to ya."

"Look, Sergeant, I'm not a doctor, not even the PhD kind. My report couldn't be used in any court, and besides, my skills are rusty. I did a lot of corpse verification at one time, but it was years ago. Your assistant, inexperienced as he is, has the formal qualifications. He can handle it, if you can keep him upright, and Dr. Dinkins can write the formal report when he returns from sick leave."

"But, Mom, you were so good back in K.C. that when the FBI called the Medical Center there for help on local cases, the pathologists suggested you." Matty was showing her off. It was the last thing she wanted.

"Dinkins can review your write-up when he gets on his feet. Hey, I'll even buy lunch after, if you're up for it. We can go across the street to Cafe Poca Cosa for the famous chef 'especial.'" Griffin's smoozing only hardened her resistance.

"I'm flattered, but we do have to run. Let us know if you need any more information from Matt." The elevator arrived in the nick of time. Pushing Matty gently inside, she pounded the "G," and breathed a sigh of relief until she saw the reproving look on his face.

When they reach the parking garage, he let her have it, "How can you refuse to help Sergeant Griffin? Somebody killed that poor sucker! I thought you had more cajones, Mom."

"Time out, amigo. Self-righteousness doesn't suit you. I changed careers, remember? I'm out of the body business, and you of all people should understand why. By the way, where's your truck? Did you drive it down the mountain or did the cops bring you?"

"They wanted me to ride in the squad car, but I convinced

one of them to come back with me in the bomber. It's over there in one of the reserved spots. Look, I know you could do this without hurting either of us. It isn't like you'd be involved forever. I've seen you tackle problems that send other people running for cover. Why are you being such a slacker now?"

"This conversation is over. I've got parents coming and a full afternoon of work at school. I'll see you at home this evening. Comprende?"

"What about me? I found the damn guy!"

"Matty."

"Okay, okay, I'm late for practice as it is."

"Don't speed on your way back. The ticket you got last month already cost us plenty. Coach will know what happened, Ron took the phone call from Griffin in his office. You'll be the talk of the team, again."

"I'm outta here."

Linda watched her contribution to the future drive away with a mixture of vexation and pride. She had a full plate of guilt without his adding dessert. Avoiding responsibility might not sit well at the moment, but the moment would pass, and so would Matty's attitude. With a lump of said guilt in her throat, she swung the Ranger down Sixth Avenue through the City of South Tucson.

This municipal artifact always puzzled her. Sitting in the geographic center of the valley and surrounded by metropolitan Tucson and its suburbs, South Tucson owned its political independence with a citizenry descended mostly from families who came north with the Spanish military in the 1770s. Its high school dropout rate was high, yet its crime rate per capita was low. It boasted the finest Mexican restaurants in the American Sonora, yet its dilapidated neighborhoods lacked all but the most basic facilities and services.

She stopped for a takeout lunch of machaca and fresh tortillas at Pico de Gallo, a tiny whitewashed cafe with a single table on a stamp-sized front patio. She should have asked Matty to meet her here for one of his monstrous midday meals, but his irksome behavior and his basketball schedule put her off. The lump was growing. By the time she reached her classroom, it had stolen her appetite. Letting her son down was not something she did easily or often. She stowed her food in the faculty refrigerator and invaded Ron's empty office. Then she phoned the Tucson police department, apologized to Griffin for her lack of cooperation, and offered her assistance.

"That's just great, Linda. Come on down. I'll have Greg and a fresh white coat waitin' for you. Anything else?"

"Just set up for autopsy procedures. I'll be there in less than an hour. Understand, I'll only be observing and helping Greg with odds and ends. I cannot be involved in the cutting if you expect the findings to stand up in court. I'll write up a report to supplement Greg's."

"You got it. Hey, I still owe you that lunch."

The lump began to shrink. She rang off and then dialed her message machine at home to leave Matty word of her change in plans. She was surprised to hear his very own voice. "Hi, kid, decide to get some grub before practice?" She tried to sound nonchalant and nearly succeeded.

"Just a couple of tamales and a burrito from the stash Mrs. Ramos gave us. Did you need to talk to me?" His tone, on the other hand, sounded a mite defensive.

She told him about her new schedule.

"All right, Mom! You're just the woman."

"Yes, well, it's going to make for a busy afternoon. Ron will rearrange my conferences for sometime next week, and you may have to stay after school one day and help me finish putting up the room decorations."

"No problema, the least I can do for such a super parent. Will you get back for dinner?"

"Let's not paint it on too thick," she began, unable to suppress a giggle. "Surely a routine prelim won't take all afternoon, but we'll have to look for another entree in the cupboard since you just consumed what I had planned." The boy's penchant for eating and his lean frame were living contradictions.

"I'll help grill chicken or something. Around six? I thought I'd head over to Peg Grazia's house after practice, if I ever get there, and see if she wants to go to homecoming." He seemed to be trying the idea out on Linda first.

She made it a rule not to influence her son's decisions, and she saw no reason to alter that policy now. She did find it interesting that he had chosen his chum over Ron's daughter, the femme fatale. "Sounds like a busy day. You can tell me how it comes out."

"Right, and Mom, I'm sorry I jumped your case back in town. No es pissed off?"

"No, sweetie, we're fine. See you for supper." The lump evaporated.

Just as she thought her phone chores were over, the ringer jarred in her ear. The caller was Griffin and his tone was officiously jubilant.

"Linda, glad I caught you. We have a few developments. My partner, Hal Hughes, went out to the crime scene with one of our new rookies. They pretty well combed the site and came up with the victim's wallet not far from where Matty found the body. Money and credit cards are missing, of course, but the driver's license and other identification appear to be intact. Our corpse is that of Mr. Benton Brody." Griffin made the announcement as if he expected Linda to recognize the name.

She did not and said so.

"The guy was a well-known business tycoon," explained the Sergeant. "In fact, he is, or was, the partner and brother-in-law of Clay Eastman, the big developer. You've probably seen the guy's kisser on television. As president of the family company, he does all the talking, but Brody was the brains behind the throne, I'm told. Technically speaking, he held the position of first vice-president. We're trying to contact the family now. Funny, he probably bought the farm yesterday late, but no one saw fit to report him missing. The family may have thought he was out-of-town. The company has interests all over the state. Anyway, looks like a robbery, which, along with the ID, should make your job easier — analysis of wound, description of weapon, specific cause of death, and some samples for the chem lab ought to do it."

"Fine, I'll be right there." Linda was as certain that this murder did not result from a botched robbery attempt as she was of Matty's birthday.

She retrieved her lunch and set out on her second trip into town in as many hours. Eating the spicy shredded beef and homemade tortillas with her fingers proved a messy undertaking, but she thought it safer than trying to use a fork and hang on to the steering wheel at the same time. The eating was important, since she could not be certain what effect the coming chore would have on her digestion. Matty might have to go solo come supper. She licked her fingers before wiping them on a paper napkin, and washed the whole thing down with a long drink of milky white horchata, the rice-based punch loved by the Spanish-speaking population here. "Thank God for Sonoran cooking," she intoned to herself.

Clumsy culinary enjoyment soon gave away to a vague anticipation and a nameless foreboding. Linda had vowed that she would never dissect human flesh again, yet she was about to assist in a process she loathed and had come to fear with the antipathy of her ancestors. Native peoples did not carve on their dead. They burned them or buried them or hung them in trees. Then the living sang to the souls of the departed to help them complete the journey into the next world. A tiny voice echoing from the furthest corner of her conscience told her she should not do this thing. Another voice, full of suppressed elation, whispered to her to go for it. Those anthropological tapes, put on "pause" long ago, suddenly began to play the mystery polka.

When Linda Bluenight arrived for her second visit with Sergeant Griffin, she found him sitting in the office of the Assistant Police Chief with an impeccably dressed middle-aged man whom she recognized from television interviews as Clay Eastman. His most recent appearance on public television's *Arizona Newsmakers* had turned contentious when a reporter attempted to grill him about one of his more ambitious and controversial development proposals for a resort near Bonita Canyon. Tim Johanson, editor of the *Southwest Monthly*, had elicited an aggressive response from Eastman when he suggested that Tucson now sported so many golf courses that foursomes of the future would include gila monsters and horny toads.

Eastman looked more like a stockbroker than a real estate tycoon in his black tasseled loafers and dark grey double-breasted suit from Brooks. His forehead was just beginning to lengthen, but a thick crop of dark hair cut to perfection reduced the effect. He had De Niro eyes and their expression alternated between impatience and affability. At the moment, they were suffused with grief and barely controlled anger.

He and Griffin were seated on a black vinyl sofa to the right of the office door, and the Sergeant spoke in quiet tones, telling Eastman what the police knew of his brother-in-law's death. He rose when he saw Linda and put a hand on the other man's shoulder. Eastman also struggled to his feet. His unsteady stance reminded her of how Matty looked just a couple of hours ago. She felt a pang of sympathy and extended her hand when Griffin introduced them. Eastman seemed not to see it for a moment, then grabbed for it in a distracted way.

"Ms. Bluenight here is going to examine your brother-in-law. We're hoping that she can provide us with more information. The perpetrator was probably an amateur. We should have him by nightfall." All semblance of the good old boy had disappeared from Griffin's voice.

Linda checked her inclination to disagree with this assessment and offered her condolences instead. Eastman was unresponsive. "Shall we get started?" she asked, turning to Griffin with a wondering look.

"Yes, but first I need to take Mr. Eastman down for formal identification of the body. Will you accompany us? Dr. Lund should have the lab ready by now." Griffin rolled his eyes a bit as he emphasized the word "doctor."

The three stood silent during the dismal ride in the dingy elevator. It did all the talking, emitting the creaks and groans of aging metal that always set Linda's teeth on edge. When they hurried off and walked quickly through the heavy morgue doors, Eastman shivered and went pale.

"This won't take long," Griffin assured him. He brushed by Greg Lund, a slightly built Swedish-looking young man who hovered beside the doors. Linda gave the rookie pathologist a sympathetic smile. The sergeant slid the drawer marked "B.B., D.O.A." from its encasement in the wall and gently pulled back the plastic to reveal Brody's form.

"Yes, that's Benton," Eastman said lowly, his jaw working. Suddenly he broke into furious sobs, sputtering something about a fucking kidnapper. "Why didn't the bastard just take the money, or demand more in a ransom note? Why kill the man? God, my sister, how will she survive this, in addition to Holly's problems and our mother's cancer? He was a good man, a family man, a contributor to his community." Then he whirled on Griffin. "You find the son-of-a-bitch for me."

Griffin wisely made no reply and instead directed Eastman toward the doors. Lund looked doubly stricken. Linda watched the two men ring for the unsympathetic elevator, then she reached for the lab coat hanging on the wall. As she pulled it over her shoulders, Griffin returned, having left Eastman to his grief for a moment. "You should know that we found Brody's Mercedes in one of the more remote cul-de-sacs of the apartment complex parking area. It was in the space reserved for Apartment 9C. That particular unit is unoccupied, so the car wasn't in anyone's way and no one reported it. The boys are going over it now for prints."

Linda thought a moment, "Will Mrs. Brody want to see the body before we cut on it?"

"Eastman says to go ahead. Evelyn Brody is visiting a fat farm in Albuquerque. He's sent someone to fetch her. That explains why Brody wasn't reported missing last night or this morning. No one was at home to notice. His wife has been out of town for several days and his daughter has been staying with friends."

"Here goes then. Check with you when we finish."

Looking around, Linda saw the old-fashioned small-town approach to police pathology, not yet upgraded to keep pace with the upsurge in violent crime that had so recently arrived in newly urbanized Tucson. The autopsy equipment rested on a cart beside the double doors. The work on the corpse was to take place right on the spot, since no holding facility existed for the purpose. The lab assistants ferried samples for lab analysis a few blocks to the University of Arizona Medical Center. That arrangement alone made Linda glad for Lund's presence. Turning on the small tape recorder, she nodded to her companion.

"I'm sorry for my unprofessional behavior," he said, starting a half-rehearsed apology.

Linda stopped him. "I filled my shoes plenty of times before I got used to this," she reassured him. "Let's have at it."

They proceeded to conduct a thorough, regimented examination, speaking in measured tones and using carefully chosen clinical language. Linda was relieved at how quickly the procedures came back to her. She watched closely as Greg deftly took epidermal, blood and various tissue samples and extracts vials full of saliva, urine, and feces, and then inspected all orifices. As she had predicted from her previous look at Brody, he proved a very easy victim to analyze. He had received excellent lifelong medical and dental care and had attended to his body meticulously. As a result, he did not show any physical deficiencies or maladies beyond the one which had caused his death.

That led them to the wound. To her great surprise, they did not find the bullet in the body. Her hurry during her first visit had prevented her from seeing the perfect perforation around the left nipple where it had made its exit. Only a sleek and efficient snub-nose could have torn so neatly through bone and heart muscle, probably a foreign-made modified 38-caliber. That's what lab analysis was for, she thought with her old appreciation of teamwork. She directed Lund to carve out small slices of all areas perforated by the bullet. These might yield a sliver of casing that would determine where it was made since the homicide detectives would have little chance of finding the slug at the crime scene. A night of collecting by pack rats and army ants would have picked the area clean.

Brody had been a bit on the pudgy side, but that in itself gave him a fair amount of strength. The killer knew that, thus the decision to shoot the victim through the back. Linda entertained a hunch that the "perp" had planned his approach to the act, and she doubted any trace of him would be found on the victim's person. Still, they clipped samples from Brody's fingernails to check for foreign skin or hair. Likewise, they pored over the man's clothing which Greg had removed when the corpse was first brought to the lab. With great delicacy, he searched every article and brushed every inch of fabric, scanning for any trace left as the murderer propped the victim between the boulders after snuffing out his life. Linda quickly concluded that the perpetrator must have taken the same precaution. The Italian suit and handmade silk shirt yielded little evidence. Fearing DNA identification, the killer touched his victim as little as possible.

Her conviction that the event had been done with malice aforethought, as the law books say, grew stronger by the minute. She was also certain that the crime had not involved a professional hit. A contract killer would not have been familiar with the obscure trail head. Nor would he have bothered to try to hide the body. This killing had been carried out by someone without experience, but with the skills and cunning required to pull off an execution-style slaying. The fact that the body had been moved at least a short distance to the boulders told her the murderer was a male. A female would have had to be a weight-lifter to drag Brody's lifeless heaviness and wedge it between the giant rocks.

Further examination of Benton Brody reverted to routine coronary detail. None of the procedures really involved any of her forensic skills. No shortage of remains, no lack of identification, and no uncertainty as to the method of murder provided the adrenaline rush which had kept her former career stimulating despite its often gruesome requirements.

She labeled the samples and placed them in their transport case while Lund marked each item of clothing from the Avanti tie to the French silk briefs, and returned it all to the sterile plastic bag which lay beside Brody's tagged toe. All details of the exam were recorded on tape before they shut off the machine.

"It's meant a lot to have you here for my first 'cut,' Ms. Bluenight," said Greg appreciatively.

"I was glad to do it," replied Linda, meaning every word. If nothing else came of making this little foray into police work, she had helped this competent young man through a difficult moment. "You look like you could use some fresh air now. Hasta la vista."

She stood a few moments before the dead man, thinking of his life, consumed in a flash of gunfire like so many others before him, sacrificed on the altar of gun worship which seemed to have become the civil religion. As she removed her lab coat, now spattered with the substances that had formed a living, thinking organism, she decided to tell the sergeant once more that this crime was no armed robbery, but a well-planned assassination committed by a male who had known Brody well enough to convince him to take a walk in a deserted canyon at the end of a workday still dressed in his best clothes.

Perhaps the killer used the pretext of having Brody meet him at the Paradise Hill Apartments for some business purpose. Once there he would have persuaded his victim to rendezvous at one of the empty units, maybe even 9C. She decided to ask Griffin to check Brody's calendar for the day and to interview his secretary to see if he had any late meetings scheduled. A check of that unoccupied flat would also be a good idea.

She looked for Griffin back in the central pool. A harried middle-aged detective at the next desk was taking a statement from a distraught Hispanic woman. The woman pleaded with him to find her esposo who had left their home on the south side for work three days before. She had not seen him since. The detective was grumpily sympathetic, perhaps thinking of his own wife and her eternal misgivings about his safety. He was about to seek help from one of his Spanish-speaking comrades. "No entiendo, Senora, just wait here un momento, Por favor."

The woman, who Linda intuited to be an old but attractive thirty years of age, wore a calf-length faded denim skirt, white blouse, and red plaid shawl. She rocked back and forth in her chair, crying silently.

Turning to the sergeant, she handed him the audiotape. Then, taking a deep breath, she related her theory.

Griffin was skeptical. "Well, now, guess I got even more help than I bargained for. Your findings may lead to that conclusion on the face of it, but we better hold off speculating about degree of murder till all the evidence is in. We still got people out at the site searching for clues. You know your stuff, I reckon, and we'll give your views every consideration." The drawl had crept back into the slow voice.

"I'm not speculating, Sergeant. By the way, can I call you Phil, since we're on a semi-first name basis? My conclusions are based on my forensic findings as well as insight from nearly a decade with one of the toughest departments in the country. You can check with KCPD on my record of accuracy. It was upward of 85% as I recall."

"Now, Linda, I wasn't doubtin' your objectivity fer a minute. I just need to get all the data in the file before I go off on a definite line of inquiry. You understand my position on this thing, don't you, hon?"

"I do." She wanted to add that frankly, hon, she didn't give a damn, "If you'll find me an empty office and a typewriter or a PC, I'll write my report. I'm afraid I can't concentrate with the din of this room in my ears."

"Sure thing, you can use Assistant Chief Mitchell's office,

where we were before. He's down in Nogales on a public relations gig, won't be back till late."

Linda pounded away on the old IBM Selectric which she lugged to the center of Mitchell's wide wooden desk from its place in a far corner. She had reluctantly learned to use this antiquated instrument as a freshman in high school when her greatest ambition had been to become a professional babysitter, and it brought back fond memories of "Liquid Paper" and love notes to a red-haired boy friend.

Contrary to old Phil's desires, her report included her assessment of the nature of the crime and the criminal. She wrapped it up quickly and then sat a moment looking out the tenth story window of one of Tucson's few tall buildings north toward the Catalinas where Brody had met his end in one of her favorite places. A walk through Ventana Canyon had always been like a visit to church. One of nature's cathedrals, it inspired reverence and revitalized the spirit. Now murder had contaminated it, had made it alien and unsafe. She knew that Matty would think twice before he ventured another trip to the maiden pools. She hated the murderer for the despoliation of their peace of mind almost as much as for the heinousness of his act.

Her thoughts returned finally to Brody. Linda could not help but be curious about the motive behind his slaying. Perhaps it was money, his own or someone else's. She had heard stories of the cowboy mentality that pervaded both the business and political establishments throughout the state. The Charlie Keating fiasco of a decade ago had provided a crash course in corporate greed and corruption. Maybe sixguns were another part of the commercial strategy in making land deals.

A crime of passion must be included on the list of possibilities. Brody might have had an affair with an employee or the wife of an acquaintance whose husband discovered them and decided to do away with the threat of a richer, more influential rival. From the brief mention of Mrs. Brody and Brody's appealing economic stature and reasonable looks for a man at midlife, the idea might not be farfetched.

Finally, it might have involved a matter of power, a political killing by a competitor who grew tired of being beaten in the race to occupy, pave, or otherwise alter every square foot of ground that could be acquired by private developers. Since their mass entry into the Southwest during the middle of the last century, Anglos had purchased what they could afford and took by force what they could not. Native lands had been usurped early and often. Untold numbers of miners had been found stuffed down their own shafts with their brains bashed and their claims jumped. Bank robbers as late as the 1950s had made their getaways on horseback, shooting pedestrians and passersby from the saddle as they rode south to Mexico and unextraditable freedom.

In recent years, newspapermen, clergy, and just plain folks had lost their livelihoods and sometimes their lives trying to expose and prevent abuses ranging from illegal grazing and dumping to desecrating historic and prehistoric cemeteries, while on the other side of the ethical stage, mining corporations, land speculators, and political kingpins had played Monopoly with the public trust.

It occurred to Linda Bluenight that Tucson might be experiencing another version of the "Strike it Rich" syndrome that had characterized the "Land of Little Springs" since before it became the last of the continental forty-eight states in 1912, and that Benton Brody might have had the misfortune to be just another casualty of the economic "O.K. Corral." The case might be out of her hands now, as she wanted, but even so, her palms itched.

—••⊱⋅⋅⋅⊰••—

<>>>> Three <<<<>

Meeting the Man

The following morning found the Bluenights bellied up to the breakfast table at their little rancheria. Saturday was Linda's favorite day of the week, and she felt as much like a kid out of school as Matty.

Deprived of the barn and outhouses that originally adorned the property, their old stone ranch house faced the San Xavier Mission and its village community. Lying only a hundred yards away and across Los Reales Road which fronted their property, the glistening white church gleamed in the sun on a day so clear that Linda could see beyond the Santa Rita Mountains east of the reservation to catch a glimpse of Old Mexico when she went outside to retrieve the morning newspaper.

Their sprawling living room looked south from the wide picture window to the right of the heavy oak door. A stone fireplace along west wall warmed the room in winter. This gave way via an arched opening to a hacienda-style dining

43

area complete with wood-burning stove. A doorway to the far right of the living room led to a narrow hallway which branched off to the bedrooms and the belatedly built-on bath with its ancient brass fixtures, claw-leg tub and hand-held shower. The long kitchen where they sat ensconced with coffeepot, juice pitcher, and newsprint stretched across the rear of the house. Its breakfast area abutted the back wall and a window by the table faced north toward the Catalinas which this morning were bathed in blue.

Ron Verasca had helped Linda acquire her "homestead" from the county after its former owner had died intestate and impoverished. A testament to the overgrazing that savaged the Southwest for a hundred years, Len Lister had been forced to sell his several sections one at a time to pay taxes on a herd that could not earn its own keep. The house with its remnant acre and a half had fallen into the public domain, and Linda had purchased it for back taxes. Every day she thanked Iitoi, the Tohono O'odham Creator, for the opportunity to live so close to the reservation that she and Matty could walk to class. No matter the red ants that camped in the drains come summer or the plumbing that talked in the night. This was her place in the sun, and she enjoyed the long hours required to make it habitable and keep the critters at bay.

Passing sections of the *Tucson Tribune* back and forth between them, Matty soon monopolized the sports page while Linda got the scoop on Benton Brody. She had spent a fitful sleep dreaming that she had become lost in the Saguaro National Monument, a park twenty miles west of the city. When the Department of Interior declared the saguaro an endangered species in the 1970s, the reserve was created to protect it, and the place was one of the first she and Matty had explored.

Stopping for directions, none of the people she encountered in the dream could tell her how to find the entrance that she remembered being just around the next bend in the road. Then a vulture with the head of a dog told her that the road had no exit, that it circled the base of the Tucson Mountains like a lasso with no knot, and that she would have to remain forever among the great green symbols of the Sonora. She replied, "Not till I find Matty," and woke herself. When she fell back to sleep, she saw an instant replay, except that this time a king snake was the messenger. After the third playback, she decided to keep the sun company as it rose over the Rincon Mountains.

Her dark hair, braided down her back at bedtime, had come loose of its white ribbon and fell across her shoulder. It was almost long enough to stir her coffee with, and she tossed it back impatiently. Like Matty, she was tall and angular, with large prominent features highlighted by towering cheekbones. Her deep-set brown eyes and almond-colored oval face carried that hint of ancient Appalachian towns surrounded by mist and maize fields.

The headline on the front page read, "Eastman Inc. Executive Found Murdered North of City," and the lead began, "Benton Brody, senior vice-president of Eastman Enterprises, was found dead in Ventana Canyon in the Santa Catalina Mountains just north of Tucson yesterday. Police say a single gunshot killed the prominent executive. Death was reportedly instantaneous." The article continued to describe the circumstances surrounding the discovery of the body, but it only mentioned Matty once, and for that she gave thanks even though he muttered a disappointed epithet.

Linda skimmed through the familiar facts to the biographical data on Brody and his business. He and Clay

Eastman owned one of Tucson's largest real estate companies. Over the past fifteen years, they had engineered a series of successful and controversial residential and commercial developments. The two men were close friends as well as relatives and financial partners, and they had earned a collective reputation as the go-getter team from Connecticut, where Eastman's father, the late Jordan Eastman, had built a fortune in suburban tract housing.

The next few paragraphs reviewed the growth of Eastman Inc.'s fortunes and the vociferous objections that seemed to shadow its every project. A decade ago, riparian areas on the west side near the Tucson Mountains had been ripped apart for Ranchland Estates. This upscale imitation of Santa Fe, with home prices starting at $250,000, had aroused the ire of native Tucsonans who resented the "build now, preserve later" attitude of these New England upstarts. Riparian habitats were a sore point with many Westerners who viewed them as oases in a sea of sand, providing respite, food, and drink for both four and two-legged visitors.

Eastman's condominiums downtown were seen by the history-minded as further encroachment on the Old Presidio which had already suffered extensive damage. The addition of posh inner-city dwellings had increased congestion in an area which had been designed for the commercial use of a dispersed population.

In yet another venture, access to archaeological sites along the southern face of the Rincon Mountains had been cut off by Eastman's new retirement village which featured accommodations affordable to only the most affluent of senior citizens. Academic research on a cluster of 800-year-old Hohokam dwellings, a hillside full of lava rock petroglyphs, and a series of irrigation canals contemporary with them had been declared off limits even to the University of Arizona's archaeology department. Now these invaluable records of the region's prehistory sat unexamined and unprotected from pothunters. The state historical society and the university faculty had protested vigorously when the county approved the zoning permit, to no avail.

Linda was familiar with the story from her contacts in the Anthropology Department, whose chairman she had contacted shortly after her arrival in Tucson. She had even signed a petition to the County Board of Supervisors opposing the project. Although the brouhaha had eventually subsided like desert dust in winter, there was now a quiet attempt to introduce legislation in the state senate to force Eastman Inc. to provide a dirt road to the ruins.

The company's newest plan was also its most elaborate and ambitious. A massive resort would block the entrance to Bonita Canyon on the northeast side of the Catalinas, much as had happened at Ventana to the west. Billed as the most luxurious and pricey of its genre, it had also become the focus of the most heated debate. Media, environmental groups, and residents decried another restriction to a lovely hiking area. Copies of the project's blueprints had been mysteriously obtained and published by *Southwest Monthly*. They included not one, but two 18-hole golf courses, a 500-room hotel, a full range of townhouses and apartments, custom homes built to specification, and a double set of country club facilities.

Public outcry was heard halfway to Phoenix. "Another Blow to Wildlife," had been the title of the *Naturally Tucson's* next cover story. The Sonora Wilderness Society was threatening to sue to halt construction, citing the threat to several already endangered species of plants and animals. Public demonstrations at the canyon sponsored by one of the more militant environmental groups, Santa Tierra, were a possibility.

The project had also run into objections from the business community.   Most open in his opposition was a native Tucsonan named Barron Kingley.   Anyone living in the Sonora for more than six days had heard about his flamboyant adventures in land speculation and development. While his own deals were nearly as controversial, his resentment of "outside" investment posed a greater obstacle to Eastman's Inc.'s latest scheme than any environmental or civic concern.

The article was a wish list of motives for first degree murder, and Linda hoped Sergeant Griffin was checking it twice. At the top of hers was for the murderer to be found "yesterday" as Matty was always saying. She felt a twinge of apprehension as she looked across at the boy, invisible behind his sheet of basketball scores from around the solar system.

When she turned to the obituaries, Benton Brody smiled confidently back at her. The extensive biography beneath the picture filled two columns in the paper's daily description of death. Benton J. Brody was born and raised in New London, Connecticut, the only son of a successful contractor and state senator. He was educated at Yale with a bachelor's degree in literature and an MBA. He married his wife, Evelyn Eastman Brody, 25 years ago. They had one daughter, Holly, 22, "of the home." His widowed mother, Jane Brody, lived on the family estate.   The funeral was set for Tuesday at St. Andrew's Foothills Christian Church.   In lieu of flowers, donations could be sent to Sonora Rehabilitation Center. Linda noted that Sonora Rehab did experimental and costly treatment of substance abuse.

Linda was as deep in thought as Matty was in his statistics when the phone hanging on the wall beside him rang and made her jump.

"Chill, Mom," he said in a coddling tone as he picked up the receiver and handed it to her.

"Hello, Ms. Bluenight? My name is Morris Peters. I'm the police lieutenant in charge of the Benton Brody murder case. Sergeant Phil Griffin passed me your preliminary report and told me how helpful you were yesterday. I want you to know we appreciate it." The voice was deep, with a tinge of Chicago.

"Hello, Lieutenant, it's nice of you to call. I hope you'll be able to make an arrest soon."

"We've got practically the whole squad working on it. It's a major case, what with Brody's position in the community and all. I wonder if I might talk to you sometime today. I understand your son found the body, and that you have some ideas about the personality profile of the killer."

"Lieutenant, my son gave Sergeant Griffin all the information he could. I'd really like to keep him away from the case from now on. He's already been named in this morning's newspaper, we may have television crews at the front door before long, and I don't want him in the public spotlight any more than necessary. As for my input, my report was complete and thorough. Besides, I have open house at school this afternoon, and Matty plays a basketball game this evening."

Matty was again giving her that "Do your duty" look over the juice jug. She squirmed and the action made her old wooden chair squeak.

"I certainly don't want to cause you any more trouble, but it would help my investigation to hear your views on the case. I could even run out this afternoon and we could chat after your school event. I haven't been to San Xavier in years. Has it changed much?"

"Not the village itself, but Tucson is knocking at our door," Linda answered with a telltale sigh of resignation. "I guess I could spare a few minutes, five o'clock all right?"

The rest of the day kept Linda too busy to think about her appointment, since she was forced to combine the social function of the afternoon with the rescheduled conferences. A few of the children were having difficulties. The individuality and competition demanded by the educational system was often at odds with the communal nature of village life. Then they were tagged as "learning disabled," a term Linda had always resisted. She did not intend to see Alicia Mendoza or Sergio Garcia suffer such a fate, so she spent extra time with their parents, listening to their concerns and offering strategies to coax out each child's talents.

She had dumped as much of the standard curriculum as she could to emphasize subjects which would put her fourth-graders in touch with their own culture in addition to the so-called mainstream. She was also attempting to bring the language of the Tohono O'odham into her classes. For the past year, she had been studying with Martha Morena, an octogenarian who lived in one of the more remote villages on the "Big Res."

The last of her students proudly showed her mother around the room as the mission bell struck five. Little Angela was eager to display her handmade flute constructed from an empty paper towel roll and colored paper. She demonstrated it for them, whistling under her breath to imitate the music which the cardboard would not yield.

"You're ready for powwow," laughed her mother.

Following them out of the classroom, Linda took the last of the cookies and punch to the small cafeteria across the hall, and hurried to the front of the building to meet Lieutenant Morris Peters. He was waiting for her just outside, looking around at the church and at a sloping hill which rose gently beside it. A white crucifix stood atop the hill, guarding the village from the ravages of Apaches and drought. A shrine to Our Lady of Lourdes was hidden in a side crevice.

With her endless penchant for physical description, Linda noted that the lieutenant stood a shade under six feet and was built like a man who drank beer and then worked out to sweat it off. His skin was ruddy, his sand-colored hair was thick, and his blue eyes were restless. He greeted her warmly and shook her hand with both of his. "Glad you could see me. I came a little early so I could take a look at this old place. The restoration is coming along fine. Read about it, but this is my first chance to see it up close."

"Yes, the people here are very pleased with it. The Italian artists we hired are doing one section each year for the next several. They are also teaching the tribal members how to clean and maintain the altars and statues so the process can be continuous. This is the first remodeling the church has seen since the building was completed in the 1790's."

"You seem to be right at home here. Have you taught at the school a long time?"

Linda felt immensely complimented. "This is my eighth year. Shall we walk over to the market and sit a few minutes?"

They crossed San Xavier Road and the wide windswept plaza to the walled courtyard which housed several small shops full of handcrafted jewelry and leather goods. A fountain and several tall mesquite trees offered a shady sanctuary from the sun which even on a November day could burn a brow.

This was her favorite time of day. During the week, life slowed down after the children exploded through the school door and scattered to their homes. She often lingered in the village, catching up on local news, preparing the next day's lessons, or sitting quietly here or up on the hill, savoring the stillness of a late afternoon.

They reviewed her findings, and he asked a few clarifying questions. Then his serious face, about forty years on it, she guessed, became intense. "Tell me what you think about the guy who did it."

"Well, he was strong, clever, and fairly young. He knew Brody at least casually, and was careful not to leave any trace of his presence." Linda cited the evidence from her examination to support her statements. "I'm sure the murder was planned and that it was committed by one person. I don't think the killer was a professional, though I could be wrong about that. I think you should check apartment 9C at Paradise Hill for clues."

"As we speak." Peters studied her face. "I interviewed the Forest Service employee, Andrea Winser, nice girl. She was very upset and wanted to know how your son was doing, but she couldn't help us much. The two of them just missed the body on their way up the trail. I also called the Kansas City PD to get some background on you. I hope you don't mind. The department there couldn't praise you enough. Can I call you if we get a lead relevant to your expertise? You have a detective's instincts."

She did mind, but kept quiet for the moment. "I'd rather not get involved any further. That part of my life is buried back in the Midwest, and I'd like to leave it there." She saw a frown line his face and thought of Matty, "On the other hand, if you really get stuck, I'll do what I can, though what I didn't put in my report ain't out there, as my lab buddies used to say."

Linda attempted a reassuring smile which led him to ask a few slightly personal questions about Matty and herself. She answered them as briefly as possible and rose to leave, "I'd better run home and throw something on the table for Matt. His game begins at 7:30."

"Your car in the lot?" Peters asked as he swung open the black iron gate at the entrance to the market.

"No, it's at our house, just over there, off Los Reales. I walk through the fields to school when the weather's nice." She laughed at her conditional tone.

"I'll drive you across, save you some time. Bet it's been awhile since you took a spin in a squad car."

Not long enough, thought Linda to herself.

During the short ride, he volunteered that he was separated from his wife, about to divorce in fact.

She murmured a vague condolence and jumped out of the regulation-equipped sedan as if a bomb had gone off in it. "Thanks for the lift, and good luck," she called, heading swiftly for the safety of her front door. Linda Bluenight was definitely not in the market for a man. Still she threw a last glance at Morris' retreating car as it kicked up dust going east toward town. He was somewhat attractive and semi-available. The biggest negative in his resume was his career as a cop.

Matty's father had been an upcoming officer on the force in Kansas City. It had been heartache from beginning to end, except for the Matty part. A brief, torrid love affair, a pregnancy, and a bloody scene on a dark highway where she had cradled his head as he lay dying, shot by a suspect he had stopped for a routine traffic violation. No marriage, no partner for parenting or for life, just a souvenir badge, maternity leave, and a small pay raise from the department to help her care for the new baby. No more of that, ever.

---·••:÷:••·---

<>>>> Four <>>>>

Test of Faith

Linda rose with the Sonora next morning and claimed sole possession of the coffeepot as well as the Sunday edition of the *Trib*. Matty slept on after leading the varsity to a rare victory and celebrating at a party with the Grazia girl. The team's lack of success was becoming easier to swallow now that Peg had accepted his invite to the homecoming fete.

Pleasant thoughts of her son's new love life evaporated when her eye caught the morning headline: SUSPECT APPREHENDED IN MURDER OF REAL ESTATE EXECUTIVE!

Incredulous, she read on. "A part-time custodian at Las Canyones Resort just east of Ventana Canyon was arrested last night and charged with second-degree murder in the death of real estate magnate Benton Brody. Police say the suspect allegedly kidnaped Mr. Brody in a parking lot at the resort.

Arresting officers also allege that he then forced the victim to drive his car, a late-model blue Mercedes-Benz, to a spot near the seldom-used trail behind the luxury apartment complex built by the Brody family's company, Eastman Inc. The suspect allegedly robbed and then shot the victim, taking his valuables, but leaving his vehicle behind for fear of recognition. Police say credit cards belonging to the developer were found in the suspect's locker at the nationally renowned foothills resort, where he works as a custodian. In addition, a fingerprint on Brody's car appears to match those taken from the accused who has been identified as Ramon Morena, 22 years old, of San Xavier Village on the Tohono O'odham reservation southwest of Tucson."

"Ridiculous!" Linda shouted, then clapped a hand over her mouth, so as not to interrupt Matty's snoring.

"Morena is a graduate of Mission High School at the historic parish established by the seventeenth century missionary priest, Father Eusebio Kino. A background check indicates that Morena has no criminal record. The accused starred on his high school's varsity baseball team as its second baseman. He was also a member of its honor society, and last year received an Associate of Arts degree in hospitality management from Pima County Community College. His father, Felipe Morena, is a member of the Elders' Council at San Xavier. The suspect is being held without bond in Pima County Jail. Arraignment is set for Monday at 1 P.M. A public defender will be assigned."

Fuming at the absurdity and unfairness of the situation, Linda rushed to her room to rummage through her closet for something to wear. She pulled out a long blue denim skirt with a ruffle at the bottom and a white cotton Western-style blouse. When Matty was small and she was in a rush to get him to school and herself to work, she had mastered the art of thirty-second dressing. The trick was to shed a nightgown with one hand, slip on a bra with the other, simultaneously get into a pair of shoes, and hold on to the day's wardrobe all at the same time. If she hurried, she could just make eight o'clock Mass. The entire village would have already heard the news through what she called its "Oral Internet."

Ramon's younger brother, Rudy, was Matty's classmate and one of his best buddies. Ramon's grandmother, Martha, was her language tutor and lived out on the big reservation. Her plan was to race over to the church to get more details. Then she would come back to the house, check on Matty, and call the County Detention Center to finagle a visit with Ramon. Maybe Peters could help her gain entry, or perhaps she could sweet-talk Sergeant Griffin.

She wondered which unpleasant bureaucracy would handle Ramon's case. The crime had been committed outside the city limits which explained why Ramon was sweltering in the county facility, but the Tucson P.D. had been dispatched to the murder scene because it took Matty's call from Las Canyones resort. The two departments might now wage a turf fight over which would take credit for the "collar." She worried momentarily that her work with the city's homicide squad might put her at a disadvantage with the sheriff's office, and she vowed to asked Father Flynn if he had any contacts.

She gave her hair a few brush strokes as the Ranger raised a cloud of dust down Los Reales and pulled with a slight skid onto the dirt track which provided a shortcut between her house and San Xavier Road. She parked in the church lot beside the ramadas where women cooked fry bread for the tourists, and she saw a crowd inside the iron entrance gate of the walled courtyard which fronted the building. As she made her way inside, she noticed that every window was open to ventilate the nave and the main altar. Two middle-aged Tohono women with sorrowful gentle eyes moved to create room for her in a side pew toward the front.

Virtually every citizen of San Xavier had come to learn about this latest encounter with "white man law," but the overflow was attributable to the horde of visitors who descended on the mission like sparrows in the wind, especially as winter drove them south. Normally, they were tolerated with patience and humor, but today they were seen as intruders, unaware and uncaring of the calamity that had befallen the community.

Father Brian Flynn, the Franciscan friar who had spent his fifteen-year career in ministry at the mission parish, seemed perceptibly upset as he recited opening prayers. His Irish face contrasted with his impeccable Spanish and his fluency in the Tohono language. Flynn had worked hard to acquire acceptance as the village's first Anglo clergyman. His impassioned defense of the people's land, water, and mineral claims in federal court, his midnight trips to town to fetch their members in trouble with the police or needing medical attention, his accommodation to their traditional ceremonials and customs had earned him respect and affection. This morning he abandoned his prepared homily to address the predicament of Ramon Morena. His tone brought a hush even to the New Yorkers who had been pointing to the murals on the nave walls. The only other sound emanated from the clicks and hums of numerous cameras which Linda speculated belonged to reporters who would be stalking the place now.

The priest's first message was one of comfort. "The parishioners of San Xavier wish to offer the Morena family all the material, emotional, and spiritual support we can provide in this time of trouble. The parish staff will do everything in our power to see that our brother, Ramon, is treated with equity by the law enforcement agencies. I ask the Morena family, their neighbors, and our villagers for their forbearance and hope, and I plead with our young people to put aside their anger. I remain confident that with the assistance of the elders in our community, we can find answers to the questions and discontent this misfortune will cause for the tribe."

Sensing that the media and thus all of Tucson might be listening, Flynn elevated his tone so that it filled every space and ear, "I entreat the keepers of the legal system to extend fairness and justice as they carry out their charge in this tragic matter. Let us not permit the sins of the past to repeat themselves."

Finally, his voice trembling and soft, he prayed, "Merciful God, extend a loving hand to care for and protect Evelyn and Holly Brody. Keep them, along with your desert people, in your care, as we move through our grief toward the light that is Your Love. Amen."

The sound of muffled weeping alternated with low angry muttering. It filled the pauses between his words and seemed to rise directly from the statues that peered down from the nooks and crannies lining the walls from vestibule to sacristy. Linda knew that the tears would be replaced by resolve, which was as much a part of San Xavier's history as those patron saints whose images had withstood the ravages of time and conflict.

When the service ended, Linda caught the priest as he shook hands and greeted parishioners outside the front entrance. He wore sandals and a brightly-colored serape over his vestments, and his face was densely freckled. Bushy red brows shaded eyes of ocean blue. "Linda, I was hoping you would be here. I was about to call the Morenas, but let's talk first. I saw Matty's name in the paper."

They walked toward the side chapel, a tiny white structure between the church and the school where hundreds of candles were offered by the relatives and friends of the sick and dying. It was a place of pilgrimage and hope. Brian Flynn turned his fair face to the morning sun as they stood in the little cactus garden in the chapel courtyard, "Tell me how Matty happened to find Benton Brody's corpse. On one of his treks, was he?"

"Yes, I nearly went with him, wish I had now." Linda summarized the events of the past two days, including her work with Brody and the visit from Peters, "I just can't accept this business about Ramon. All the evidence points to a premeditated killing. I know the credit cards implicate him, but there could be an explanation for that."

"I was just thinking about how quickly the police made the arrest," replied the priest, pacing around a tall ocotillo. Another of the Sonora's unique cacti, its stick-like branches looked dead until moisture turned them a verdant, if temporary, green. This morning they were in full color. "You know more about these matters than I do, but don't they usually try to accumulate more evidence before they go about charging people with murder?"

"That's right, but with all the notoriety in this case, they needed to have someone behind bars fast. I'm going into town now to try to see Ramon. I'll stop off at headquarters first. I'd like to know what the detectives are saying about him and have another look at the body, just in case I missed something."

"You're getting into the thick of this, Linda. Does it

bother you to be so close to police work again?"

Brian Flynn was remembering her first year of teaching when Linda had sought him out as she questioned the wisdom of her decision to change careers. Her long years of study followed by her professional status as a forensic expert left a temporary vacuum after she arrived to start over as a "schoolmarm."

"Yes, Father, it does, but I owe the Morenas a lot. Matty's eaten many a tamale in their kitchen, and my Tohono O'odham would be far the worse if it hadn't been for Martha. Nap s-ma:c mo he'ekio d a'i g 'o:la?" She gave him a reassuring pat on the arm and showed off her skill by asking him the time.

"Almost 9:30. I'd go with you, but the village counsel is meeting in a while to talk about how to deal with the youth. The members will have their hands full. The teenagers are angry, the children bewildered, the parents frustrated. They may call a meeting for the high schoolers to let them vent. I need to make an appearance, then I'll go by the Morenas and see what I can do there."

They stood together silently, thinking of the heartbreak afflicting that house in its grove of creosote off Mission Road. Felipe Morena was an auto mechanic. His wife, Mendina, drove out to Sells three times a week to work as a practical nurse with the Indian Health Service. Ramon was second in a flock of seven, and the whole family was active in parish and village affairs. Ramon's ancestors had been subchiefs in their traditional lands out west. He had moved into Tucson last year after graduating from Pima College, hoping to break into the hotel business, but had been able to find only menial work. The recent slump in tourism was passing slowly, and jobs were especially tight in the resort industry. Then again, the darker the skin, the harder the market.

Linda looked up at the priest and saw an expression alien to his features. "Think I'll light a candle before I go," she said.

He nodded and cautioned her, "Be careful with yourself, Linda, and let me know what you find out. Vaya con Dios."

She popped in to check on Matty and found him burrowed under a pile of pillows. Standing over him for a moment, she thought of Ramon, separated from his family, perhaps forever, and of how easily loved ones could be lost. A sense of urgency led her to forget about phone calls. She placed the article about Ramon strategically atop the sports page and scribbled a note, "Not to worry, am checking it out. In town for a few hours. Do homework. Love, Mom."

She was disappointed to find the TCPD homicide office deserted except for a Sunday watch officer who told her his partner had dispatched himself to Bowen and Bailey's for scones and latte. It amused her to imagine Tucson as the rare American city where the police patronized a 1960s-style coffeehouse. The remaining officer informed her that Ramon's paperwork had been completed, and that the arresting officers, Griffin and his sidekick, Hal Hughes, had taken the day off. Peters had checked in earlier, but he had departed as well. Linda referred the officer to her report and requested clearance to visit the morgue again.

"Sorry, Ms. Bluenight," he emphasized the Ms. "The victim's remains have been released to a funeral home in the foothills at the request of his family."

She stuttered in disbelief and then tore into the uniformed desk clerk before she could stop herself, "What kind of store are you guys running here? I can't believe Griffin or Peters approved of such an amateur stunt."

Puffing out his barrel-chest and running a hand through his thinning blonde hair, Sergeant Foley assumed a contentious tone, "From what I understand, the Chief received a call from Mr. Eastman and the minister from St. Andrews yesterday late. They asked that the body be handed over for religious reasons. Since you so kindly assisted our man with the autopsy, and since only a few lab results remained to be completed, the Chief acceded to their wishes. Arrangements were made for the body's transfer after the suspect's arrest, and once the officers on the case and the city attorney decided your report was sufficient. Is there anything else I can do for you?"

"Please. I'd like Sgt. Griffin's and Lt. Peters' home phone numbers. Maybe they can tell me just why private citizens have more to say about police procedure than the *Police Department Procedures Manual.*"

"I'm afraid the Manual in this department prohibits the distribution of home numbers to outside parties. They'll both be here tomorrow, I'll have them call you first thing. Just put your number on this pad." Foley's face was alive with color.

Linda tried to cork her temper. "They have my number," she replied, "but I need to speak to one of them now. Besides this business with Brody, I also need permission to see the Morena boy. Since I don't know anyone in the Sheriff's office, I was hoping you people would clear the way."

"Well, now, we have a mighty good working relationship with county law enforcement. I'm sure if you just go on over there and mention your connection with the case, the folks in charge of day duty will give you a few minutes with the kid. You live out there on the reservation with him, don't you?"

She ignored the question and the hint of a sneer behind it. "I hope I can expect more cooperation from that department than I'm getting from this one." She turned on her heel and marched out, slamming the door smartly behind her. "My last visit to that dump," she thought, giving her eyes a Betty Davis roll.

She used the short drive across town to calm down and plan what she wanted to say to Ramon. She realized that his contact with his family since his arrest could only have been brief, so she would try to convey their love and encouragement. Most of all, she wanted him to tell her what had happened at the time of his arrest, and she wanted to look into his face as he described what, if any connection he had with Brody's murder.

Without the city's weekday traffic to battle, a feat which Matty often called "the daily desert car fiesta," the trip west to Silverlake Road took only a few minutes. The Tucson Mountains loomed before her. She would have loved to drive through them, across Gates Pass and down the back range to the Sonora Desert Museum. Right now, she would welcome spending an hour sitting on the stone bench in the aviary .

New houses at the top of several peaks looked down arrogantly on the valley below. Linda frowned at these encroachments on the area's already stressed and threatened wildlife, and the fact that they interfered with her own view of the gently sloping Tucsons, so different in size and shape from the more dramatic Catalinas.

Linda parked the Ranger in front of the two-story building marked Pima County Adult Detention Center and braced herself for the possible confrontation ahead, but as she entered the foyer and approached the information desk, she found the place in a state of near pandemonium. A female officer stood behind the desk frantically ordering an ambulance over a speaker phone. Two uniformed guards in a far corner of the room argued about someone's responsibility, spiking their accusations with generous shots of invective. A great commotion came from a corridor behind a set of heavy doors which she figured to be the entrance to the holding cells.

The woman, whose name tag identified her as "Denise Dobbins" banged the receiver on its pad and swallowed hard. "Pardon me," began Linda, "Is there an emergency? I'm not a doctor, but I have some medical knowledge. In fact, I've been helping the city homicide unit in the Benton Brody case. I'm here to see Ramon Morena, the suspect in that case, but if there's something I can help with..."

The woman caught her breath and gave Linda a stricken look. A siren sounded in the distance. Linda took a faltering step back. She knew without being told that Ramon Morena was dead in lockdown.

<>>>> Five <<<<>

Enter the Nightmare

Linda's mind began to career like a "Tilt-A-Whirl." Reeling from two deaths that so intimately affected both herself and her son, she cursed the fact that after years of avoiding such soul-searing violence, she still had found no escape. "Get hold of those cajones Matty mentioned," she reprimanded herself. Her eyes were deep dark pools of fury and confusion, boring holes into the duty clerk's badge. Officer Denise had taken off her large-frame glasses until she could contain the moisture about to wet her cheeks. She was perhaps twenty-one years old, and this was most certainly her first on-the-job crisis.

Struggling with her own self-control, Linda pulled her shoulders erect and addressed the entire room. This included a man she pegged as the officer in charge, who had just emerged through those metal doors to her right. "My name is Linda Bluenight. I'm a forensic anthropologist. The Tucson Police Department requested my help in the examination of Benton Brody, the man Ramon Morena is accused of killing. I came here to interview Morena about the murder informally. If there is a medical emergency, please, admit me to the

67

inmate facility so I can be of assistance."

"This way," replied the man, a Sgt. Bud Collins. Linda hurried through the barrier of cold steel he held open for her and was struck at once by the sour odor of caged humanity. The harshly lit hallway was lined with large holding tanks, but only the one to her left contained prisoners, several disheveled men who stood in the shadows of their lives. Charged with crimes ranging from petty larceny to drunk and disorderly, their confinement might last for hours or weeks. At the moment, their normally passive faces were alert with fear.

She rushed on through a set of gates into a section containing individual windowless compartments. About half were occupied, all were eerily silent. At the end of the corridor, a door stood ajar. Inside lay Ramon Morena, sprawled on the floor, his head resting on his right shoulder, snapped at the neck. He wore only a white T-shirt and jockey shorts. He was a small man, about 5'6", slightly built. His quick hands and graceful movements had made him a natural infielder. He had been a freshman in high school when Linda and Matty had settled at San Xavier, and she remembered his easy laugh and droll jokes when he had come next door to the grade school to pick up his younger brothers and sisters after the final bell. Linda choked up and covered it by pretending to cough.

Sgt. Collins saw right through her, "We can go back outside and wait if you want. Denise has called the Corrections Superintendent, the emergency unit at Tucson General, and homicide over at Tucson P.D. Those guys are really gonna be pissed." His own anger appeared to be directed at Ramon. Collins looked like a man fed up with the world and its inhabitants, dead and alive. Stout and red-faced, about five years from retirement, he just wanted to get it over with, this case and his unfulfilling career.

Linda sized him up and said slowly, "I'm all right. It's a suicide?"

"Right, look at this." Collins pointed to an air-conditioning vent which had fallen from the ceiling and rested on the floor near the body. Ramon's pants were fastened to it.

"Damned creative way to make a noose. Looks like he tied one pant leg around his neck and the other around a rim on the vent. The guard who found him noticed earlier that it had come loose of the screws that held it up. The contraption took the kid's weight just long enough to separate his head from his spine before they both fell. If he'd been twenty pounds heavier, all he'd have for his trouble would have been a few bruises. This cement floor didn't help. He took a shot to the head when he landed. He might have even suffocated on his own blood. See the puddle under him?"

"How long ago?" Linda walked delicately around Ramon's prone figure, gauging the distance of his fall, trying to determine whether he had been able to move after he landed or whether he was unconscious from the moment his neck broke.

"Couldn't have been more than an hour. Lunch was delivered just before you arrived. It comes early on Sundays. The guard found him when he brought the trays. The other inmates swear they didn't hear a thing, more likely they didn't want to. I'd just run back here myself to take a look when you showed up. You know this kid?"

Linda could tell that Collins was wondering why a lab specialist would want to interrogate a suspect. "I teach at San Xavier. I know his whole family. After I saw the paper this morning, combined with our examination of Brody yesterday, I needed to talk to him about what happened. If I'd just come a little sooner..."   She halted in mid-sentence when she noticed the expression on Ramon's still face. It wore the same frozen look of surprised terror worn by Benton Brody in his last moments. She dropped to one knee for a closer look. There it was, the same incredulity, the same profound shock. Maybe they had in common merely the final realization that their lives were about to end. Still, in her decade of forensic lab experience, she had seen this expression only on these two men, joined in life by crime and in death by a fearsome astonishment.   "Did he have any other visitors?"

"Just Morris Peters earlier this morning. He stopped by to ask Morena if he wanted to volunteer a statement. The kid refused to call an attorney or anyone else when he was collared last night. He just kept repeating that he didn't kill anybody, over and over. I told Denise to call Peters at home if she didn't find him in his office. This place will be crawling with folks in a few minutes."

They heard an low aggravated moan from one of the cells. The prisoners had been listening to every word.

Linda examined the pant leg around Ramon's slender neck and then his hands, checking his nails for skin scrapings. There were none. He had made no last minute attempt to loosen the instrument of his death, he had not panicked or changed his mind. She refrained from touching him further, knowing that the paramedics would resent any interference with their work.

She stood and looked around the cell. No one should have to die in pit stops like this, she thought, with no light or fresh air. The cubicle was woefully inadequate. The toilet in the corner was foul-smelling and noisy, and a slow leak from under the grey sink beside it had dampened the area underneath, inviting roaches to come for a drink. The iron bed was chained to the opposite wall only at one end. Ramon had been able to pull the other to a spot beneath the vent. He had then apparently stood on the metal frame while he constructed his own gallows.

"Did he seem despondent when you saw him this morning? Was there any indication he was thinking about harming himself?" Linda's questions sounded more like demands for information than she intended.

"I can't tell you much about his state of mind." Collins was straining to be civil. "I came in at 7:30, but I generally don't hold Sunday church in here unless there's been a request for services. The guards take care of the care and feeding. Bill Jackson is one of the two you saw having words in the office. He was in charge of this section. We'll be interviewing him as soon as we get the body out of here." He seemed anxious for her to finish her inquiry and be on her way.

As they walked back toward the outer office, she had an urge to put questions through the walls to the men who had been Ramon's invisible last companions. Had he said anything to them, had he cried or prayed or appealed during the hours of his confinement here? She asked Collins to get statements at least from the prisoners in the cells closest to Ramon's. He insisted that it was a waste of time, but finally agreed once the officers' reports were finished.

The paramedics entered at a run until Denise stopped them to say there was no need for hurry. They brushed past her to check for themselves and disappeared down the corridor, carrying their emergency equipment on their backs. "Coming' through!"

Peters was right behind them. He looked shocked and pained and uncertain, "I just left here a couple of hours ago. How the hell could this have happened? He was all right when I saw him, upset naturally, denying everything, pretty uncommunicative, but for sure he didn't act like someone on the verge of suicide."

"One of those things, Mo. Look, my guys are clean on this. They did the job they always do. No way they could know the kid was going to waste himself before the prints they took off him were dry." Collins tried not to sound defensive.

"I understand that, Bud. If anyone should have seen it coming, it's me."

The two men conferred on procedures. Ramon's body would be taken to the city morgue. Peters looked at her with a silent question on his worried face. She shook her head quickly and walked across to the bank of windows near the door. She would not watch the coroner cut on this boy who had made her smile, whose kinsmen were her neighbors.

The windows faced south toward San Xavier, several miles and a world away. The two were about to collide with a vengeance, Linda thought, biting her lip. Casualties had already been heavy, and she feared more. The grief she had witnessed in the village that bright morning was nothing compared to the heartbreak the news of such a loss would bring in the afternoon. The lump was back, this time in her stomach, a leaden ball that grew heavier each moment.

She whirled to face the men when she heard mention of Ramon's family, "I'll break it to them, please. His parents and brothers and sisters will be shattered. I'll get Father Flynn, the pastor at the church, to go with me. In fact, he may be with them now."

Peters looked at Collins, nodding. Then he walked toward her, his voice soft with sympathy, "Okay, Linda, but someone from the department will have to go with you, so the report can say the notification was official. I'll follow you out and we can see them together."

They left Collins to his grim task and headed for the dusty parking lot. In a perverse way, the momentary lapses Linda had noticed in Peters' professional composure helped her maintain her own, and she used it to interrogate him. Was he sure of Morena's guilt? Why the quick arrest when there hadn't been time for even a preliminary investigation? For what seemed the fiftieth time, what about the lab findings indicating premeditation? And finally, how could homicide have turned over Brody's body for disposition when it was barely cold?

Morris Peters took a deep breath and began to explain, "The maintenance supervisor at Las Canyons called Sergeant Griffin with a tip on the kid, said he saw Morena poring over a batch of credit cards beside his locker. He knew the boy didn't have the financial clout to afford even one piece of plastic so he figured they were stolen. He says he didn't confront Ramon himself because he's 'wary of Indians.'" Peters grimaced in disgust. "Knowing Brody's wallet was stripped, Griffin got an emergency warrant on a 'what if' notion and nabbed Morena as his shift at the hotel was ending. Some of the evidence was in his locker. Two of them, an American Express and a Visa Gold Card, he had on his person, in the back pocket of his jeans. It pretty well eliminated giving him the benefit of the doubt. He wouldn't explain how he got them or tell Griffin where he had been the day of the murder. He just kept repeating that he didn't do it until the squad car sounded like an echo chamber. By the way, I had Griffin check that empty apartment like you suggested. It showed no evidence of being entered, much less used for an impromptu cocktail party.

"I was going to call you this afternoon to explain what

went down. I just wanted to see the kid myself first, to ask him to come clean. I thought I might even suggest the possibility of a plea bargain. He seemed rational enough for someone that young whose just been arrested on murder charges, not for a minute the type who'd string himself up. As for Brody's body, that was the chief's decision. He's a political animal, probably got calls from City Hall as well as Eastman. You know how things work in these departments where appointments mean everything."

"Yes, that's why I teach school."

"Linda, I'm sorry as hell about Morena. Did you and Matty know him well?"

"Well enough." She told him about the links between the families.

He watched her face sadden and her lip tremble. Reaching for her hand, he said softly, "Nothing like this has ever happened on my watch. I'm pretty stung by it for a lot of reasons, but most of all because it's hurt you. Let's go talk to the boy's people now. I've had to do it many times, it never gets any easier."

She appreciated the offer and said so. Peters appeared to be a man with something to give, but she realized how much more the family would suffer if the news came from a stranger. The O'odham felt, with good reason, that the "milgahn" tended to speak of the dead inappropriately, without respect, invading the realm of personal existence as they had the traditional homelands. The idea of exposing private suffering to the outside world had never set well with the Tohono community, and Linda wanted to spare the Morenas what humiliation she could.

She explained this to Morris Peters with a rare display of diplomatic skill. He seemed to understand, though she detected disappointment in his eyes as she asked him to leave the task to her and to fudge on the technicalities. He continued to watch her as they talked, interested and curious and looking for a way to approach her.

"I don't have any problem with that," he conceded, "but I would like you to call me after you finish, to let me know it's done. I'll be at the office the rest of the afternoon, cleaning this thing up. There will be a mountain of paperwork. The chief will probably show up for a powwow..."

Linda's back stiffened, and Morris picked it up immediately, "Bad choice again, I can't seem to get it right with you."

"Thanks for your help on this, now I've got to get going. If they should receive the news from the wrong source, I'll never forgive myself. Matty's got to be told as well, he'll be almost as hurt as Ramon's family. Of course, I'll call you when it's over." She withdrew her hand from his and moved toward the Ranger.

She watched Morris Peters in her rear view mirror as she turned down Silverbell. He was standing quietly, looking after her, but she had no space for him now. Her every thought focused on the heartbreak ahead. A slow creeping fear that somehow the life she had struggled so hard to create was about to slip from her grasp tore at her insides. She felt an urge to see Matty, to assure herself that he was all right. She jammed the Ranger into fifth gear, hurdled it down I-19, and uttered a collective prayer to all the patrons of San Xavier.

<>>>> Six <<<<>

Unspeakable Sorrow

Matty wandered into the kitchen, found Linda's note, and poured himself a pint of orange juice. Groggy with sleep and sore-armed from a dozen trips to the free-throw line, he picked up the front page to find the reference in his mother's message. As he read of Ramon's arrest, his mouth fell open and he sloshed liquid on the newsprint. He scanned the article quickly, then threw the paper across the room and bellowed loudly enough to rouse the family cat from its morning nap in the window beside him.

"Sorry, Mouser," he crooned. Mouser was an escapee from coyotes and humans that Matty had rescued on one of his hikes through the "Big Res" some years back. Of indeterminate age and line of descent, the cat's silver-grey coat hid several layers of feline flesh, and he chased mice only when his master enticed him with a mixture of threat and encouragement. Now, he nodded tolerantly at the boy and dropped off to sleep again.

Matty grabbed the phone and dialed Tommy Orozco's number. "Dude, you're up? Good, get dressed. We need to get over to Morenas' to check on Rudy. Did you see the paper? His brother's been thrown in jail for killing that guy I found. My mom's down there now, trying to get him out, I guess. I'll pick you up in ten."

Rudy Morena was the same age as Matty and Tommy, and the three had several classes together. "Best buds" since grade school, they ran together, and like pack animals everywhere, they protected their own.

Tommy mumbled something about a hangover.

"Jesus, man, did you go drinking after I left you to take Peg home? I thought you went on to bed like a good boy. Your dad will bench you for a thousand games if he finds out. Can't take you anywhere, can I?" Tommy's drinking habits were developing fast, and they worried Matty more than he let on, "All right, meet me there as soon as you get your head rearranged."

He fretted over both his friends as he slipped into a dark green T-shirt with the words "Mountains Matter" printed on the chest and stepped into his "weekend" jeans with the holes in the knees. Then he snatched the first sweatshirt that came to hand and tied it around his waist. Sockless running shoes completed his look and he ran his hands through his mid-length dark hair to get it all flowing in the same direction. As he slammed the kitchen door behind him, he remembered promising his mother that he would rehabilitate his room, but he knew she wouldn't kick about it, considering the emergency. On his way to the Morenas, he made a quick detour to the church and dashed over to the little chapel to light four candles, for Ramon, Rudy, Tommy, and Benton Brody. He wondered if the events of the past few days were a sign that his adulthood was pending. He felt a heaviness now and then that led him to believe he might have to grow up after all.

The Morena place was a modest grey cement block house sitting back and barely visible from San Xavier Road. Pre-Hispanic Tohono O'odham villages consisted of a small central plaza which served as a meeting area and dance platform, and as a place for ritual and social activity. Homesteads were set away from it some distance, accessible by packed-earth walkways which the women swept clean each day with branches from the desert broom. The layout of San Xavier resembled this ancient settlement pattern.

Several thatched ramadas, shady and open to the desert air, stood in a scatter around the yard. One was a carport, two others sheltered worktables and chairs for the many outdoor chores, a last supported a couple of hammocks.

Horses whinnied in the corral whose living ocotillo fence stretched across the courtyard from the main house. When they were all much younger, Matty had helped the Morena boys install the thorny branches that formed the corral wall. Most took root until the enclosure eventually took on a life of its own. Ramon and Steve Morena, the oldest brother, had also taught Matty to ride horses there when he was nine years old. He had only fallen once before he got the knack of staying on bareback, clinging to the sides of the animal with his knees and holding on to its mane for dear life.

To the left of the corral grew a kitchen garden. It was the children's task to tend it, and Matty remembered how the little ones had shown off their bumper crop of onions and tomatoes this fall. The salsa their mother put up for winter use was proof of their value to the household, something in which Tohono children took great pride.

Today no activity was visible outside the house that Mr. Morena had built himself. He and Ramon and Steven had even installed the plumbing and electrical fixtures. Matty and Rudy had watched as they worked one scorching July day to complete the work before the summer monsoons set in. The doors and windows were wide open to the fall breeze, and Matty could hear quiet conversation inside. He wondered if he should have come. He understood that Tohono people valued their privacy at such times, but he also knew that Rudy would need support. He rapped the wooden door frame gently and Mrs. Morena called out "Venga". The two parents and Steve were sitting with Father Flynn in the living room near the small fireplace, discussing how best to address the dire legal situation confronting Ramon. Where should they look for a lawyer? Would he be released on bail? How would they manage to raise it?

"I'm sorry if I barged in," he stammered, "I was looking for Rudy. Is he around? Hi, Father."

"Hi, Matthew. Has your mother returned from town?"

"Not yet, she left me a note saying she'd see me early this afternoon."

Mendina Morena rose deliberately, gathered the coffee mugs scattered around the room, and moved toward the kitchen for refills, motioning for Matty to join her, "I'm glad you've come, Matt. Rudy's out back and the girls have taken the two little ones for a walk while we get things sorted out here. I wish you'd talk to him, if he'll let you. He was so angry when the call came early this morning that we could hardly keep him from going to the jail right then."

Mendina Morena was about fifty years old and heavy from childbearing and a Europeanized diet of fat and carbohydrates. Her face, now strained with care, was formed in the pleasant pie-shape common to the peoples of the Southwest and Central America, and glowed a soft brown with lovely almond-shaped eyes she had passed on to each of her seven offspring.

"I'll sit on him if that's what it takes, Mrs. Morena. Don't worry about him or Ramon. My mother knows cops, she'll find out what happened. Ramon will be out here demanding his green corn tamales before you know it."

Mendina squeezed his hand and looked away. He took the back door to the yard behind the house and corral. Rudy was nowhere in sight and at first Matty thought he must have walked down the road or gone into the room he shared with his baby brother. Then he saw movement inside the grass "kih" or traditional Tohono dwelling.

Felipe wanted them to understand the lives of their ancestors, so last year he had helped them construct the desert shelter. Together the family had collected and assembled the creosote branches, the mesquite timbers, and the dead saguaro ribs, and roofed the structure with bear grass. The cool room had housed families when they left their villages in the sweltering heat of summer to forage in the cool mountains nearby. Dual residence and ingenious food-producing techniques had made their lives in this difficult terrain satisfying and fruitful for hundreds of years. The grass-frame hut was cooler than the frame houses the post-colonial culture had adopted, and it was more open to the surroundings the people considered sacred.

Rudy had taken refuge here, sitting on the earthen floor against the back wall near the smoke hole. He was rocking from side to side, puffing on a cigarette.

"Those things'll stunt your growth. Gimme one," grinned Matty, sliding his tall frame through the low entrance and settling in beside his friend. He had done tobacco exactly once before and he hated the stuff, but he decided that the occasion warranted a sign of solidarity. "Como estas?"

Rudy passed him the pack and the lighter and said

nothing. His jaw was set and his eyes glittered like pieces of obsidian.

"Listen, I know this is killin' you, but don't freak out on me. My mom is on the case. She's with the police now. If anybody can spring your bro, she can. At least she'll see to his bail, then we can find out what the hell's going on. Everyone knows Ramon wouldn't kill a man for some stupid credit cards and a hundred in cash."

Rudy was a ringer for his older brother as he looked at Matty with a child's hope and a man's anger, "We know it but how are we gonna prove it? We gonna get one of those uptown lawyers in the yellow pages to defend my 'red-skin' brother? The bastards just want to solve a big-time murder and Ramon was the closest minority at hand. Remember Leonard Peltier? He's still sweating it out in Leavenworth. Well, I'm not gonna let the state of Arizona inject Ray with any lethal drug as long as I'm alive. I'll bust him out and we'll go to Mexico. There are plenty of our people down there..." His voice trailed off as he became aware of how farfetched his plan sounded, but Matty realized that Rudy would do anything, try anything, to save the older sibling he adored. He also knew better than to argue with blind rage, so they sat and smoked and the effect was to calm them both.

After a while, they heard the younger children approaching the yard, returning from their trip to the small market down the road, their fingers sticky with candy bars. The thirteen-year-old twins tried to coax the four-year-old boy and his six-year-old sister over to an outdoor spigot to wash off the chocolate before they went inside. Instead, the little tykes swooped into the kih like birds and jumped into Matty's arms. He had become their teenage idol, and they wiped their hands on his clean-shaven face and neck as they gave him a hug. He in turn feigned disgust, "Arghh! Dog germs, dog germs!"

They clambered out, each boy carrying a smaller child. Louis, the baby of the family, was a miniature Rudy. When the bunch of them reached the house, they heard Linda's Ranger pull up in front. The adults rose expectantly as she knocked and entered without waiting. The whole family stood together, looking to her to explain the inexplicable and to help them in their need.

When Matty saw the futility and defeat in his mother's demeanor, he realized with a shock that she could do neither. Never before in his young life had she been unable to make a situation come out right. Ramon must be in deep, he thought. He took Louis from Rudy and stepped behind the others, holding the two young children in his arms protectively.

Linda bowed her head, then looked around the room as if for invisible guidance. She glanced past Father Flynn and let her eyes fall briefly on her son to help her through this moment. Then she turned to the Morenas with all the compassion one parent can extend to another, "Felipe, Mendina, tu hijo es muerto. He died in his jail cell this morning. The officers in charge think he took his own life. I arrived just after. I saw him. Lo siento, Ahnih sho'igchuth hekaj ahpih."

Steven bolted the house, ran to the corral, jumped a horse, and rode away west toward the midday sun and his ancestral home. The twins clung to each other, crying. Felipe held his wife as her legs gave way. They began to sing the ancient and holy Tohono O'odham death chant heard too often in these times for the young. Father Flynn looked helplessly at Linda and went to the children. Matty's heart broke for all of them. He carried the little ones into a bedroom, distracted them from their unknowing confusion with a few toys, and then returned. He approached Rudy who sat like a stone in the dining area off the living room. He put an arm around the narrowed shoulders and searched for a word of comfort.

Rudy began to speak in a monotone in the careful formal manner he had seen in his elders when they met in counsel, "My brother called yesterday to find our father. Our father was working at his job. My brother told me he found plastic money in a trash can on the second floor of the Las Canyones Hotel. It crossed his mind to use them, or to at least ask for a reward for returning them to their owner. He told me he was bitter about having to work as a janitor in the white man's bathrooms, this after he studied for a college degree to do better.

"My brother told me he put the cards in his locker while he thought of what to do. He decided at last to give the plastic to his manager when his shift ended that night. My brother must have been arrested before he got the chance. The law does not hear pleas of innocence from its Indian servants. My brother has never had trouble with the law or its enforcers. And now my brother commits suicide? On a Sunday? With no note for our mother, and no goodbye for us? And now my brother is dead? For what? My brother, my brother..." Rudy collapsed onto the table in front of him, his head in his arms, sobbing uncontrollably.

Matty clung to his friend, tears streaming down his face. The room was full of tears.

Only Linda sat quietly across from Rudy, listening, committing every word to memory. When he finished speaking, she went to the two grief-stricken boys, laid a hand on each, and whispered mother words to them. Looking at her through his pain, Matty asked, "Oh, Mom, how can my friend's brother have done this to himself, and all of them?"

"I don't know, dear," she answered, "I don't know."

———···••••···———

<>>>> **Seven** <<<<>

Journey West

An hour after making her tragic announcement, Linda found herself driving toward the sun. Her destination was the village of Pitoikam on the "Big Res," the location of the Morena family's ancestral lands, and the home of the its female elder, Martha.

At a distance of just sixty miles, the trip still meant two hours on State Highway 86, a well-groomed two-lane that belted the midsection of the two-and-a-half million acre reservation. Turning south at Sells on Indian road 19, which she picked up at the site of the tribal headquarters, she passed Topawa and found the dirt lane which swung back ten miles to the village.

She enjoyed her forays into the heart of Tohono country, and despite the pain of Ramon's passing, its stark beauty soothed her sagging spirit. As she approached Iolgam, the O'odham name for Kitt Peak with its white-domed astrological observatories, the Baboquivari Mountains rose dramatically to her left. Their rounded tops were turning a

soft pink as the sun's gradual descent began to toss colored
shadows across the Pimeria.

Iitoi, the Creator of the Tohono peoples, had forever
lived atop Waw Giwulk or Baboquivari Peak in the center of
the range. From there, He watched over His people and the
land He created for them. Long ago He had given them rain
with the help of Gopher, Hummingbird, and Coyote, and He
had told them He would always be near enough to hear their
cries for help. Linda wondered how many were calling Him,
their Elder Brother, on this day.

Back at the Morena house, she had helped Matty care for
the children until neighbors and relatives arrived. Then she
had volunteered to make the trip to Pitoikam as Felipe called
the one house in the village with a telephone to ask his cousin
to break the news to the boy's grandmother. She, along with
her sons, would preside over the traditional burial ritual after
the Catholic funeral Mass was finished. Linda also had
promised to keep an eye out for Steve, though she held little
hope of locating him in the vast expanse which provided
endless camouflage for a young man who chose to exercise his
grief alone.

The bumpy road circled the 7,700-foot volcanic cone that
was Baboquivari and ended abruptly at Pitoikam. Making a
terrific racket, the Ranger rattled and clanked to a halt in the
tiny central plaza. Martha had lived here for most of her
eighty years, in the arms of her husband's lineage, saying that
she needed to see the place of the tribe's origin each day in
order to properly conduct the affairs of her large family. His
premature death had left her a young widow with six small
children. Refusing to marry one of his brothers as was the
custom, she nonetheless remained near his family in his honor.

Linda stood a moment looking at the diminutive Catholic

chapel which neighbored the traditional dance platform and its border of benches. A traveling Franciscan based at San Xavier came through once a month to say Mass. Otherwise, the villagers ventured to Topawa for church services or provided their own. From the fresh paint and decorations, Linda concluded that they were getting on just fine.

A few earthen ornos gave off wisps of smoke from their morning use. Women baked early on Sundays for the large family dinners in the evening. Other than that the plaza appeared deserted and peaceful, its residents hidden behind groves of palo verde and mesquite.

Linda left the Ranger and entered a path to the right of the tiny church. Fifty feet back, the trees gave way to a clearing with a small adobe house roofed with mud-thatch, fronted by a large ramada where most of the day's activities took place. A table stacked with dishes, pots, and pans leaned against the front wall by the door. Low chairs and stools dotted the floor and utensils as well as flower baskets hung from the ceiling. A twenty-gallon water barrel guarded the far edge of the shelter to catch the runoff from the meager rainfall. A hearth for open-air cooking was removed a few yards from the house to keep the smoke at bay.

A woven hammock occupied one end of the area, and it was here that Linda found Martha Morena, intent over the medicine wheel she held in her miniature hands, murmuring soft incantations designed to protect the living from the restless spirits of those who had died by violence. Scarcely five feet tall, with enormous intelligent eyes and a silver braid as long as her body done up in a bun, she wore a black cotton ankle-length dress, guarachis, and a dainty silver squash-blossom necklace.

Linda loved this woman like the grandmother who had

left her long ago. She came for regular visits to study the
Tohono language, to learn the art of fry bread cooking, and to
cut her fingers stripping fiber for the baskets Martha was
teaching her to weave. Most of all she came to hear the
stories, legends, and history of the O'odham, and for the
personal friendship that had grown between them. Martha
Regina Morena, symbol and siren of her family, showed Linda
the patience that Linda denied to herself.

Recently the older woman had commented on her
increasing frailty. Linda feared the blow of Ramon's death
might further weaken her health, but as she watched from the
shade of a pastel paloverde, she saw that the vitality had
returned to the woman's once nimble hands, and that in her
children's need for protection she had found a reason live on.
For her, the evil that had befallen their house was not an
event, but a presence to be challenged and driven out by right
thought and deed, and by the proper performance of ritual.

Her soft swinging as she rocked slowly back and forth
seemed to provide her with physical solace, and to bring
emotional strength for the journey ahead. One of the few
pieces of furniture to adorn a traditional Tohono house, the
handmade rope hammock served from birth to death as cradle,
resting place, marriage bed, and sometimes coffin. Martha
looked up, nodded, and their conversation began with the
expected and formal inquiries into the other's well-being.
Linda was still a bit self-conscious about her pronunciation,
"Martha, sa: p a'i masma?"

"Ah, Linda, s-ape 'an, a:p hig?"

"'A:ni 'an ba 'e:p m 'a'i s-ape."

"My girl, we may be less well than we have just claimed,
but we will improve if we trust Iitoi and stay loyal to our own
hearts. I am ready to go with you. Just help me carry my

bundles to that motorized gila monster you call transportation." Martha let herself down from her perch with a graceful tilt and extended her hand to Linda.

They entered the four-room house where seven people had lived contentedly and in relative comfort during her decades of child-raising. Grandchildren often came to stay, helping with chores too strenuous for their "bahb".

The two women talked in low tones about the circumstances of Ramon's death. Martha did not cry or mourn for her grandson. The survivors were her priority at the moment. They must be shielded from death's contamination and from the harm to their souls caused by excessive grief. The children must be taught and their parents reminded that going in and out of life, even at such a young age, was a necessary part of the circle. Still, anger flashed behind her eyes as they walked down the path with their bundles of clothing and food. Martha had packed her funeral dress and veil in a faded leather valise. In a cardboard box she had stowed the last of the summer harvest of saguaro jam and some dried venison her nephew had brought from a hunting trip to Mexico. "Until the lifetime of my sons and daughters, the O'odham did not take their own lives. Only when they were directly threatened as with the Apaches did they take the lives of others. Now they say my grandson did both. I cannot accept it until I hear you tell me it is true."

She turned her wide all-seeing eyes upon her student, and so obligated Linda to give an answer. "I cannot say it is true, my Mother. I don't believe he did the murder of the milgahn millionaire, but I can't say more. Perhaps whatever Ramon knew about the killing drove him to suicide, or perhaps one of the other prisoners taunted him with it and in his desperation, he succumbed. I simply don't know, but I intend to find out."

Their conversation on the drive back to the mission was conducted in Martha's language since there would be no time this week for a formal lesson. They spoke of the land and its markings, commenting on each outcrop's features or significance in the lives of the people. They talked of Ramon's final ritual.

"The boy should be buried on his father's people's land, but his mother's devotion to the Christian god is deep." A hint of complaint bordered this remark. "I will respect her by allowing my grandson to remain near the santos. His uncle will see to the piece of ground that will hold him. The Christian service is only a formality, and it must be finished by sunset on Tuesday. Life is filled with responsibility and opportunity, so the period of mourning must be brief. The period of remembrance on the other hand, must never end."

Again the familiar anger, the anger Linda had seen so often this day, flashed briefly across the aged face. Until this day, Martha's lineage had been spared the cycle of despair, alcoholism, and suicide that plagued so many O'odham. When they arrived at the Morena residence, the older woman pulled something from her large woven bag and handed it to Linda. It was the dream catcher Linda had given her when they first met. "You put your own in your classroom for the children," explained Martha. "This one you should return to the place above your bed."

Linda took it in gratitude, but as was customary, without comment. She would need its help to trap the nightmares soon to come. "My Mother, ka:a, nt o a 'ep m-nei."

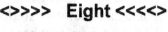

<>>>> Eight <<<<>

Teaching and Learning

When she arrived at school for Monday morning classes, her students insisted on discussing Ramon's death. Their earnest, fearful questions were those of all children. Where had he died? What was it like to be in jail? What could they do for his brothers and sisters? Did it hurt when his neck broke? Would he go to heaven if he killed himself? What happened to make him unhappy enough to want to leave his family?

Linda answered as best she could, but the last one stumped her. After a painful silence, Julio suggested a group visit to the shrine of offerings. The gesture seemed to put their minds more at rest. When her stint as playground monitor ended, she munched her sandwich and reviewed the newspaper article on Benton Brody. It suggested enough suspects to fill every cubicle in the county jail, she thought in disgust, but none of them had even been questioned, much less investigated, only Ramon with those damnable credit cards.

She walked to Ron Verasca's office and phoned Dr. William Radcliffe, assistant curator at the Arizona State Museum. "Hello, Will, how have you been? I haven't talked to you since the museum's centennial celebration last month. It went well?"

"Very well, Linda, but I missed you. You didn't come to any of our events." During his forty-year career, Will Radcliffe had excavated Inca tombs in Peru, built an archaeological field school in central Arizona, established relationships with the native American tribes in the region, developed the finest ethnographic library in the country, and doubled the size of the state museum.

"I know and I'm sorry. Between my teaching and Matty's schedule, the time just got away. Living out here tends to isolate me a bit, I'm afraid."

"We'll have to do something about that. Doris and I are throwing a dinner party next week, and I expect you to join us. Ned Hansom will be the guest of honor. His father was on our faculty and he's an alum as well. He's raised a lot of money for our collections over the years."

"I'd love to come. Doris puts on a great spread, and I'd like to see if the guy is as good-looking in person as he is on camera. Do you have a few minutes for me this afternoon? I need your sage advice about Eastman Inc.'s projects and their impact on your work at the museum."

"I can fill you in on all the unpleasantness, if you've got the stomach for it. Let me make a few phone calls to see if there have been any developments with the lawsuit the department filed against the company last year."

"After the weekend I had, I'm very proud of my stomach." Linda related her experiences and hinted that questions about Benton Brody's murder were part of her agenda.

"I read the whole sorry saga. I thought to call you when I saw Matty's name, but I didn't know about your lab work on the case. Can't escape our anthropological destinies, can we? Come in after the bell rings and we'll have coffee over at Pony Espresso. Say four o'clock?"

"I'm looking forward to it. See you then, compadre."

At 3:15, Linda locked her classroom and crossed the walkway between the elementary and high schools. She caught Matty in front of his locker making plans with Peg, Tommy, and Tommy's girlfriend. "Sorry to interrupt your conference, folks, but I need to speak to the man here for a minute."

"Got to get to chemistry, Mom. You can walk me. See you later, dudes and dudettes." If Matty was embarrassed by his mother's presence, his demeanor did not reveal it. "Wha's up?"

"I need to run to the university this afternoon, but I should be back by supper time. I'll bring something from town."

"No problema, make mine chicken enchiladas. I'll be tied up at practice till six or so. Vaya con cuidado, Mamacita."

As she left the building, Linda found a cluster of animated kids outside, talking and gesturing with great intensity. *Wha's up*? The phrase was still ringing in her ears.

"We want to go over to the Morenas' and see the twins. They babysit us sometimes so we made some cards for them just now. See?" Little Trina showed off some colored papers folded in half with heart-felt messages inside. One read, "I'm

sorry for Ramon. I'm sorry for you." Another simply said,
"You are loved."

"But my sister says we can't all go, there's too many of us,
and we'll make too much noise."

Trying to hide how moved she was by their generosity,
Linda put on her negotiating face. "Why don't you all go as
far as the courtyard and wait there while two or three of you
deliver your cards? They're very nice, and I'm sure the
Morenas will appreciate them."

They squealed their agreement and scurried away in the
direction of the Morena house, deciding as they went who the
ambassadors would be.

Late afternoon performed a one-act play of shadow and
light cast by a chorus line of fifty-year-old palm trees that
stretched from the front gate down to Old Main on the
campus of the University of Arizona. Built of native stone
and two stories high, the second story of Old Main was
surrounded by a wooden veranda. From here in 1890, the two
dozen members of the academic community had witnessed the
arrival of the cavalry and the approach of an Apache war
party. Today, the university's president could watch the
arrival of 35,000 students in pursuit of degrees ranging from
architecture to zoology. Fronting the building were cactus
and flower gardens and a round stone fountain with benches
and Inca doves.

Below it stood the oldest and most stately red brick
buildings on campus. The Arizona State Museum fronted a
manicured flower bed and a grove of Russian olive trees.
Across from it, the Anthropology Building had recently been
renamed for one of its most revered occupants. Inside,
cultural exhibits of Sonora's native peoples attracted visitors

from around the world. Each year Linda brought her students here to show them the history of their region. To the rear of the building were faculty offices, classrooms, and storage facilities for precious artifacts.

This day she turned in the direction of the museum, admiring its simple but elegant lines, the huge arched windows, and the entrance lined with orange trees. Riding the elevator to the third floor, she was greeted by Sheila Rodriguez, Dr. Radcliffe's secretary who looked up from her littered desk with a busy smile. Will appeared a moment later and they descended the marble staircase. At sixty-five, he was still a specimen of a man, of medium height and build with broad sturdy shoulders and a receding hairline that only accentuated eyes that reminded her of the Caribbean. He stooped as they walked to scoop up a scrap of paper and to dust a railing with the sleeve of his tan suit jacket. He loved the place as one of his children, and he cleaned its face in a fatherly way when the dirt began to show.

Exiting the main gate and crossing the street, they strolled down University Avenue to the coffeehouse to order tea and sweets. Will launched into his narrative as they found a table in a semi-quiet spot, and he confirmed that Eastman Inc. was thoroughly despised by the academic community for blocking its research in the Rincon Mountains. Protests had begun after the zoning board had cleared the way for construction of the "Golden Sonora" condominiums. Higher administration, encouraged by the school of engineering which had received sizeable grants from Eastman-backed foundations, was ambivalent about the project, but after it became obvious that archaeologists and geologists would be kept away from their research sites, a civil suit had been filed, supported by the U.S. Forest Service which maintained the wilderness area where the ruins were located.

"The plot thickens," Linda interrupted sarcastically.

"You ain't heard nothin' yet." The curator's slang was rusty. "A couple of years ago a lightning fire damaged the sites badly."

"I remember," recalled Linda, "Matty and I were visiting my parents in K.C. It was a major blaze and it happened just as the monsoons set in."

"Exactly, and that clinched it. The anthropological community and Eastman are forever enemies. Professor Allen Linton in particular hates the whole breed of developer that Eastman represents. He and his most promising graduate student were denied a one-time opportunity to excavate a virgin site, and to obtain truly original findings. I understand they were close personal friends and that she's had some trouble since then." Radcliffe looked at her with sudden enlightenment, "God, you're looking for a murderer. You don't think the Morena boy killed Brody!"

"Will, my examination of Brody reeked of premeditation. With the company's penchant for making enemies, I see no reason to ignore that evidence just because the police caught Ramon with Brody's stuff. Aren't the environmental groups also put out by the ecological impact of Eastman's developments?"

Radcliffe nodded, "Several of them are cooperating to prevent this latest Bonita Canyon fiasco. That new outfit, Santa Tierra, seems to be leading the charge. Lee Sims is its president, and he is acting as spokesman for the whole movement. The S.T. crowd are an innovative, noisy bunch. Because they have very little money, they use a lot of extralegal tactics and civil disobedience to get their point across, which makes for colorful news stories and a degree of unpredictability. The more moderate organizations are a bit embarrassed by them, but Sims is a master of publicity and he does get results. The coalition's office down on Fourth Avenue is serving as "Dump Eastman" headquarters for the time being."

Linda was out of her chair, looking at her watch, "I wonder if it might still be open."

"The place is going night and day, I'm told. I'm sure you'll find someone to give you an earful. Anything else I can tell you?"

"You've been wonderful, as always, Will," Linda said, leaning down to peck him on the forehead, "I'd have been one lonely anthropologist if you and Dr. Lowie hadn't opened office doors and made introductions for me back when. I'll try to get to your shindig next week, but kiss Doris for me in the meantime."

She walked the eight blocks down University Avenue to Fourth and turned south to a small two-story frame building. Its beige plastered stucco was aged but in good repair, and the open front hallway was designed to educate the visitor on the nature of environmental threats, local and worldwide.

She entered the office with its hand-me-down desks and potted plants and saw several workers preparing to close up shop. "Sorry," apologized a man of about thirty sporting a goatee and a Western shirt with string tie. "We're on our way out for an early dinner. There's a strategy session back here at seven o'clock if you're looking for information about our movement."

"I wish I could make it," Linda explained, "but I live out of town. I just wanted to find out how the work is going."

The staff there began to shoot information at her so fast she could hardly keep up without taking notes. Each of them coordinated a specific area of activity. Don, the goatee guy, was conducting the petition drive against the Bonita Canyon project. Signatures were coming fast and furious and would be presented to the city council, the county supervisors, and the state legislature within the month.

A woman of about forty wearing horn-rim glasses and a visor was recruiting volunteers to show up at all city council and county supervisor meetings. The group feared the last-minute introduction of more new zoning permit requests.

A boy of eighteen, a freshman in environmental studies at the university, was mounting a publicity campaign to alert the community to the ecological consequences of the Bonita proposal. Dozens of students and faculty were writing letters to the editor, phoning local talk shows, and inundating media with requests for coverage of environmental impact issues.

An elderly woman with a bandanna wrapped around her white hair had just completed a monster list of telephone calls soliciting people to come to a public demonstration outside the Eastman offices next week.

Linda listened intently and asked if Lee Sims might be available to talk for a few minutes. They looked at each other and Don shook his head.

"Lee left for Phoenix a while ago, be back sometime tomorrow. He's meeting with environmental groups from other parts of the state to enlist their help against Eastman. We need money and bodies if we're going to win. Eastman's high-priced lawyers are pushing to begin construction in Bonita Canyon come early spring. Lee said we might even have to bring in militant organizations like Daily Planet, and we were just discussing how to keep folks like that in the fold. We're already having problems with the Santa Tierra contingent."

"Really? I hear they're effective, dedicated folks." Linda's ears tingled at first mention of in-house dissension.

"True enough," answered the woman in the bandanna, "but we'd like to get this thing done without having our mug shots taken in the meantime."

"Don't you think Brody's death might alter Eastman's plans for the new resort, or at least give you enough breathing room to consolidate community support against it?" Linda asked the question tentatively.

Don answered, "Well, of course, we hope, but we can't quite believe, that Clay Eastman will back off. After all, it was only his brother-in-law and lifelong partner." Apparently, no one in the room was spent with grief for Benton Brody. In fact, a collective if unspoken sentiment hung in the autumn air that made Linda go a little cold.

She wrote Sims' home phone number in the notebook she always carried, a holdover from her previous career, and then she headed for La Indita, a Sonoran cafe further down on Fourth. She bought a heaping plate of Tarascan tacos and the requested chicken enchiladas and walked quickly back toward the Ranger. She considered the atmosphere in the office she just visited, energetic and determined, but also tense and palpably venomous in its hatred of all things Eastman.

When she arrived at her beloved homestead on Los Reales Road, she found Matty in a glum mood, and they began their meal in silence. Then, as he warmed up with the green chile salsa which he poured with gusto over the entire surface of his plate, the boy's natural talkativeness surfaced, "I tell you, Ma, this is about the roughest day I've had since we moved here. In every damn class, kids made heavy remarks about white injustice. I share their feelings, but it was still pretty uncomfortable. The funeral is manana, you know, and my class is going to support Rudy. That won't be any easier."

The pain in her son's face made him look older, and it pulled Linda's heart around in her body. She distracted him by describing her visit with Will Radcliffe, especially the following week's dinner party for Ned Hansom, and she asked Matty to be her escort. She refrained from telling him that Brody's killer was not Ramon. She needed some hard data first, and besides, a vague sense of danger lurked behind her theory that she was not yet ready to face. She left messages on Lee Sims' and Allen Linton's answering machines. Then she prepared lessons for the substitute teacher who would replace her at school the next day so that she too could attend funeral services, a pair of them. "El Dia del Muerte" had come early this year.

———••❖••———

<>>>> Nine <<<<>

A Time To Mourn

St. Andrew's Christian Church hugged the Santa Catalina foothills just west of Ventana Canyon. Built by one of Tucson's noted architects to serve the growing numbers of affluent faithful in the city's northern suburbs, its exterior decor melted into the surrounding desert. Gardens and fountains adorned the three courtyards within the stucco and tile walls. Offices, meeting rooms, and Sunday school facilities opened onto a central plaza in a 'tasteful' imitation of mission architecture.

Not, Linda thought privately as she wheeled the dusty Ranger into a parking lot filled with expensive foreign models. Running late and with the church on the opposite side of the valley, she feared that the crowd Benton Brody's funeral was expected to attract might leave her standing outside.

Inside, the only empty seat was in a corner of the choir loft, high above the proceedings, but it provided her with a perfect view. A long narrow table covered with Spanish lace served as the altar, and overstuffed chairs embraced it from both sides. The ceiling towered to fifty feet, vaulted by monstrous oak beams. The real eye-catcher, however, was the floor-to-ceiling glass wall behind the altar. People attending services could look beyond the minister to the heavens and to the mountains which rose to meet them.

Turning her attention to the crowd, Linda saw Benton Brody's widow, Evelyn, in the front pew. Shoulders slumped with grief and hands folded serenely, her head rested lightly on the shoulder of her brother, Clay Eastman. Her absence from the scene the day after her husband's death had been widely reported, overlooking the fact she had gone directly to the bedside of her mother to break the news and to lessen the shock.

Her brother, now alone at the apex of the Arizona's largest land company, looked the worse for it. He was noticeably gaunt and thinner than when Linda last saw him. His profile revealed a man who obviously believed himself offended by life.

Eastman's wife, Lois Cabot Eastman, was a fair, haughty-looking woman and was dressed to the nines. Rumor had it that she was distantly related to "the" Cabots of Beantown. She, too, wore an offended look, but in her case, the discontent seemed to arise from unwanted public attention.

Beside her sat the Brody daughter, Holly. She looked older than the twenty-two years assigned to her by the newspaper account. She also displayed the demeanor of someone struggling to maintain contact with reality. Her slim-fitting dark green dress was a size too small, and her black pumps were a bit high in the heel for a funeral service.

A young man on her other side supported her and looked distinctly uncomfortable about it. Linda guessed he was the boyfriend, that he felt no particular fondness for the family, and that the feeling was mutual. She also surmised that his excessive thinness and the dark circles under his eyes, which she could just detect from her position, pointed to either insomnia or heavy drug use.

An obvious empty space in the middle of the pew was apparently to honor Eastman's mother who was near death in a Sun City hospital. Until her health had failed, she had been as responsible for the success of Eastman Inc. as her male heirs. Some observers were already questioning the company's ability to maintain its current position once her absence became permanent. Brody's own mother was also too ill back in Connecticut to attend the funeral of her only son. Relatives dotted the rows behind the immediate family. None of them appeared spent with sorrow.

The section behind them was occupied by the board of directors at Eastman Inc. whose tasks consisted mainly of gophering. The family made the important decisions and set policy for the company's developments. Assorted business associates, most noticeably a group of bankers with controlling interests in First Arizona and Southwest Regional, had arranged themselves according to the order of their financial stake in the Eastman empire. Each was accompanied by a sophisticated woman.

The other half of the church was jammed with company employees. Interspersed among them were reporters, acquaintances, and even Eastman rivals, like Barron Kingley. Linda conceded to herself that he made an outstanding appearance at six feet-six inches tall, and that he carried the finest Stetson she had ever seen. She also noticed that he was watching the proceedings with as much eye to detail as she.

A few plainclothes officers were nonetheless conspicuous

in the crowd. They had probably been given the assignment for security reasons, thought Linda with a frown. She noticed Morris Peters among them, studying the crowd. Linda was aware that he had seen her arrival as she climbed over other late-comers, all banished to the rafters, and now he caught her eye, nodding with affectionate concern.

As the organ beside her played softly, she spied the vicar of the Presbyterian Diocese of Southern Arizona sitting just off the main altar in a low padded chair. Other officials from Tucson's major denominations accompanied him. Linda could not help but wonder how many were beneficiaries of the Eastman family's charitable contributions. The pastor's short sermon addressed forgiveness and, from his position in the pulpit, he admonished the congregation to forego the inclination to vengeance and prejudice. "Justice is the province of God, but mercy is the measure of man," he concluded as his audience nodded in less than unanimous assent.

In spite of his words, Linda could feel an undercurrent of fear in the hall of affluent mourners. Violent crime had struck like a dreaded apparition in their midst. Just as they could not keep the scorpions from using the water faucets in their million dollar homes as drinking fountains in the summer, so they were unable to confine the sound of gunfire to the barrio.

After the service Linda watched the crowd file out, and she was struck by how little these people had to say to one another. They knew each other's business affairs and probably their marital ones as well. Still they were unwilling or unable to share themselves even under these tragic circumstances.

She found a spot for the Ranger in the line behind the long cortege as it traveled down the foothills toward the center of town. Her clunky four-wheeler looked like a junkyard refugee between the silver Jaguar ahead of it and the burgundy Peugeot behind.

A massive cemetery occupied a large tract of land on the east side of the city, stretching north to south along a street strangely called Oracle. As the line of cars turned in among the grave sites and snaked its way past rows of silent markers, she observed that newer sections were distinguished by the economic means of their residents, while the older areas were divided into areas with stones engraved with names all Hispanic or Anglo.

As the mourners gathered round the well-groomed interment area, she stationed herself at its periphery. Rev. Tinsley had only just begun the burial prayers when Holly Brody's eyes closed and her ankles gave way. She swooned and collapsed into the arms of her boyfriend who carried her to a waiting limousine. He looked as if he were relieved to have an excuse to make his getaway. Evelyn Brody looked at her daughter with contempt and motioned for the clergyman to continue.

The onlookers looked uniformly embarrassed and many shuffled their feet audibly. Clay Eastman stepped forward in an effort to keep it all together and get the family through the ordeal without further mishap. He requested the prayer book from the pastor and read with a steady voice from the Twenty-third Psalm and from the Book of Job. Then he closed the book, stood quietly for a long minute, and thanked the crowd for its support in the family's hour of need. Finally, extending his arms to his wife and sister, the trio walked slowly through the crowd to the black Lincoln Town Car which awaited them with open doors.

"Pretty smooth," said Morris Peters from behind Linda's shoulder.

"Yes," replied Linda, turning to him with a small smile. "A dramatic moment or two, but it might have been worse if he hadn't shown such moxy. I can see why he gets his way with the county zoning board."

"Too bad about the Brody girl though," Peters observed with a frown. "She's had a drug problem for years, prescription barbiturates mostly. She's been trying to kick it lately, but the boyfriend isn't much help. She's created a public spectacle or two, mostly at their country club, and she's done a stint in the rehab center that was listed in her father's obit. Her mother's been preoccupied with her own middle-aged predicament, her weight problem, and rumors that her husband was bored with her. That hasn't left much time for poor Holly. I think Brody planned to phase out of the company soon so he'd have more free time. He shouldn't have waited."

Linda was listening closely, trying to put the pieces of Brody's family life in order. "On the whole I'd hesitate to describe them as close-knit."

"Not exactly," agreed the lieutenant. His dark suit favored his complexion and complemented his square build, making him almost handsome. "Still, he and Eastman had a profitable business and personal relationship for nearly twenty years. There must have been some family feeling in the group, though nothing like what you see among your Tohono neighbors."

"Right about that," said Linda, starting for her car. Her voice sank, revealing her spirits, "I have to get on to the services for Ramon out at the mission. This is not a banner day for the living or the dead."

"I know, I'm going too. My conscience has been bothering me all weekend. I should have seen the signs that the poor kid was on the edge, but I suppose I was too preoccupied with solving the damn case." His voice dropped, "Can I follow you out there? We could have coffee after."

"Thanks, but I've got appointments with Lee Sims and Dr. Allen Linton later. I'll have to turn around and come right back to town, I'm afraid." She told him about her visits to Will Radcliffe and the "Dump Eastman" headquarters. "I'm more convinced than ever that Ramon had nothing directly to do with this killing."

Peters was surprised, but seemed receptive, "After what happened with Ramon, I don't have any right to deny the possibility. Do you suspect anyone in particular?"

"No, I need to poke around a bit, interview these two guys if they'll let me. I know your chief has stamped 'Case Closed' on Brody's file, so I promise I won't involve you unless I have to."

"All right. Linda, I don't have to worry about you, do I? You'll be careful and call me on your first suspicion?"

"Sure, in fact, I'll call you this evening after I get Matty fed and watered. Don't worry, I'm a coward at heart."

He looked after her and knew better. A dust devil followed her Ranger as it left the cemetery.

———···❖···———

<>>>> **Ten** <<<<>

Last Words

In the sacristy at San Xavier Mission church, Brian Flynn donned his vestments and prepared to conduct Ramon Morena's funeral Mass. As he dressed in the garb of his profession, he found himself wishing he had entered the insurance business with his late father, or that he had followed his brother's advice and studied architecture, or that he had become a gypsy, anything but a Franciscan friar.

To put this boy who had scarcely reached manhood into the cold ground was his most wrenching priestly chore. Flynn had buried a child thrown from a horse and a teenager drowned in the Santa Cruz during Las Lluvias as the Hispanic community called the summer storms, and on both occasions he had told himself they were the last his faith could endure. This morning he resented both his job and his faith.

With a sigh he walked slowly through the sacristy door and into the small, ornate sanctuary. The faces in the dozens of statues, carvings, and oil paintings beamed down their encouragement. The reredos or main altar was adorned with life-sized images of Matthew, Mark, Luke, and John, witnesses to the history of their church. Standing directly above the tabernacle was a fully-costumed statue of San Xavier, whom the Tohono O'odham often equated with both Francis of Assisi and Father Kino. Tohono lore claimed that the spirit of one of the three performed Mass continually when the living priest was about his other duties. Brian Flynn wished that one of them would step in this morning.

"Bart, are we all set?" Flynn asked Brother Bartholomew Berdini who was looking very picturesque in his brown monk's robe, rope belt, and sandals. The Franciscan brother was busy lighting candles and arranging the chalices on the marble Mass table before the main altar.

"Sure now and we are, Father." Unlike his friend from the coal towns of rural Pennsylvania, Bart Berdini's roots were in the Sicilian neighborhoods of Chicago, yet the two men shared an ethnic humor that made their days together comradely. Berdini's vocation had come to him after a life-changing stint with the Green Berets where he grew disillusioned with strategies for killing. Now his world consisted of assisting but never performing pastoral duties, advising but never administering the schools next door. "Always the bridesmaid," he often joked. Today his jokes were forced, his thin, olive-shaped face was strained with suppressed rage, and the muscles of his sinewy arms and legs were taut with tension.

Brian Flynn was concerned about his amigo's intense involvement with the political affairs of the tribe and its impact on the other man's volatile temper. Over the last year, toxic chemicals from nearby construction sites had found their way onto the reservation. Berdini and the tribal leadership had concluded that the culprits were subcontractors of Eastman Inc. They also believed that the company was aware of the problem, but found it convenient to look the other way. The brother's anger had mounted now that illness had begun to appear in children from the west side of the village and in a remote northern section of the "Big Res". Ramon's death had put an edge on him that Flynn had not seen before.

"Are the boys here yet?" Bart asked his friend and boss.

"Nosotros aqui," answered Matty, who had entered through the sacristy door behind Flynn with Rudy Morena on his heels.

Felipe Morena had phoned the rectory last night to request that his son and Matty serve as altar boys at the funeral Mass. It would be good for his wife to see a living child on the altar while having to witness the last rites of another.

"Are you up to this, muchacho?" Bart asked Rudy.

"Yeah, Brother, I'd rather be doing something up here than just watching from a pew." The O'odham were active participants in their own religious rituals, and the passive spectating involved in Christian worship was not easy for them.

People were beginning to stream in, so the two clergymen and their assistants hurried to the front door to greet them. Flynn had roped off every pew and marked each one "Reserved" to prevent the bevy of reporters and the merely curious from monopolizing the seating in the relatively small central nave. He glanced up at the painting of the Last Supper on the wall to his right which had survived two centuries of Sonoran weather and human occupation. The faces of its dinner guests wore stressed, intense expressions, much like those of the mourners coming through the front door. Judas, the traitor, the murderer, lurked in the background. Flynn felt sure that someone like him was at that moment in Tucson, taking his silver while Ramon's parents drowned in shame and grief.

Linda Bluenight had as much as told him that someone else was behind the murder of Benton Brody. The priest had no trouble believing that, but he dared not mention it to Bart. There had been one violent episode in the rectory already, when the monk, powerfully built, had thrown a chair ten feet across the room when news came of Ramon's death.

He stood to the right of the double doors with Rudy protectively at his elbow, while Bart held court on the other side, backed by Matty. When the Morena family arrived, Rudy and Matt escorted them to the front pews and proceeded to the altar. Classmates of Ramon's other siblings entered and sat together. Distant Morena relatives from as far away as Mexican Sonora were distinctively dressed in their more traditional campesino costumes. Six of Ramon's friends carried the plain wooden casket across the courtyard, into the church, and down the aisle, bringing Ramon's body from the house of his birth where it had lain since the police released it yesterday morning. The young men had kept constant vigil on it and now they placed it on a rough wooden rectangular table which had been set up before the altar.

Inside the coffin which Ramon's uncles had made from pinon hastily cut from the forest atop Iolgam, the young man's remains lay wrapped in a hammock, the one in which he used to lounge outside his father's house. His mother and grandmother had bathed and dressed him in the traditional garb of his people. There had been no visitation since the O'odham did not believe in gawking at the dead.

Flynn stopped to greet and bless the family, then began the service. His eyes caught Matty's and picked up an inquiry. He turned back to the crowd and scanned it with a swift, practiced glance. Linda Bluenight was not present. Matt had told him of her attendance at Benton Brody's funeral.

He conducted the service entirely in Spanish, the burial would be done in the native tongue. The choir, mostly older women of the Legion of Mary, sang a version of the Ave Maria just before the Gospel. When he read the passage, "Suffer little children to come unto Me," the shoulders of several family members began to shake. He made his sermon brief, a reflection on consolation which he said would surely come in its time as a gift from God. In his heart, he knew that for some it never came, and for these people it always ran late.

Steven Morena, back from his self-imposed exile on the reservation, gave the eulogy. His anger dissipated by two days alone beside a flowing stream in the Coyote Mountains, he spoke quietly of the nobility of his ancestors, of the courage of his family here before him, and of the endurance of his people. Looking at his mother, he proclaimed that the duality in Tohono faith would provide a double strength to help them in their struggle for understanding. His tone was almost conversational, and when he felt he had said enough, he simply stopped and returned to his seat.

Brian Flynn noticed that Linda had entered the church. She appeared embarrassed at her tardiness and seated herself in the last pew. As he took the wine and water from Matty during the offerings portion of the ceremony, he gave the merest nod in her direction and smiled when he saw the relief on the boy's face.

After the final Mass prayer, he circled the casket, sprinkled it with holy water, and intoned the blessing for the dead. Then he led the way to the front door and stood aside as the box was carried out, followed by the mourners. His part in the ritual of death was finished. A procession formed and began the short journey west down San Xavier Road to the burial ground.

He and Berdini raced to the sacristy to don their civies and hurry out to join the villagers. The crowd was solemn but not silent. People talked quietly, inquiring about one another's families, sharing news, and discussing what could be done in the days ahead to support the Morenas.

Linda dropped back to greet the two, "I'm sorry I was late. The services up in the sky country took longer than I anticipated. Funny, this ceremony is out of the same religious tradition, and yet it feels completely different."

Berdini gave a disgusted snort, "Those foothills Protestants should be praying for their own souls, not Brody's. The mortgage note on that church of theirs was paid off with blood money from his land schemes."

Brian Flynn turned to Linda, "Did you find what you were looking for?"

"You know me too well, Father. The Eastman clan is not exactly the Brady bunch. I felt kind of sorry for them, actually."

Berdini nearly shouted at her, "Excuse me? Let's save our sympathy for our own people. They're the ones losing their young to nooses and poisons, not to mention alcohol and prisons. As far as I'm concerned, the Apaches had the right idea — pick'em off as they come. Brody may have been the first, but I'll bet you the altar wine he won't be the last."

Flynn was shocked at the viciousness in his companion's tone. Linda was alertly curious, "You think someone other than Ramon is responsible for Brody's murder, that it could happen again?"

Berdini became instantly evasive. "I can't say. I just know Ramon was no killer."

"Bart, you've got to turn away from this hatred," Flynn put a hand on the other man's broad shoulder. Berdini went silent and turned his face toward the procession before them.

"Do either of you know a man named Lee Sims?" Linda asked. "He leads a group called Santa Tierra."

The priest shook his head, still upset over his friend's outburst.

The brother gave a mild nod, "I've met him a couple of times. He came out here to examine the results of the dumping, to see if the groundwater might be contaminated. They think it is, probably with PCBs. That could be what's causing the anemia and skin infections we're seeing in the kids. I heard that his wife is thinking of leaving him because his one great love seems to be his cause. I get the idea that he relates to issues better than people."

Berdini's insight impressed Linda. "Well, I have to dash back to town when we're finished here to meet with him. I'm also supposed to see an archaeologist named Allen Linton at UA. Any skinny on him?"

Again Flynn shook his head, and so, this time, did Berdini. "Those bone diggers are about as popular out here as snake bite. No offense," he grinned, in reference to her background, "you're one of us now."

The burial journey reached its end at a gated cemetery. For three hundred years Tohono O'odham had placed their dead in the sandy soil with the shadow of the mission on one side and the view of Baboquivari on the other. Felipe and his brothers intoned an appeal to the ancestors to receive their child, born of water, bathed in sunlight, now returned to the earth. Clan and family members, even little Louis, helped with the digging, lovingly creating the space which would house the remains of their Ramon. The coffin was covered with the same care and attention, but without eulogy. No words were required to tell what Ramon Morena meant to his family and community. Soft singing underlined the simple ritual, its

melody a low-pitched chant which soothed the spirits both
living and dead.

In all the faces, Brian Flynn saw only three he did not
recognize. One belonged to a young woman of about twenty,
short and pleasant-looking but much aggrieved and leaning on
the arm of a middle-aged man who Flynn assumed to be her
father. The woman with them bore a striking resemblance to
the girl. Perhaps they were Yagui or northern Akimel people
from up around the Gila River, those the Spanish called Pima.

Bart, on the other hand, recognized them and went to
offer greetings. Friends of Ramon's, wondered Flynn to
himself, a girlfriend from Tucson maybe? As his friend
chatted with them, the girl began to cry and the father's face
became stern. Bart put a hand on them both in a reassuring
gesture and walked with them toward the mission parking lot.

"Curious," mumbled Father Flynn, not really meaning for
Linda to hear him.

"Yes, Brother Berdini is a very angry man, and more
knowledgeable about this case than he's admitting," remarked
Linda. "When things settle down this evening, would you
mind asking him again how he can be so sure about Ramon's
innocence?" She had also witnessed the scene and wondered
vaguely whether there might be some connection between the
dead boy and the living girl, but she was in too much of a rush
to give it more than a passing thought.

"I certainly will," he replied, "but do you have to leave
right away? The village women are preparing dinner. They'll
be serving in the cafeteria within the hour."

Matty was coming toward them. "Mom, glad you're
back. Tommy's mother wants you to help make horchata for
the kids. She's got her hands full with the tamales, and I mean
literally."

"Gosh, Matt, I just can't. I have to get back to town for

some meetings. Would you ask Mrs. Verasca to help out, and tell them both I'm sorry?"

"Okay, but why are you running back and forth? What are you up to?"

Flynn watched Linda's reaction to this interrogation. She obviously wanted to avoid a detailed discussion. "I can't go into it now, Matt," she answered, her voice edged with impatience, "but I promise to tell you what's going down when I get back. Would you ask Mrs. Orozco to wrap up a couple of those tamales for me?"

"All right. Tommy and I are going to stay with Rudy a while after we eat, so I'll meet you at home later on. Vaya con cuidado." He gave her a quick hug and dashed off to meet his buddies.

"That goes double, Linda. I worry about you conducting what looks like police work."

"I'm just going to ask a few questions, Father. I have a wrenching in my gut that won't go away until I know about Ramon. Don't you feel that way?"

"Yes, but unlike you, I don't know where or whom to start asking. I agree though that Bart might have a useful idea or two if we can manage to have a sensible conversation."

Linda nodded with understanding, "Tom Orozco mentioned something to me about the soil pollution problem. That agave patch he was about to harvest has withered after more than twenty years of growth. It's near one of the dump sites."

She looked toward the parking lot in sudden remembrance, "Do you know a Lieutenant Morris Peters from Tucson homicide? He was at the Brody funeral and said he was coming out here for Ramon's service. I haven't seen him. Have you?" She recited an automatic and detailed description of Peters' physical appearance. "God, I sound like a police blotter."

Flynn was intrigued by the interest he detected in her voice, "I don't know exactly who you're talking about, but I'd probably recognize a detective. I've unfortunately had to extract a number of people from the clutches of Tucson's finest. I don't recall seeing anyone resembling him in the church."

"Right. Well, I need to run. Be in touch with you tomorrow."

Brian Flynn walked deliberately to the whitewashed rectory and entered through the carved Mexican doors. The house was completely quiet because of the staff's attendance at Ramon's services. He crossed the parlor and exited through the rear doors onto a balcony which looked across an expanse of desert. A hundred yards in front of him were the parade grounds where the spring powwow was held each year, and where traditional tribal dances took place at regular intervals. Beyond that were fields of grass and alfalfa grown collectively by the villagers for their horses. If he turned to his right, he would see Linda Bluenight's house across and behind them. In the distance was the city of Tucson. Every day it seemed to move closer, another house, an extension of road, more traffic. He wondered if the mission and its inhabitants were to be engulfed by Anglo expansion like the nearby Yaqui Pascua Pueblo.

He heard a step behind him and recognized it. Without turning around, he asked the dreaded and necessary question, "Compadre, did you kill Benton Brody?"

<>>>> Eleven <<<<>

A Bit of Digging

Sitting at a table with a view of the front door and the traffic on Fourth Avenue, Linda Bluenight waited for Lee Sims at Rosa's Cantina in the heart of Tucson. She had shopped at the consignment shop across the street and purchased a pair of liquid-silver ear cuffs. She had browsed through the Penny Ante Bookstore next to the cafe where students often pinched a paperback from the boxes littering the sidewalk and then stole into Rosa's for a Mexican beer and a quick read at one of the rickety tables. She had even spent a reluctant fifty cents for a couple of dog-eared Tom Robbins novels. Now she waited with some impatience for the very late Lee Sims.

This section of Fourth Avenue stretched from University Avenue on the north to the underpass which lead downtown.

Its stores offered funky clothing and curios, music and margueritas. Rosa's pink stucco storefront was decorated inside with potted palms and cacti. Paper mache parrots hung from the ceiling while watercolor matadors and their bovine victims stared down customers from the walls.

Sims' tardiness did not surprise Linda. She knew of no function sponsored by a left-of-center organization that had ever started on time. Though she was familiar with his reputation as an organizer, there was still a seat-of-the-pants feeling about Santa Tierra's operation. The movement was long on inspiration and short on cash, leading her to wonder if Tucson's preservationists would get it all together in the face of opposition by the forces of cornucopia.

Preservation versus cornucopia, Matty had explained to her a while back, were two antithetical philosophies toward the land which at present commanded center stage in the morality play facing twenty-first century America. It had not been difficult for Linda to lure him into a lecture. "Mom, it's like this. Across the country and the hemisphere, the results of advanced industrialism, pollution, and population explosion are threatening to snuff us. Cornucopians favor letting market forces correct the situation. They hope that technology will eventually solve the problem. After all, waste can be burned, buried or sent to vacant lands, or planets. Populations will decline as the standard of living rises and causes families to want to live in comfort. Development of resources and jobs will guarantee affluence, which will also motivate couples to reduce the size of their families. Entiende?

"Preservationists, on the other hand, insist that this laissez-faire ideology is a recipe for disaster. Soil, water, and air have been dirtied by human hands and by human hands they must be cleaned. Runaway populations are nails in the coffin for each child born as forests disappear, fresh water dries up, and ozone declines. Family planning must be encouraged, perhaps even legislated, to ensure a future for those already alive. Above all, what remains of a clean planet must be saved. Every tree, animal, and stream must be placed beyond monetary value and seen as precious in and of itself. I don't have to tell you which position I take," the boy ended with a deep breath and a slight bow.

Linda was anxious to see what preservation strategy Sims advocated, if he ever arrived. She stepped outside to browse a bit more and found Sims there, soliciting the shop owner for a donation to the Santa Tierra rummage sale. The woman agreed to contribute four boxes of dollar novels, knowing that he would triple the price and make out like an eco-bandit.

Linda recognized Sims from a picture in the newspaper a few months ago. He and several other S.T. members had been arrested after they barricaded themselves in a development-doomed riparian area. In the end, they were carried bodily to waiting police vans after they used said bodies to block oncoming Eastman bulldozers. The company had won a dubious victory as several protestors, including Sims, suffered minor injuries when the dozers nudged them off the road before the police could, or some said would, intervene. Despite the physical violence, it was the Santa Tierra zealots who were ordered to stand trial for disturbing the peace. They in turn had filed suit against both Eastman for inflicting bodily harm and Pima County for failing to protect their civil rights.

Lee Sims stood a robust five feet, ten inches, and was fair

of complexion with hazel eyes and a moustache to match. Intelligently aggressive, he spoke in a soft compassionate voice as he persuaded the shop owner to part with her paperbacks, a voice which belied a willingness to risk his own safety and that of others in a just cause.

"Lee? I'm Linda Bluenight." She was anxious to get this interview under way since her next one with Allen Linton was fast approaching.

Sims extended a friendly and enthusiastic hand. "Linda! Good to meet you. Sorry about the time, I had a few stops to make, lining up goodies for the sale next month. Eastman raises his capital by the bank full, we get ours from the slim wallets of the citizens. Shall we go inside?"

They walked the length of Rosa's small interior to take a table in the open-air patio at the rear of the place, where their only company was a pair of red-headed house finches feasting on tortilla chip crumbs. Sims ordered two bottles of dark ale from Mazatlan and sat back, but before she could question him, he launched into a recitation of environmental problems threatening the delicate integrity of the Upper Sonora.

"One of Santa Tierra's major concerns is the depletion of groundwater and the resultant 'CAP crap', as I call the Central Arizona Project." He leaned across the table toward Linda, hands clasped in front of him. "Two decades ago, it became obvious that the exodus to the Southwest was about to outstrip the desert's ability to provide drinking water from its slim aquifers.

"At that point, politicians struck a deal to divert the Colorado River into canals which would fill the irrigated fields and faucets of farms and homes in Arizona. Now people are drinking the runoff that the 'Water Gods' see fit to flush down here from the river's pitiful leftovers, but even fish can't live in the stuff. The authorities arrest guys who throw a line into the canals to catch a bass or two and say it's to protect them from falling in. They don't want people to know the canal fish are so contaminated that anyone who eats them may start dreaming in four dimensions. To complete the fiasco, they've priced this imported water so that it's now as expensive as Perrier, so local governments are refusing to buy it. The upshot is that the population continues to drain the wells, the water problem is worsening by the hour, and the taxpayers are getting it in both ends." Sims' hazel eyes popped with rage.

"Eastman Inc. lobbied hard for CAP. The company figured the assurance of water would lure even more new-comers to the desert. Now it's socking Joe Citizen with the bill. You know, over in the Salinas Valley, they're having a problem with seawater seeping into the aquifer because it's been so badly depleted. Down here we won't have to worry about salt, we'll be drinking sand instead."

"Doesn't Clay Eastman worry that these well-publicized controversies might drive away business and turn off buyers?" asked Linda.

Sims shrugged, "The company has a battery of public-relations officers who run around the country lying about how sensitive Eastman is to ecological considerations. In fact, I believe poor old Brody was in charge of that area." His tone was less than mournful. "You should see the slick brochure he put out touting the valley's air quality. It reads like a nursery rhyme, 'How now brown cloud.' It even claims the winds coming down from the surrounding mountains blow the car exhaust away, keeping the city cleaner than other urban areas. You can imagine how appealing that pitch is to the smog-ridden residents in L.A. and Chicago. Far be it from Eastman to replace fact with fiction, but the soot we breath is a fairly lethal combination of fireplace smoke and diesel fumes combined with car exhaust emissions. People with lung problems used to move here on the advice of their doctors. Now physicians around the country have begun to recommend southern Colorado or northern New Mexico."

"I haven't seen the advertisement you're referring to," said Linda, "but I did pick up a tastefully-designed flyer describing the new Bonita Canyon project. The picture on the front showed a fairly pristine area at the canyon entrance and depicted some of the more colorful birds of the area perched on top of tall saguaros."

Sims' jaw tightened and his face began to glow, "There won't be a saguaro standing or a cactus wren chirping by the time Eastman gets through at Bonita, but I can promise you he'll do it over the prone bodies of every S.T. member between here and Albuquerque. The annihilation of wildlife habitats we've seen in the rush to build resorts and shopping centers on every corner in Tucson is the best mobilizing tool we have. Hell, our fastest-growing age group is sixty-five and over. People who have lived here all their lives seeing yellow grosbeaks and hummingbirds around their patios now have to net their roofs to keep the black pigeons from roosting. Small animals have less food and are becoming scarce as well. We'll lose everything in another twenty years if we don't take action now, and, by God, we're going to make an example of Eastman Inc. to demonstrate our commitment."

Linda told him about her work at Wa:k, as the Tohono O'odham called the site of the mission, and asked him what he knew about illegal dumping on the two reservations.

"We have a team working on it. You can bet the Eastman people are aware of the use of Indian land as a trash heap and give it at least tacit approval. That kind of disposal is free of charge except for the gasoline it takes to haul the filth out there. We're trying to find the drivers now. From what I gather, the refuse involved consists of assorted industrial solvents, all mixed together, which makes them even more harmful. We're not just talking about PCBs, but about thousands of gallons of lead-based paint, chemical cleaners by the barrel full, petroleum distillates, phosphoric acid, even M.E.K."

"I'm sorry?"

"Methyl ethyl ketone, about as hellish a flammable as you can imagine. Besides the way it poisons the ground and of course the people who come into contact with it, there's also the danger of combustion, especially come summer. With a strong wind to feed it, half the reservation could resemble a giant piece of fry bread in a matter of hours. The final ingredient in this little caldron of toxic soup is the trichloroethylene that the Hughes Corporation and the other aircraft companies poured into the ground out there years ago. That caper has never even been formally acknowledged, much less cleaned up. The T.C.E. has been creeping into the area's groundwater ever since, and what remains in the soil will form a contaminant mattress."

"What will it take to clean the places, and how long will it take?"

"If you can convince the EPA there actually is a problem, you might get some help in five years or so. After our friends in Washington gutted the superfund, the agency cut back the number of waste sites it approved for cleanup. There are hundreds more than its pitiful staff and budget can handle. Your people may be on their own, at least in the short run, and the short run is what counts. Then, of course, there's still the groundwater to worry about."

"No wonder Brother Bart was so furious. He knows the tribe can't undertake a project of that size."

"He's in good company. Eastman and his corporate henchmen have enough enemies to fill your address book ten times over."

"I was going to ask you about that. When you first read about Benton Brody's murder, before Ramon Morena was arrested, did you have any ideas about who might have done it?"

Sims looked at Linda in a way that might have alarmed her had they not been in a semi-public place. "Are you asking me if someone in the Tucson environmental movement could have killed the bastard? Or someone in Santa Tierra? We may be into deep ecology, but we're not into homicide." He did not attempt to hide how threatened he felt by her question

Linda wondered whom he might be protecting. "I just feel that Ramon could not have done such a thing. I've known him and his family for many years."

"You think he was going to be the goat? It's possible. It wouldn't be the first time expediency came before justice, but you'd better look somewhere else for your suspect. My people are not in the habit of knocking off the opposition."

"You have knocked off a few cows though, am I right? Wasn't that your northern branch up on the Mogollon Rim last year that retaliated against the ranchers for declaring open season on the elk when they started to take some pasture?"

Sims slammed his empty bottle on the table and rose from

his chair, "We do happen to know the criminal as well as the moral difference between shooting four-legged and two-legged mammals, lady. I need to get down to the office. Anything else?"

"No, and I'm sorry if I sounded accusatory. I'm trying to find answers, and I'm running into a wall with no door."

"Well, I can tell you this," Sims' anger resembled the throttle on a runaway train, "Personally, I wish all developers were dead or in Detroit. The land Brody and his brother destroyed with their stucco monsters is too sacred to hold his rotting bones. I think the guy who did it ought to get a reward, and if it was Morena, he deserves a posthumous medal. I'll get the check as I leave."

Linda thanked him for the beer and watched him disappear into the dim recesses of Rosa's front room. Despite his protestations, the barely contained violence behind his little temper tantrum convinced her that Lee Sims was fully capable of inflicting bodily harm in his crusade to uphold preservation.

Sims' tardiness prompted a dash to Professor Allen Linton's office at UA. He had agreed to see her with some reluctance, and Will Radcliffe had mentioned that he would not relish talking to a stranger about the Rincon debacle. He had also hinted that Linton was a moody, embittered borderline misanthrope. Linda guessed that having his career stalled at the moment of its greatest potential had not improved his disposition.

The professor's resume revealed a man of high energy and keen intellect. He had conducted his doctoral research in the Mexican state of Quintana Roo, excavating early Mayan temples near Coba where he was better known for his gun battles with antiquities poachers than for his artifact analysis. He had been forbidden by the Mexican authorities from returning to the region after he strolled out of the jungle lugging the dead body and stolen booty of an infamous grave robber. Back in the United States, he had written a brilliant dissertation on the cultural impact of changing ecological conditions in the Yucatan jungle on the Mayan elites.

He easily obtained a faculty position at the university where he acquired tenure and changed the focus of his research to the nearby and more accessible prehistoric Hohokam. Over the years, he had championed the cause of preserving Native American burial sites, although he was a less than popular figure among the Tohono O'odham because of his arrogant manner. He had also initiated numerous encounters with developers over salvage archaeology on construction sites. On the personal side, he had acquired a reputation as a womanizer, especially among the ranks of the female graduate students. All in all, he was not a man to be trifled with, or stood up.

Linda parked the Ranger along University Avenue and walked quickly through the main gate, turning toward the Haury building. She skipped up the steps and entered through the museum portion of the structure.

She loved the smell and feel of the main exhibit hall, lined with artifacts, life-sized models, and miniature depictions of cultures from San Pedro Sobaipuri to Mexican Tarahumara to Chiracahua Apache. A special exhibit, "Along the Yellow Ware Road" was mounted in the center of the large room, four centuries of Hopi pottery with demonstrations of manufacturing techniques and explanations of domestic use and value.

As she dawdled a moment to admire the artistry and functionality of these graceful cultural symbols, she noticed Will Radcliffe across the way, chatting with the clerk at the information desk. Linda waved a greeting, then pointed toward the corridor leading to the faculty offices. Will nodded in acknowledgment of her hurry but motioned her over anyway.

"On your way to see the Man?" he asked with a worried grin.

"Yes, and I'll be late in about two minutes. I wouldn't want him to start class without me."

"Okay, dear, but put on your tap-dancing shoes for this one. There was a huge uproar at the faculty senate meeting this morning. Your friend, Dr. Linton, stood up during the open session and announced his intention to resign and take every one of his grants and graduate students with him if the university authorities and the senate do not support the suit against Eastman Inc. with more vigor. Then some dodo from engineering got up and said the administration ought to go easy on Eastman because of the tragedy in his family. Allen shouted at the guy and accused him of being on the company payroll. Before you know it, the two of them were swinging at each other. Luckily, no punches landed before yours truly and a few other foolish souls pulled them apart, but the dignity of our institution came very close to being sullied by a fist fight within its hallowed halls. If Allen hadn't had such a murderous look in his eye, it would have been comic."

"Sounds like quite a spectacle. I'd love to have seen it, especially you in the role of referee."

"Allen has been locked in his office ever since. I went to check on him, heard him pounding furiously on his PC, and decided to let discretion be the better part of valor for a change. Just be a little careful when you knock, and stay low."

"You're a sweetheart. If you hear a racket on the stairs, it'll be me, coming down head first." Linda gave her friend's hand a squeeze and raced through the corridor leading to the departmental offices.

In contrast to the grace and dignity of the adjacent museum, the anthropology digs were regulation ugly. Cramped cubicles housed the country's finest scholars, and badly designed classrooms served the next generation of ethnographers and archaeologists. All were painted an eye-numbing olive. "This place makes my little work area look like Harvard Yard," thought Linda.

She rang for the creaky elevator to take her to the fourth floor where Linton was quartered, though it would have been faster to walk. The metal doors opened with a clank and she stepped inside to find the graduate student adviser, Herb Lowie, in serious dialogue with the department chairman, Len Wissler.

Both were distinctly Anglo-Saxon, middle-aged, and dressed in identical Panama shirts. Lowie was short, balding, and sported a pleasant paunch. Wissler's features were quizzical and his thin lips disguised a surprisingly wry smile. They were discussing what to do with the raucous professor, and they looked slightly embarrassed when Linda acknowledged their problem, "Gee, guys, haven't had this much fun since the sixties, have you?" She laughed as the elevator ascended with an arthritic scream, "I'm headed into the combat zone now. Any coded messages to relay?"

"Just stay low," they recited in unison. Apparently it had

become the new departmental slogan.

She found Dr. Allen Jasper Linton's door slightly ajar, so she watched him for a minute before announcing her arrival. His profile glared at the screen of his computer. Possessed of huge hands and a large head with great protruding ears, he reminded her of Paul Bunyan. His face was covered with a full beard and, as she would soon discover, he had a booming voice to match. Combined with a six foot four inch frame, all this made him too much man for the corner cubby-hole to which he had been banished him for one too many displays of temper.

She cleared her throat and rapped the door at the same time. Linton looked up quickly, and his dark eyes flashed over her. She shivered slightly, "Sorry if I'm late, I'm putting on a lot of mileage today."

Her attempt at light conversation fell on deaf ears. "Sit down, please, and tell me what's on your mind. You're an anthropologist of some sort, aren't you? Not one of those damnable contract diggers, I hope." Contract archaeology had become big business in the Southwest. With his penchant for pure research, Linda was not surprised that Linton condemned it. She noticed that he seemed to take pride in his lack of social skills, and turned the supposed defect to his advantage by using it as an instrument of interpersonal power.

"No. Matter of fact, I gave up professional anthropology to teach elementary school out at Mission San Xavier some years back."

Linton looked at her as if she were speaking some ancient and unfathomable language. Ignoring this, Linda took a deep breath and plunged on. Doing a lot of that today, she thought to herself. "I've been following your dealings with Eastman

Inc. and I realize you've had some setbacks..."

He gave a "Harrump!" that reverberated through the open door and up the hall.

"I'd like to know how you see Benton Brody's murder. Do you think the Morena boy killed him? If he hadn't been arrested so quickly, might you have guessed or suspected that the assailant was known to Brody? He and his brother-in-law are reported to have had any number of enemies. I've even heard that of you..." Fearing she had said too much, Linda faltered.

Linton did not. "Hey, lady, I wish I had killed him. I thought about it a time or two, it's just that you can't get away with that sort of justifiable homicide in this country. I'd have started with Eastman though, the grimy bastard. Did you see the article in the paper a few days ago where he claimed that the gilded concentration camp he built in front of our sites in the Rincons was a service to the elderly community of Pima County? Those condos from hell start at $100,000!

"I had three grad students with dissertations in the making who needed to excavate the village ruin to verify their theories about why 1350 A.D. is such a widely-shared date for the devolution of Hohokam civilization in this area. One of them was especially close to finishing a brilliant piece of work." Linton ground the words between his teeth.

Linda took this as a statement of personal as well as tutorial involvement.

"Yeah, I could name a dozen candidates with reason to plug the son-of-a-bitch, including some of his company weasels. He hired and fired them as often as he changed ties. Then there are the environmental folks. Don't let them fool you. They're tougher than they look. They all apparently lucked out and the kid got to him first. Didn't he?" He asked the question with genuine interest.

"I'm having trouble with it," Linda answered, and told him why. Linton looked her over again, sizing her up. "If you want to rule out the Indian, which I'm not sure about, my guess would be that another developer hit him. They're all a bunch of cannibals. Get the bio on Barron Kingley. He wants that Bonita Canyon project in the worst way. He might just get it now, too. You see, Ms. Bluenight, Brody and Eastman are merely gunslingers with briefcases. Like the movie says, there's always somebody faster — a bigger deal, a larger bid, a better blackmail. As far as I'm concerned, the bullet did everybody a favor. Now if you'll excuse me, I have a letter of resignation to write."

"Sure," Linda was relieved, but frustrated by what she had and had not learned. "Forgive my forwardness, but I'm surprised to see you quit in the middle of a good fight. Those sites mean a great deal to you, don't they?"

The idea of her questioning his mettle made Linton's eyes smolder, "Darlin', I've stood shoulder to shoulder with the people in this department through budget-slashing bouts with the state legislature. We've struggled together to protect academic freedom and defend our students from curricular meltdown. In another life, I faced jaguars and vandals with my bare hands. I'd meet Eastman or his henchmen at the OK Corral at sundown, but there's no hope without the backing of the few institutions Eastman does not already control, and believe me, their numbers are dwindling fast. Good luck." With that he returned to his computer and Linda was left to let herself out.

As she descended the staircase across from Linton's

office, feet first, she concluded that the professor was a man dangerous to his enemies, loyal to his colleagues, patron to his students, and passionate about his work and his women.

She passed Herb Lowie's office and he called to her through the open doorway. She smiled at the secretary as she passed through the tiny outer office and bowed to the halo-haired man seated behind a stack of correspondence, "Here I am, vertical and unbloodied. Surprised?"

"A bit, but glad to see you made it out of the lion's den. You're a brave woman."

"Just foolhardy. Herb, do you think our man Linton really killed that poacher in Mexico? It sounds too Indiana Jonesy to me."

"Well, there's no smoking gun in a literal sense, although gunfire was heard coming from Linton's camp the day before he emerged with the corpse and the loot." Lowie searched for his pipe on the cluttered desk in front of him, "Excavators in the next century may uncover the bones of pothunters dispatched by our burly friend."

Linda looked at her watch and jumped, "Look at the time. Matty will be calling the hospitals. Thanks, I hope the guy doesn't resign. The dust he stirs up in this place keeps the rest of you from rusting out."

"And sends us running to the antacid counter," laughed Lowie, "See you later."

As she twirled the Ranger out of its parking niche, she considered what she had seen and learned this day, and she wondered how much of it would ultimately help her. Both the men she had just met were filled with a hate strong enough to unleash violence, as Linton had demonstrated that morning.

As for Lee Sims, his organizational tactics were becoming

more extreme with every protest. Denials to the contrary, his tendency to deal with a problem through action rather than negotiation kept him in the picture as a potential killer.

She also thought of how tired she was, and how eager to get home to Matty and Mouser and a warm bath. She stopped at Rosa's again and bought half a Sonoran pie, in case Matty did not get his fill at Ramon's funeral dinner. She was tempted to pick around the edges of the pastry as she drove across the desert. The aroma of spices, corn, and shredded beef was causing her stomach to talk back.

As she approached the Valencia Street exit along I-19, the mission church appeared in the distance, its towers spread like a dove's wings in the gentle light of dusk. She was grateful for the lingering sunset, as she was for every moment the Sonora bestowed, and she slowed the Ranger to enjoy the soft baby-pink glow of the Santa Ritas on her left.

She took Valencia west to Indian Agency Road and dropped south to Los Reales and home. The house was dark when she pulled off the black top and down the long drive. Matty might still be with the Morena boy. Perhaps he and Tommy had taken Rudy to town to distract him from his grief. On the other hand, he might be in the kitchen at the back of the house, sitting by the window with Mouser, watching the sunset on the Catalinas across the valley.

She fumbled with the screen door, holding it ajar with her foot while she balanced the pie in one hand and her keys on their heavy ring in the other. Finally she found the right one and twisted it into the front lock. Then she turned the handle and swung open the heavy wooden door. She stepped through to find Matty crouched on the sofa in the darkened living room. His eyes were wide with fear. She nearly dropped the plate in shock.

"Close the door!" he whispered hoarsely, "We've got company."

———••⋅⟶⋅••———

<>>>> Twelve <<<<>

House of Fear

Linda crossed the room, sat down on the sofa beside her son, and put the plate on the floor with a clatter. "Matty, boy, que sucede? Decime que paso?"

"I'm too freaked out to remember my Spanish right now, Mom." The boy's face was the color of fresh ash. He gripped a flashlight in his right hand and a tennis racket in his left, but that did not prevent both of them from shaking. A kitchen knife and a tire iron lay on the floor beside his feet. Mouser was wedged into the corner of the sofa behind his back and looked distinctly annoyed about it. Glancing around, Linda could see that the furniture had been pushed against the windows which were low to the floor, and that the telephone in the living room had been taken off the hook. The only curtain left open to the evening light was the one beside the large plate-glass pane near the front door that gave a full view of their driveway, the road, and the mission beyond.

Matty's eyes were glued to it. "God, I'm glad you're finally here. I was beginning to feel like that dumb kid in 'Home Alone.' Some SOB's been making threats. He started calling a while ago, right after I came home from the funeral meal. Rudy's folks wanted them all to be together tonight so Tommy and I split. I was gonna catch up on some history assignments, but the phone rang as I walked in."

"Oh, dear, I'm so sorry." The apprehension that Linda had tried to ignore now seared her insides like grease from a burning vat.

"Geez, Mom, the first time he said, 'Where's your mother?' and hung up. A few minutes later, he rang back and asked, 'Is she home yet?' Then, on the third call, he really got nasty and said, 'Maybe she's not coming.' That time I hung up. The damn thing rang at least half a dozen times so I dumped the receiver. Just when I thought the whole thing might be a sick joke, someone began driving past the house and shining a bright light toward the porch. The glare kept me from recognizing the vehicle or the driver, except it seemed like a car rather than a truck or van. He made two or three passes, but I haven't seen him for about fifteen minutes. When I realized you were late coming back from town, I began to really get the creeps. I was about to try getting a dial tone and then 911 when you pulled up. I watched the driveway to be sure no one was following you. Mouser and I were going to nail the bastard, weren't we, boy?"

Mouser managed to climb out of his hole, and meowing loudly, made his escape to the kitchen.

"Dear God," Linda felt as if oxygen had been sucked from her body. The lump was back and this time it was the size of a bowling ball. She put her arms around Matty and held him tight for a long minute. Then she rose and began turning on every light in the place. She also returned the phone to its cradle, in case they needed to ring for help.

"You didn't recognize the voice, I'm sure," she said as she tried to sort out who could do this evil thing.

"Nah, he had his hand or maybe a cloth over the receiver." Matty paced the floor now, swinging his weapons back and forth. His foot caught the edge of the pie plate and sent it skittering across the floor. Mouser, looking amused and curious, came back in for a look. "Damn! Sorry Mom, I guess I'm a little weird with all this."

"No foul," Linda said, as she retrieved the thing and checked for damages. "At least you didn't plop down in the middle of it. Let's eat this before Mouser does."

They fell into a thoughtful silence as they arranged the kitchen table and thought about who might hate them enough to invade their domestic tranquility. Turning to each other at the same time, they asked each other the same question, "Who do you suppose...?" They laughed and tried again.

"I can't come up with anybody," complained Matty, shaking his head and furrowing his brow. "I haven't had any trouble at school or anywhere else for that matter. Besides, it was a man's voice, deep and husky. I don't know anyone my age with a croaker like that." His fear was being replaced by frustration. "How about you?"

Linda took a long look at the man-child in front of her, wondering if he could handle the idea that Benton Brody's killer might have come calling on them that evening. She decided to hold off, mostly because she was having trouble believing it herself.

A number of people knew that she believed Brody was assassinated. Both the men she had met that afternoon knew they were on her list of suspects. Sims would have had plenty of time to pull such a stunt if he considered her a threat.

Linton might have been a bit more pressed, but if he had left his office just after she did, he could have beaten her to the house, especially since she stood chatting with Rosa after she purchased their dinner. The calls could have been placed at a public phone or from his cellular along the way.

In either case, the caller might have meant to leave a warning for her, knowing she was en route. When he reached Matty instead, he could have altered his plan, thinking she would be even more frightened if the danger included her son. He was right.

The magnitude of the incident hit her like a punch to the stomach. She began to shiver with anxiety and sat down heavily at the kitchen table. Think, she reprimanded herself, turning toward the window and away from Matty who was rewarding Mouser for his support in time of crisis by feeding him some Mighty Cat. Who else might do this?

Both county and city law enforcement had been apprised of her lab report which clearly stated her hypothesis. She felt sure that the county agency was mightily miffed by it. If an innocent young Tohono man had been driven to suicide by maltreatment, the detention facility and the sheriff's department would suffer immensely from the publicity.

Even the newspapers now had a copy of that report according to the article in the *Tribune*. She did not believe that the reporters themselves would harass her, but she knew that developers like Barron Kingley courted the editorial boards of Tucson's major media. If an enterprising columnist had passed her findings unknowingly to the person who responsible for the killing, she could be a sitting duck.

Bringing her speculations closer to home made them even

more distressing. Could one of Ramon's friends or relatives have blamed her for his death, believing she could have saved him somehow? If the caller was from the village, perhaps he had convinced himself that she was lying about Ramon's suicide. Mistrust of the Anglo police was so rampant that the person might believe Ramon was beaten and then hanged and his murder covered up in a ruse to protect the police.

Then again, a traditionalist might have decided that she had been contaminated by her close contact with violent death. If so, she now posed a threat to the health of the village, especially its children. She was not Tohono O'odham, and not subject to the culture's cleansing rituals.

Of course, it was possible that the threat had nothing to do with the Brody case. There were a few people in the village, more on the "Big Res," who considered her an interloper, even now.

Finally, there was the chance that alcohol might have fired up one of the village residents. One night not long ago, a member of the village council had chased his wife out up a ladder and onto the roof of their house. There he had announced to her that he had received a message from the Creator Who had directed them both to join Him at his vacation home in Guevavi. With that the man had approached her with a rusty saw, too dull to do more than bruise the skin. She in turn knocked him off the roof. He had broken an arm but had no recollection of the incident.

"Yum, Mom, this smells good," exclaimed Matty, pulling the steaming pie from the oven and sliding it onto the table in front of her. "Believe it or not, I'm still hungry."

"I believe it." Grateful for the distraction, Linda cut a huge wedge and heaped it onto Matty's plate. Trying to reassert a semblance of normality, she pushed it toward him and made a little face as she saw that he planned to drink an entire quart of Grapade with his meal.

She took a tiny sliver of the casserole that so had tempted her an hour ago and picked over it with a total lack of appetite. They made small talk tentatively, distracted by an irrational fear of sound, but the phone remained quiet in its cradle, and the few vehicles that traveled Los Reales Road after dark passed them by.

Matty explained that the whole village and half the "Big Res" had turned out for the dinner that afternoon. Every person brought food, even the little kids who carried an ear of corn or a wrapped tamale.

"I wish I'd been there," said Linda, with regret in her voice. "All of us need to feel that we belong..."

"Specially when life gets scary." Matty finished her sentence and put down his fork. His plate was already clean of every morsel. "What were you doing in town all afternoon?" he asked.

She told him that she had consulted with Will about additions to the university curriculum for Native American students. The bowling ball gained weight with every word of her white lie, but he seemed satisfied, so she grabbed their plates and headed for the sink. "Help me with these, will you? Then you'd better get to those assignments. I'm going to monopolize the bathroom for an hour."

The warm water lulled her almost to sleep as she rested body and mind in the antiquated tub, sitting on its claw legs high off the floor. She had just begun to relax when the ringing began. The sound pierced her like a shot and she sat straight up, splashing the cat who had chosen an unfortunate spot beside one of the tub's legs for a nap.

"Mom?"

"What Matty?"

"Shall I get it?"

"Yes, but if it's him, hang up before he can get more than a word out."

"Right."

He answered with a halting "Hello," then breathed a sigh of relief that she could hear through the walls. "Mom, it's Father Flynn. Shall I say you'll call back?"

"No, thanks, sweetheart. Just tell him to give me a minute."

The adrenalin rush from the false alarm had made her a bit lightheaded so she took her time getting out of the water. Wrapping herself in the baby blue terry-cloth robe Matty had given her for Christmas, she made her way into the living room. She could not help but keep an eye on the road as she talked. "Hello, Father, is your day finally over?"

"To tell you the truth, dear, I don't know yet. Any luck downtown? I'm still worried about you poking around in this thing by yourself."

"It seems we may have real reason to worry now." She told him about the mystery caller and admitted her nervousness about staying alone with Matty that night. The idea that she no longer felt safe in her own home infuriated her.

"Dear Lord! Linda, I want you and Matty to come and stay here at the rectory. You can have Conchita's room off the kitchen. She had to go home to Santa Rosa to nurse a sick sister. She left enough tortillas and beans to feed the staff for a week, and there are several priests' quarters Matty can use. I can't bear to think of you there with some pervert prowling around. I must tell you though, this place is by no means tension-free." Brian Flynn described his encounter with Bart

Berdini earlier in the day. "Perhaps I was too impetuous when I asked him about the killing. It was a downright accusation, but I was sure from his remarks that at the very least he was taking ferocious satisfaction from the man's death."

"You certainly took a chance, Father. What if he had said yes?"

"The point is, he didn't say no. He stood there looking at me, not as if I'd betrayed him, but almost as if he felt sorry for me. Then he turned without a yea or nay, walked out of the rectory, got into that old Plymouth of his, and drove away. I haven't seen him since. I still don't know that he's guilty of any wrong, and now the idea of his pulling the trigger doesn't make any more sense than the notion of poor Ramon's doing it."

"There's one difference, Father."

"What's that?"

"Ramon didn't own a gun. The Morenas have hunting rifles, but Ramon didn't take one when he moved to town. Brody was killed by a small-caliber handgun anyway. Unless the boy stole one or purchased one the day of the killing, the police have a hole in their case. Of course, it doesn't matter now. They will say they would have found it if Ramon had lived to come to trial. And the truth is that Bart does have several firearms, doesn't he?"

"Yes, he does. Aside from his practically uncontrollable temper when it comes to the victimization of our people here, that's another thing that made me wonder if he could have been involved? But how did you know about his collection?"

"Matty's friends have mentioned that he has taken them hunting out west. Do you know whether it includes a .38 of any kind?"

"I'm sorry, I can tell a pistol from a shotgun by the length of the barrel, and that's the extent of it. Now, why don't the two of you pack a kitbag and come on over."

Linda was suddenly energized by her outrage, "I'm not leaving here on a bet, Father, but hold on a minute, will you?"

She turned from the phone and called to Matty. He came in carrying his history book. "Father has invited you over to his place to spend the night. I think it would be a good idea."

"You coming?"

"No, dear, I'll stay with old Mouser here. We'll be fine. I can always join you if I get spooked."

"Tell him, thanks, Mom, but I'll hang out with you. We'll throw up some barricades and give that guy all the shit he can handle."

She relayed the message, sans epithet, to the priest who begged them to call or just show up at his door if they should change their minds.

She made certain the house was lit up like a candle and rechecked all the locks. Then, remembering something she had seen in a bad movie, she placed dishes and silverware on top of the furniture Matty had stacked in front of the windows.

He was stretched across his bed when she looked in, his schoolbooks and weapons spread out on either side. He informed her that he was going to sleep in his clothes, and he asked her to leave her door open. She bit her lip to keep it from quivering, bent over to touch his cheek, and returned to the kitchen.

She prepared each of them a sack lunch for the next day, the standard sandwich, fruit, and cookies. Then she stowed them in the refrigerator and heated two mugs of milk. On her way back to the bedrooms, she stopped in the living area to unplug the phone and tuck it under her arm.

She slipped through Matty's doorway quietly and placed one mug on his bedside table. The other she carried across the hall into her room. She stuffed the phone under one of her pillows to muffle the sound in case the worst should happen. Pulling down the covers and wondering how all the events of this endless day could have taken place in just twenty-four hours, she crawled between the white cotton sheets with a pleasured groan. Sipping her soothing childhood drink, she opened a volume of poems written by a Chickasaw friend and began to read.

A few minutes later, the sound she had dreaded made its ugly way through the foam and feathers. She snatched the receiver before it could send off more than a half-ring. The guttural male voice, muffled by a handkerchief as Matty described, said, "Think of your kid and your students. Don't go off the reservation."

<>>>> Thirteen <<<<>

At Death's Door

L inda awoke at dawn to find Matty curled up like a great puppy at the foot of her bed. His mouth was slightly open, and his breath came softly as his chest lifted and fell in the regular rhythm of innocent rest. She wished her own had been as easy.

The late-night call had convinced her she had nothing to fear from the people in the village or out west. No member of the tribe would use demeaning language like "Don't go off the reservation," nor would a Tohono man mention the tribe's own schoolchildren as possible targets of reprisal.

The threat against the defenseless and the loved echoed in her ears, and it left her two choices. She could accept the status quo and pretend that Brody's murder was the result of a crime spree by a disgruntled Native American. The police, the media, and the people of Tucson had already made their peace with that idea. Or she could follow her conscience and her professional instincts, and seek Brody's killer to clear Ramon's name and expose the corruption and civic distortion within Tucson's economic and political sectors.

If she chose the first option, the calls might stop. Still he would be out there, looking over her shoulder, watching her son and her charges, an unknown force with power to touch their lives any time he wished. The other option put her directly in harm's way. The caller might be bluffing to intimidate a lone woman into silence, but more likely he meant business. His behavior the evening before had been too obnoxious to be taken lightly. Someone sick enough to harm the people she loved was lurking in the shadows of her life. That brought to mind a third choice. She could run. She could take Matty in one hand, her car keys in the other, and set out for a new place. She had done it before. She could land a teaching job in British Columbia among the tribes of the Northwest coast. Looking down again at the boy's peaceful expression was enough to tell her that Matty would never accept another move. She could not avoid this predicament, and she could not abandon these people or her work here.

As if his dreams had told him her thoughts, he opened his eyes. "What's on for today?" he mumbled groggily.

"Let's drive to school together this morning," answered Linda, "We can figure it out on the way."

They left the house earlier than usual, taking the precaution of locking Mouser inside. They also searched out the seldom-used keys for the dead-bolts on both doors. The metal turned hard from lack of frequent use and Matty's effort to secure them required a few minutes of real effort. "The cat burglar of the month couldn't get in this place now," he said, shaking his fingers.

Linda accompanied him to his homeroom despite his protestations.

"Humor me," was her only reply.

Rather than informing his teacher, Linda confided in Ron Verasca whom she found down the hall reviewing attendance forms. As principal of both schools, he also had a tiny office in this building.

As she related the events of the previous evening, he listened with a calm face and alarmed eyes. "I'm glad you didn't tell Mrs. Lena right away. I'll call a meeting of all Matt's teachers during morning study hall and let them know what's going on. That way we can provide a presence when he's in the school. I'll get hold of Big Tom Orozco, too. He can work out something for basketball practice.

"Linda, this is getting too dangerous, and I don't mean because you're a woman. Scumbags like this can be unpredictable as hell. They can fade into the woodwork on a moment's notice or ...they can be a lot of trouble. I think you should call the police pronto. I know they haven't responded the way we hoped, but they'll look out for you now. This might even convince the milgahn detective squad to reopen Ramon's file."

"Let's hope so, compadre," replied Linda, "because it's the only way to end this thing. I'll see you next door."

She got Peters when she phoned the homicide unit at morning recess. "Linda, the first priority here is to protect you and Matty from this creep. Most of the time, these guys are too cowardly to do more than talk, but there's no sense taking chances. I'll see the chief soon as we hang up. Then I'll call the sheriff's department. We'll have your area patrolled as often as we can, but you're awfully remote out there on Reales. I'm not surprised that you didn't take Father Flynn up on his offer, but I wish you would think about it for tonight. If the rectory isn't your cup of java, maybe some friends can help until we have a chance to 'round up the usual suspects.'"

"I understand, Mo, but Matty and I will stay put for now. Our house is pretty secure, and Ron says the village council may do some patrolling until things calm down, even though technically we're not on reservation land."

"I'll call this evening to check on you." Peters sounded pleased to finally be on a first name basis. "Don't jump too high when the phone rings."

Linda felt better at having partially confided in her friends. As she stood looking out Ron's window toward the cross on the hill and Our Lady's shrine below it, she wondered how good a friend Peters might become.

A flash of memory took her mind off romance. She picked up the receiver again and punched in the number for Eastman Enterprises. The taped voice did not reveal a method for speaking to the president, so she waited on the line for a real person.

Finally, the woman who in pre-electronic times had monitored callers' requests firsthand twanged "May I help you?" and then informed Linda that Clay Eastman was tending to his family. She was naturally reluctant to share his home number with a stranger, but after Linda enlightened her about having met Eastman and about her official work with the police, she skeptically relented.

Linda was surprised to hear Eastman's own voice over the wire when she rang. "Yes, Ms. Bluenight, I do remember you. I've been so busy with the funeral and family affairs that I haven't had the opportunity to thank you for your work with my brother-in-law. My sister was adamant about having the services take place without delay."

"I was glad to do what I could. Mr. Eastman, could you spare a few minutes to talk with me this afternoon? I have just a few questions more about Mr. Brody." It did not trouble Linda that the ambivalence in her speech gave Eastman the idea that she was in pursuit of police business, since she knew he would not agree to see her otherwise. They made an appointment for 4:30, then she rang off and hurried to class.

At lunchtime, she ran over to the high school again and found Matty with Tommy and some of the team in the small cafeteria. He looked at her curiously when she told him that she had been called to town again, but he did not question her in front of his friends. Thankful once for peer pressure, she asked him to go to the rectory or to Coach Orozco's house after practice and she instructed him firmly not to come home until she called to give him the okay.

After the bell sounded afternoon dismissal, she sped north on I-l0 toward the Catalinas. Twenty miles from the reservation, she took the exit to Ina Road and followed it east to Skyline Drive. Another few miles led her to Sunrise Parkway. The foothills which circled the city of Tucson were also its fast growing suburbs. Some subdivisions she passed consisted of middle-class track housing with row after row of repetitious pink stucco split-levels sporting double garages and pocket-size grass lawns. Others were more exclusive and were built on spacious lots, marked by distinctive landscaping and architectural styles. Higher still up the mountain range sat the perches of the powerful, at the end of hastily built dirt roads, looking majestically south, in total visual and economic command of the valley below.

She stifled a twinge of cynicism as she searched for the mountain road which separated the merely affluent from the truly monied and led to the highest house along the Catalina front range, the Eastman estate. After a steep climb, she was practically upon the villa before she noticed it. The dwelling was cut out of the mountain itself, a gash upon its face, its back and side walls part of the natural outcrop of basaltic granite. The front and roof were constructed of brick baked to a tone that made it virtually indistinguishable from the surrounding rock, and the windows were set back to eliminate glare and reduce the visibility of the place from below. The design had a layered effect, and each of the structure's several levels followed the path of the increasing height behind it. She parked on the long circular drive beside the front door, ignoring the four-car garage she passed at the lowest level.

She exited the car with a little leap, then caught the door handle as her upbringing on the prairie asserted itself. Far below her, a line of traffic resembling a column of army ants trudged toward its next assignment, and the few mini-skyscrapers downtown resembled a jumble of alphabet blocks. Tucson's human element disappeared in the distance.

The house below and to the right of the Eastman place belonged to the Brodys. It was appropriately positioned as regards the family and business hierarchy, and was slightly more modest in size and style, although it too straddled the million dollar bracket. A Hispanic woman answered Eastman's door before Linda could finger the bell. "You are the appointment for Mr. Eastman?" Her English was well-practiced.

"Si, me llama Linda Bluenight," answered Linda, extending her hand.

The woman slapped both palms on her apron in surprise, then stuck out a much-worked right hand accompanied by a small but sincere smile, "Venga con me."

They walked through a living room that paralleled the front of the house and extended along its entire length from the entrance to a set of glass doors that stood open. These led to a pool on the next level up, accessible by a set of steps lined with blood-red bougainvillea and wild grape. The house behind them was still. The maid motioned her to ascend to an area about the size of Vermont. The pool there stretched back to the mountain wall where its waters were fed by a huge waterwheel that churned constantly to freshen the enormous expanse and give it the appearance of a lake on a breezy day. A stream-fed jacuzzi with seating capacity for a basketball team sat off to the right. A full-bar and changing room were on the left. Behind them was yet another entrance to the premises. Fairly impressive, admitted Linda with grudging admiration for the setting, if not the occupants.

"If you go up those stairs to the next level, you'll come on a pond I put in for the animals, no sense in us humans hogging all the water." Clay Eastman had appeared and was standing below her. He had emerged from the living room and was pointing to a set of stairs behind the waterwheel which seemed to climb the mountain face. He wore an open-collared deep-gold Panama shirt, khaki pants, and sockless glove-like loafers, and he looked at her as if he expected her to respond to her surroundings. She decided not to give him the satisfaction, but she asked politely, "What kind of visitors do you get?"

"Oh, just about anything you can think of that roam these hills, javelina, coyote. Had a mountain lion come in for a drink a few days ago. All the little ones use it, too, the rabbits, Harrison squirrels, and such. Then, of course, it's salvation for the birds in the summer. Come on up. You don't really get wet from the wheel, just a little damp from the mist."

Eastman took her elbow and guided her to a pathway strewn with greenery and ground cover. This led to the staircase which took them up another twenty feet and ended in a grassy area that bordered a crystal blue pool about twenty feet in circumference. The far side disappeared into a canyon-like crevice beyond and formed an entry way for animals to come and go. "I'd forgotten how nice it is up here. My wife's a big nature-lover."

Linda wanted to ask, "Y tu?" but decided against it. "I want to apologize in advance for intruding on you like this. I know you and your family have been through a terrible ordeal."

"That's all right. I happen to have a little time this afternoon. The women have all gone to Sedona for a few days. There's a private resort at Oak Creek where they can get away from the publicity down here. The trash in the newspapers is especially upsetting for Ben's daughter. You know how self-conscious young women are."

"I can imagine it's very hard for her."

Eastman pursed his lips together in a subtle frown. "Sara is bringing drinks. What can I tell you while we wait?"

On the way there, Linda had determined to be direct, and so she put it to him, "I don't believe Ramon Morena killed your brother-in-law, Mr. Eastman."

His eyes narrowed and turned a steely blue. Their expression shifted rapidly from surprise to skepticism to suspicion, of her. "You have evidence to the contrary?" he asked cautiously.

She gave him a summary of the results of her examination. Then she reminded him of the circumstances surrounding Ramon's arrest and told him something of the Morena family. Finally she asked him if Brody had made any enemies during his business career. Linda was aware of the animosity Eastman's personality aroused. Brody's reputation was a bit more ambiguous.

Eastman shook his head. "I'm the one with all the enemies," he proclaimed with pride rather than remorse. "Ben was the venerable salt of the earth. We made a great 'good cop, bad cop' team. I'll miss that as much as I will his allegiance, and his friendship." His voice cracked just audibly. He turned back toward the staircase and began a slow descent, holding out a hand to her as she followed.

"And no personal or family difficulties?" Linda knew she was getting close to the line, but she also realized that this might be her only chance at a face-to-face encounter.

To her surprise, he showed no resentment. "Ben's daughter ran with a rough crowd a few years back, did a lot of drugs at one time. Her parents worked hard and have her pretty much straightened out now, though she still has her ups and downs. Her fiancé is a stand-up guy, too, he'll see her through this."

Sara waited for them by the pool with a tray of lemonade accompanied by two crystal decanters. One held vodka, the other gin. "Neither for me, please," said Linda, "but the juice looks wonderful."

"Do the police share your doubts?" Eastman wanted to know. "If so, they certainly haven't mentioned them to me."

"Morris Peters may have a qualm or two about the case, but officially the file is closed. I just can't clear it up in my own mind. I hope you can understand my misgivings."

"I've talked to Peters a time or two. He never mentioned any of this. It's just too incredible. I believe you're reaching, out of some misplaced sentiment. My family could use some sympathy." There was sudden anger in his outburst.

"They have mine, believe me," Linda replied quickly, "but I have to pursue the case, considering what has happened to my own family." She told him about the menacing phone calls.

Eastman said levelly and without the sympathy for which he had made so recent an appeal, "It could be anyone, some lunatic, someone your son has a quarrel with, a disgruntled Indian, anyone." He was very irritated now. Condescension punctuated every word, and Linda saw that further inquiry would be futile. Eastman had walled himself in, too bullheaded or too fearful to be of help.

She placed her glass on the bar. "I'm sorry to have bothered you at such a time. I'll let myself out."

He caught her arm as she walked past him to descend the stairs toward the living room doors, "I'm sorry as well. I just don't have anything to contribute, and I do think you may be looking in the wrong place for the source of your trouble. I hope whoever it is leaves you alone from now on. Have you notified the police?"

"Yes, they're doing what they can. Thank you for your concern."

As she maneuvered the Ranger down the narrow dirt track from Eastman's property to the main road, Holly Brody's fiancé' passed her. He was behind the wheel of a turquoise Lexus, and he was driving three times too fast, skidding around curves and throwing up dust. She wondered if she should contact him, and decided to decide after she had analyzed Eastman's responses.

Determined to have a home-cooked meal with Matty for a change, she hurried through the late afternoon traffic. Miles before the San Xavier exit, she dropped off I-l9 onto Ajo Way which would take her to Sells and the tribal headquarters if she followed it west. Instead, she found the northern stretch of Mission Road and followed it south to Valencia Street. Then she cut back east and south. Her circuitous route still saved her fifteen minutes through rush-hour hell. She pulled into the drive and came to a stop in front of the house, confident that Matty was elsewhere and happy that the place looked pleasantly quiet. Then she saw the coyote. It was laying crumpled beside the front door, a bullet through its brain.

———••⋅⋅——

<>>>> Fourteen <<<<>

Violations

A trail of blood stretched from the driveway to the animal whose eyes were wide with surprise at the death which had come without warning. The small red pool around its head revealed that it had been killed elsewhere, transported to the house, and deposited on the doorstep. Its body was still warm to her touch.

Linda Bluenight slumped beside it in unbelieving shock and despair. She took the coyote's muzzle in one hand, and with the other she stroked its back. He was a young male, not yet fully grown, like Matty. His coat was long and sleek, ready for the winter he would never see. His life had been stolen as a message for her, and she felt responsible for his death. The killer might as well have pinned a note to his carcass saying that Matty would be next. She gathered the body into her arms and sat rocking it while the tears came and came. The grief she had locked away flowed in a torrent down her face and onto the coyote's fur. She cried for the animal, and for the Morenas, and for the life she had worked so hard to create for Matty and herself. She wept for the innocents mangled and destroyed by the violence and malice of others. As her sobs subsided, anger began to replace sorrow, a consuming anger that overpowered loss and anxiety. For a long while they sat together, woman and coyote, while she gradually regained control.

Finally she staggered up, cradling the body like a baby, its long legs dangling before her like ropes. She stumbled off the porch and over to an area of brush away from the house where she gently laid the animal out of sight. Blood from its wound had stained the beige khaki dress she was wearing, so she stripped it off and wrapped it around the corpse as a shroud. Then she plucked desert broom plants from the sandy soil to cover it. When she was sure it could not be easily observed, she walked quickly back to the house and let herself in. Going to her room, she pulled on jeans and the dark green sweatshirt given to her by her students last Christmas. A picture of the church covered with snow was embroidered on the front.

Then she remembered that she had not seen Mouser, and the terror returned with a rush. "Mouser! Kitty! Come, kitty." She ran from room to room, remembering that the cat was locked inside when they left that morning, but unable to overcome the irrational fear that harm had come to it. Finally she noticed that the cabinet door underneath the kitchen sink was standing slightly ajar. Jerking it open, she spied Mouser crouched against the wall behind the water pipes. "Come, boy. Come on out. What's the matter, sweetie?"

The cat's sharp nose had identified the coyote, though it had not been dead long enough to give off a stink. Spooked, Mouser had taken refuge in the darkest, safest spot he could find, and he was not inclined to obey either Linda's coaxing or a direct command.

Relieved beyond measure, she crossed the room to sit at the kitchen table by the telephone and to consider whether she should call animal control. She had hidden the coyote's body to protect Matty, at least temporarily. If the county agent came to fetch it, she would have to file a complaint, and the boy would learn the hideous truth. He would surely insist on seeing the animal, and the fact that he too was in danger would not escape him. She called Peters instead, but he was away from the office, so she left an urgent message with the always affable and gregarious Sergeant Griffin. Then she located Matty at the Orozco house. Tommy's mother had invited him to stay for supper, and they were just getting it on the table. Linda could hear her friend calling through the phone for her to come on over, there was stew and cornbread enough for everyone. Linda instructed her son to make her apologizes and to come home when he was finished.

"Es todo bien?" he asked. In the background, Tommy asked whether Matty wanted milk or punch to drink with his meal, and he found himself distracted by the multitude of conversations he was attempting to conduct at one time.

"Yes, I'm fine, just another long day," lied Linda, hating the habit, but relieved to have him away for the moment. "Don't rush. See you when you get here." After they rang off, she considered calling back to have him stay the night, then realized it would only make him suspicious.

She tried to put the receiver down, but her hand seemed glued to it. Slowly, she punched the number for the tribal police office in the village as she thought up a story. She told Officer Rodriquez that a prowler had been snooping around her place. She said nothing about the coyote-killing. Since her house did not sit on reservation land, she refrained from requesting a patrol car.

"This area is seeing more transients than ever, Ms. Bluenight. The guy may not bother you again. Your place is just the other side of our jurisdiction, but we'll cruise your perimeter. Did you notify the sheriff's office?"

"I just called the Tucson P.D., and I'll ring the county when we're finished. Between the three of you, I'll feel twice as safe." The quip came hard.

She was standing before the open refrigerator door when Morris Peters returned her call. She had been contemplating a salad, but the internal bowling ball warned her to be careful.

"I hope this is a social call," he began, "I just turned in my badge for the day and I could be persuaded to buy you guys dinner if the two of you are free."

"I was just thinking I might never eat again," replied Linda. She described the latest ugliness, especially how serious she considered the sex and age of the coyote when compared to Matt.

"Sit tight and try not to worry. I'm on my way, and I'm bringing you a helper."

Linda retreated from the kitchen to her favorite spot on the porch swing facing south. On her right, the White Dove gleamed in the last light of day. On her left, the Santa Ritas pointed the way to Mexico. She wondered momentarily if she should follow their silent advice. She had to find this stalker to make certain he never laid a hand or even a word on her son.

Normally this was her favorite time of day. Evening gradually dimmed the lighted sky and stars appeared like crystals pulled out of a celestial magician's hat. The Inca doves in the stumpy mesquites near the martyred coyote's hiding place called across the desert and listened to their own song echoing back over the dry air. A pair of elf owls whispered to each other in the ironwood tree beside the front porch. Tonight she found it difficult to see the land she had grown to love, her Sonora. She hated her enemy for that, too.

If the phone calls had left any doubt, this heinous act confirmed that Eastman was wrong about the stalker being local. Coyote might be a trickster, but he was also given grudging respect in the mythology of the Tohono O'odham as a repository of knowledge. In many legends, he helped the people solve problems and get out of scrapes while he ridiculed them for their weakness and gullibility. In this society animal-killing was akin to murder when it did not involve subsistence. The malicious taking of life was incomprehensible to a people who saw themselves as members rather than masters of a living world. No member of a nation which had occupied the same territory for thousands of years was going to destroy his own resources any more than he was going to threaten his own children.

Even with an attempt at camouflage, the Anglo voice over the phone was unmistakable, and the precision of the shot into the coyote's head revealed a skilled marksman. She guessed that the bullet had come from a high-powered rifle, one with a fairly small muzzle since the lead did not slash and tear the head, but penetrated the skull, passed through the brain, and exited cleanly out the other side. At least the animal's death had been painless. These friendly scavengers had adapted easily to urban life, raiding backyard trash cans, pilfering garbage from restaurant and supermarket bins, and kidnaping unsuspecting pets. She was surprised old Mouser had lasted this long, especially after she heard about an ingenious mother coyote sneaking her way into a smoker on a suburban patio to steal a side of ribs before the outraged householder could run her off.

There was no doubt in Linda's mind that Allen Linton's familiarity with firearms made him capable of such a shot. Since he defined his opponents as subhuman, killing might have become a reasonable means of disposal. Lee Sims was another matter. His creative, often volatile, style of confrontation had resulted in injury to himself and his followers. Any man so willing to offer up his friends on the altar of ecological justice might also sacrifice his foes without compunction. The people she had met at the movement's headquarters were intense, ethical, and far less comfortable with extra-legal forms of resistance than their leader. She could conceive of no murderer among their ranks.

As she looked toward the church, she wondered about Brother Bart Berdini. He had looked into the eyes of the Viet Cong he killed as they fell before him. Combined with his temper and his ferocious dedication to his parishioners, he might even have convinced himself that he was doing this for Linda's own good.

Finally, she had to admit that Brody's murder might have

been done by a hired gun who was now attempting to frighten her off the scent. Barron Kingley might have done the hire. As Eastman Inc.'s top rival on the local scene, he had made no secret of his contempt for the upstart New Englanders. A serious threat to the economic dominance achieved by his family over three generations might have pushed him to drastic measures.

On the other hand, the board of directors at Eastman Inc. was a powerless facade. One of its members might have decided to become a major player. Killing Brody left an important vacancy to be filled. Finally, there was still the family to consider. Those relatives who drove directly from his funeral to catch the next plane out of Tucson might have financial stakes in the business or in his assets back East. She knew better than to turn to Eastman and the women in the family for information about such matters, but she wondered how much Holly Brody's fiance might be willing to share.

Morris Peters drove an unmarked Chevrolet sedan into her driveway and parked behind the spot where she had described the trail of coyote blood. He looked at it as he slammed the car door, then came to sit on the porch railing facing her. The proximity of another human being brought Linda a little comfort. Peters shook his head and looked grim, "This is getting too kinky, Linda. Where did you say you put the carcass?"

"Over here," answered Linda, jumping off the swing and brushing by him as she stepped out into the yard. Mouser stuck his head through the open front door to see who had come to call, but, catching another whiff of the dead animal, he withdrew into the house.

Peters followed close behind Linda, and together they pushed aside the fragrant branches Linda had thrown over the animal's body. "What's this covering him? Looks like a piece of cloth."

She told him about the blood-stain that ruined her dress and her impulse to give it as a burial offering to the coyote, much as the Tohono people did with their dead.

Peters stared at her in amazement and curiosity about such a scenario, a tall dark woman trudging across the desert at dusk carrying the heavy, dripping burden of death, shedding her clothes, ritually covering the corpse with her own garment, weeping over the senseless waste of the animal's life. "Come back to the house now," he said softly, "I'll put the thing in the trunk of my car and join you in a minute."

Matty arrived as they sat in the living room reviewing the incident. He was full of his day, which had gone better than the last few, and of his business, which included preparations for homecoming and extra basketball practice.

While he went to the kitchen for a cold drink, Peters took the opportunity to pull a pistol from his jacket pocket. "I don't blame you for not wanting to leave your home, but I want you to keep this handy. If nothing else, it will make you feel more secure, and if you hear anything strange, you can just shoot it up in the air. It will alert those neighbors down the road and warn any intruder that you're on your guard."

"You know that the only person I'm likely to shoot with this thing is myself by accident," said Linda, with a guileless smile. "I don't think I've ever fired so much as a cap pistol."

Matty's eyes grew big when he came back into the room with sodas for them all. "Wow, Mom, you really are spooked, aren't you?"

"The gun is my idea, Matt, and I'm sure you all won't have any occasion to use it."

Linda looked at him quickly with an almost imperceptible shake of her head. Morris picked up the signal and changed the subject, "I haven't been to a high school game since I played at Salpointe Catholic years ago. Maybe I'll run out and watch you clean Gila Bend's clock. I hear their guards are pretty quick, so you guys had better watch for the outside shot."

But Matty proved single minded, "It's pretty hard to plug somebody through the telephone. You think he's liable to show up here?"

"No, but it's nice of Lieutenant Peters to trouble himself on our behalf," said Linda as she rose and moved toward the front door. "Much homework tonight?"

"I'm on my way. See you, Lieutenant." Matty strode down the hall to his room, turned on his boom box, and shut the door.

Peters placed the gun on the coffee table and joined Linda on the front porch, "Listen, I could sleep over if you'd lend me a pillow. That sofa looks comfortable enough. Tomorrow I can talk to the chief about putting somebody out here for a few days. I've got nothing to go home for anyway."

"Thanks, but Matty will know for sure that something else has happened if you stay. I will keep the gun handy. Now that I think of it, I had to do a bit of target training when I joined the department in K.C. I suppose I can get off a round or two in a pinch. Let's talk again before you ask for a watch on the house. I have a feeling this will all be over in a few days."

"Are you up to something I should know about?" Peters leaned down to try to read her face.

Linda turned away and answered evasively, "Not really, just poking around. I'll be in touch, and I'd appreciate it if you would check on us manana. I can't tell you how grateful I am for all you've done."

"I'd do a lot more if you'd let me, Linda." He touched her face and turned to leave.

<>>>> Fifteen <<<<>

On the Skids

The next morning, while Linda Bluenight taught her fourth graders about the wonders of world geography, Jay Grayson threw his new Lexus into overdrive and began to negotiate several sharp curves on the highway leading from Phoenix to Flagstaff. He was headed for the popular resort town of Sedona, but he intended to make an unscheduled stop before proceeding to his appointment. A couple of his old California buddies had become disciples of the "Vortex," a name applied to the tall crimson boulders which formed distinctive landmarks of the Verde Valley. New Agers from around the world claimed that these formations radiated peace and spiritual insight. His friends, Troy and Tina, smoked plenty of Turkish hash to enhance their sacred experiences, and he could use a toke or two to enhance the effect of the "ludes" he had washed down with a bottle of malt liquor before setting out on his unpleasant errand.

His task was to fetch Lois Eastman and Evelyn and Holly Brody from a spa on the banks of Oak Creek, drive them back to Tucson, and install them in their respective homes. Then he was to report to his boss, Clay Eastman, for further instructions. The thought of his reunion with Holly brought him little joy. After the nightmare of the last few days, the break from Holly's eternal whining had been welcome, and he was in no hurry to see it end. Her dependence on him and her insistence on sharing his drug habit made him queasy, and whatever sexual interest she held for him had faded as his own dependency increased. Had she not been the daughter of one of Tucson's wealthiest families, he would have kissed her off months ago. Because she was, he had put an engagement ring on her finger. Now he was stuck in a trap of his own making. Those depressing thoughts had provided him with an excuse to get loaded before starting the journey north from the Sonora into this high green country.

He was unfamiliar with the hairpin turns along this section of I-17, but he needed to make time to manage a detour to Troy's place, so he gave the accelerator a firm push and let the steering wheel slide between the palms of his hands to feel the contours of the curves. His mood was more than a bit euphoric from his morning fix, and he was eager for more of the same, so he failed to notice that the $30,000 automobile was not handling as well as it should. The gears did seem somewhat slack, but he thought nothing of it until he found himself looking over the edge of a two-hundred-foot precipice. His foot searched frantically for the brake, missed it, then found it too late. He slammed the floorshift into second and felt the clutch jiggle under his right hand. Frantically, he twirled the steering wheel with his left, but succeeded only in spinning the rear of the car in the direction of the overhang. He cried out in fear as the Lexus soared into the air over the steep gulch which was to be Jay Grayson's final destination, but finally, he smiled with panicked pleasure at the view ahead of him. At that moment, his impending fate seemed less real than the vivid spectrum of color which flashed before his eyes. The deep blue of the morning sky at this high elevation, the gold and green branches of the scrub pines along the cliff down which he was plunging, and the rich rust tones of the rocks which lined the way to the bottom formed a kaleidoscope which held Jay Grayson in rapt attention until the sound of the automobile exploding around him reminded him that he was in the hands of God.

That afternoon found Linda en route to Tucson's main library to conduct further research into Eastman Inc.'s tenure in the Southwest. There she used the Internet to search out articles from local magazines, newspapers around the state, and sources as far away as the Connecticut home of Clay Eastman's progenitors. The story of the company's holdings on the American side of the Sonora formed a blueprint sketched in hues of controversy.

Frequently mentioned was a group called the Arizona Eighty, an informal cadre of bankers, real estate developers, land speculators, financial brokers, and "old money" families, movers and shakers of the state's economy and political establishment. Eastman and Brody were not card carriers, but they had cozied up with the group and won its approval for the company's projects. Indeed, one factor in Eastman's Inc.'s enormous success had been Benton Brody's talent for glad-handing, deal-making, and social climbing with Tucson's commercial elite. A family or business needed to occupy a spot at or near the top of the that pyramid before gaining admittance to the Arizona Eighty's mighty echelons. Eastman's membership card was in the mail.

Still, Linda noticed that the recent venture at Bonita Canyon had caused more of a stir within the organization's ranks than usual. A vociferous minority, headed by Barron Kingley, objected to the plan not on environmental grounds, but out of concern that one more giant vacation and conference facility would dilute business from the others.

Nonetheless, contacts with Arizona's top echelons had garnered Eastman the support of key members of both the city council and the county board of supervisors. This alliance had been reinforced by generous campaign contributions. So much for election reform, thought Linda cynically.

She came across several reports of "AZ-80" gatherings, business and social, over the years. They were always held at the newest and most expensive resorts, and at least one photograph featured the Eastman/Brody contingent.

Every bank in the city was somehow involved with Eastman Inc.'s ventures. Some held mortgages on Eastman office buildings and residential developments. Others had made large signature loans. Still others were heavily invested in company stock. All reported that Eastman's financial standing was solid, and all had a significant stake in it. Operations like Arizona First Bank and United Sonora owned branches statewide, and some had been on shaky ground as a result of poor investment practices during the fiscal frivolity of the 1980s. A healthy Eastman Inc. was vital to their survival.

Several financial companies were listed as holders of substantial amounts of Eastman-related stock. These were mostly specialists in pension and estate planning. Large numbers of middle-aged, middle-class citizens relied upon these institutions for security during their golden years, despite the growing unreliability revealed by their declining profits and periodic IRS audits.

Brody's winning ways, personal charm, and business acumen had also won the hearts and minds of a large number of small and medium-sized investors, ranging in type from young, upcoming lawyers and medical professionals to several of the state's lottery winners. Appeals were also made to snowbirds who came for the winter sun and to dream of permanent residence if they could only build up the nest egg required for the purchase of that townhouse or mobile home.

All of this meant that Eastman Inc. had become intimately intertwined with the local economic infrastructure which in turn had become dependent on the company's well-being for its own stability. The accounts Linda read made the savings and loan scandals of the 1980s look like a dress rehearsal for the debacle to come. She was sitting beside a sunny window facing east on the municipal library's third floor. Musing over her findings, she looked out to a lovely view of the Rincons. This tempted her to daydream like Jaime, the fourth-grader whose desk she had to move that morning because he kept writing the name of the little girl sitting beside him on his spelling paper instead of the words in his lesson book. Linda giggled at his insistence that he was just trying to learn to spell "Helen".

Turning back to her task, she found that Barron Kingley was as frequently the subject of her articles as the Eastman/Brody duo. He, of course, was an outspoken critic of every project bearing the company's name. Continually referring to it and its leadership as "outside interests," and touting himself as a native Arizonan, he had repeatedly charged that the firm was proceeding too far too fast. He also supported politicians who wanted to reign in Eastman with tougher zoning and environmental impact requirements.

Eastman was obviously more than a mite frustrated about attempts to place limits on his business goals or his more covert political ambitions. He had lashed out publicly at Kingley on a number of occasions, but each time, Benton Brody had stepped in to smooth matters over.

Linda left her post and located the public telephone beside the library's expansive glass doors. When she dialed the number for Kingley's offices, his secretary laughed at her request for an appointment, but when Linda informed her of the pathology report she wrote on Benton Brody, the woman put her on hold, then returned to set up a meeting for the next afternoon. Her next call was to Jay Grayson, whose number she found in the white pages alongside a Calle Ranchero address which she identified as a luxury condominium complex along River Road. Getting no answer, she stowed his number in her Apache-beaded canvas shoulder bag and headed for home.

The necessary wait to see Kingley nagged at Linda Bluenight, never one to claim patience as a virtue. She needed answers, and up to this point she had not exactly qualified as a finder of lost truths. She felt as if she was racing against time, and that with every passing minute, she and Matty and her students were exposed to the whims of someone ruthless enough to hurt them all. She also knew that her window of opportunity was very narrow. Soon she would have to alert Ron Verasca, the village council, and Matt about the coyote. After that, she would be forced to rely on law enforcement to help her sort out the facts. Considering the skepticism she had already encountered, she was not sure she trusted Tucson's finest to handle such a politically-charged case. She excluded

Mo Peters from this judgment.

She had crossed over to the high school during every class break and at lunchtime, to check that the boy was where he was scheduled to be. It was enough to catch a glimpse of him laughing with his friends in the hall, or see him hunched over a pop quiz in math class. In her own classroom, she had experienced several poignant moments as she helped individual children write their Thanksgiving essays. Self-same little Jaime pronounced in his best cursive that he was thankful for Helen. When he saw Linda looking over his shoulder, he added, "And for my teacher." Second place was fine.

Now, late in the day, she knew she should go home to start dinner, but she turned instead toward the village. Half-conscious of her anxiety about what she might find on her doorstep, she told herself she only wanted to see Matty's last scrimmage before he played the most important game of the season. He had asked her to come, claiming that it was "major."

The gymnasium was small, intimate, and smelled of teenage sweat. It was also totally without acoustics, and the noise from shouting boys and bouncing balls was deafening. The varsity and junior varsity had just finished when she entered. Matty dashed down the middle of the court, hurled himself through the other team's defense, and gave a vertical leap, elevating himself to the height of the basket for a dunk.

"And they say white men can't jump," laughed Tom Orozco Sr. "All right, that does it for today. Shower up, and go to bed early. I don't want any drag-assing tomorrow night, fellas." He waved to Linda and walked across to meet her in the middle of the court. "Think they're ready?"

"You know better than I do, but they look a little short to me," she teased.

"I told them to concentrate on the basket rather than the opponent if we're lucky enough to play offense. I also advised them to eat some macho chilies. How you doing anyway? Any more trouble?"

"We're okay, I think. Matty was upset by the calls but he handled himself pretty well. I could use a good night's sleep myself."

"If it would help, I could get send Tommy over to keep you all company. I don't how useful he is, but his mother says he's a great distraction, especially when there's work to be done." Tom's sense of humor was legendary. "Matt seems cool enough. I can always tell by his concentration at the free throw line. He was about 75% today, better than usual."

"I'm glad to hear it," replied Linda. "Anything I can do to help with tomorrow night's bacchanal?"

"Not that I can think of, the PTA has the dance under control. The officers finally convinced the senior class to hold it here in the cafeteria instead of renting a hall in town. That will cut down on the drinking and driving. The kids made decorations in study hall today, and the band they hired puts out some rockin' noise. We may have to slap a fresh coat of adobe on the place next week.

"The chaperons could always use some extra help. If we would happen to beat Gila Bend, their guys might decide to come by the dance and raise a little hell. A number of the dads will roam the perimeter. You ladies can pour punch and see that the lights stay on." Tom loved that division of labor that separated men and women but gave them both their due.

"Sounds like fun, I'll be early," promised Linda.

"Do you think Rudy Morena will come back to school tomorrow?" she asked, changing the subject. Rudy was a bench player and enjoyed his role as seventh man, third guard.

"The homecoming activities might help take the boy's mind off his grief. I was thinking of calling Mendina when I get home tonight. I'd like to see how the other kids are getting along, too."

Tom looked thoughtful, "Rita talked to her sometime yesterday. They're having a rough time. Rudy is so angry that he and Steve have begun to quarrel, and Felipe has to play referee as well as deal with his own feelings. They sent the twins to stay with Martha through the weekend to get them away from the ruckus. Mendina is about at her wits' end."

Linda understood just how she felt.

"Let me ask you something, girl," said the coach in a confidential tone, "Father Flynn was by earlier to catch a little of the scrimmage. He told me about the phone calls you been getting. I already knew about them, of course, since Matt and Tommy tell each other every detail, including how much hair they shave off their faces, but the padre also said you don't believe Ramon killed that developer. Is that right?"

"Yes, but I don't have a shred of proof, Tom, and from what I've learned, there probably isn't any."

"And do you think the calls are connected to the questions you've been asking about the case?"

"I can't say for sure, but I think so. Do you know how Ramon spent his time after he moved to town? I realize people in the village haven't seen much of him this past year."

Tom Orozco shook his head, "Ramon didn't play basketball, so I didn't get to know him as well as I do Rudy. I suspect he was pretty unhappy about not finding a good job. He did talk when he was in high school about ranching out west, and he hoped the college degree would help him earn enough money to stock some horses and sheep out on his family's land. When it didn't pan out for him right away, he got disillusioned. That pretty girl at the funeral was his sweetie, I take it?"

"Gosh, I don't know," Linda was surprised and angry at herself for not seeing it before. Of course, that explained Bart Berdini's relationship with her and her parents. Maybe she could shed some light on Ramon's state of mind, what friends he might have made in town and on the job. "Do you know who she is or where she lives?"

"Nah, I'd never seen her before, neither had Rita. She's probably someone Ramon met after he moved to Tucson. She could be Jicarilla from over on the southeast side. Brother Bart might know, I saw him talking with them."

"Me, too. Thanks, Tom, I'll ask him. In fact, I think I'll run over to the rectory now. Would you tell Matty to meet me there when he's finished in the locker room? I'll give him a ride home." "Okay, but wait a sec. Have you listened to any news today, Linda?"

Linda Bluenight closed her eyes, dreading Tom Orozco's next sentence. "No, what is it?" she asked in a low voice.

"I had on the box in my office just before I came down to practice. There was a bulletin on KOOL-FM. The highway patrol found a car early this afternoon at the bottom of a gorge off I-17 south of Flagstaff. The officers said they could hardly make out what kind it was between the fire and the fall it took. Apparently the thing was just a tangled ball of blackened metal by the time they reached it. Turns out it was a new Lexus. Now they've tentatively identified the driver as Jay Grayson, Holly Brody's intended, I believe. He was DOA."

———••◦∺◦••———

<>>>> **Sixteen** <<<<>

Possibilities

Corpses were piling up. Linda's shock erased the Berdini question for the moment, so she collected Matty and settled in for the night. Still, the accident should not have surprised her, considering the frantic driving habits she had witnessed at the Eastman place. She wondered how the Brody women would manage now, how much more pressure would fall on Clay Eastman, and whether this new tragedy would slow his plans for Bonita Canyon.

She fed Matty and carefully steered him away from the television news. Today, for the first time all week, he had not referred to "The Caller," and, with homecoming on the horizon, she found it easy to distract him from flipping the

"Trolls" as he called the remote channel changer.

He did not expect to win the game against the Gila Bend team. Those Pimas were tough competitors, he claimed, and for emphasis he listed their victories to date.

"Hey, bud, those Pimas are more accurately known as Akimel O'odham, the River People, just like the Tohono prefer their own handle to the 'Papago.' Since the two groups are so similar, language and customs and all, I should think our guys would be equally tough, or not. Sabe?"

"Yeah, yeah. This is a basketball discussion, not a cross-cultural comparison. We're better shooters over all, if we only had more size. I'm gonna have my hands full trying to keep up with their forward, that guy's built like an ironwood tree."

"The dance looks like fun," Linda said, trying another tack, but she had trouble staying with the topic.

"Some of the kids are squawking about having to hang around the village. They'd rather cruise Tucson, but it's not as easy with the baile being held at school." Matty refrained from adding that the last time he had driven into Tucson with several classmates, he came close to not making it back because the driver was tooting all evening and could barely see the yellow line.

"We haven't talked about your attire. Should we rent something, or buy a new jacket? How much are people fussing up?" She felt negligent, not remembering such an important detail until the last minute. "Actually, the team members are wearing their lettermen's jackets with shirts and ties underneath, no big deal. I hear the girls are going for the nines though. The moms are sewing their brains out to get the dresses ready in time. Aren't you glad you got me instead?" He sidled up to her with his best grin, and she gently pushed him away, laughing at his antics.

"How about Peg? Has she said anything about her outfit? You need flowers for her, right?"

"Aw, cripes, I forgot. Are you going into town manana? I got practice, and Coach has called a team meeting after."

"As a matter of fact, I do have to go in again." She was silent as to why, and the boy was too full of himself to notice. "I'll pick up something if you trust my judgment. Do you even know what colors she's wearing? Maybe I should just go for white or yellow, that's always safe."

"Yeah, but her favorite color is pink, of course," Matty smiled with what she saw for the first time as genuine attraction, perhaps even longing.

She spent a minute thinking of this new development in the life of her only child. It briefly took her mind off her confusion. This relationship with Peg Grazia was fast turning into his first major romance. Knowing Matthew Bluenight, she would not have to wait long to find out how major it was. She sometimes thought he was born talking, and his inability to remain silent meant that their house harbored no secrets. It had saved her many a worry and from being tempted to use that favored parental data-gathering method, snooping. They parted company, going to their rooms for homework. Linda had waded into the middle of her geography plan when the phone rang. She lifted it as if it were a bomb and was infinitely relieved to hear Morris Peters' voice.

"Linda, did I disturb you?"

"Not at all, I'm just a little jumpy when it comes to using Western Bell these days."

"I thought about that as I dialed your number, but I wanted to see how your day went. No more funny stuff?"

"No, thank God, we almost had a normal one for a change, that is, until I heard the news about Jay Grayson. Are you handling that one?"

"Only by proxy. I sent one of my detectives to look things over when the call came from Flagstaff around noon. He just now phoned in with his report. Apparently the kid was driving to Sedona to retrieve Clay Eastman's wife, Brody's widow, and her daughter, Holly. He had just driven past the Stoneman Lake exit where Interstate 17 switches back and forth through a few curves. The angles are not really treacherous, but he might have run into some moisture or loose gravel. Anyway, that's where his Lexus skidded out of control. It spun out over an embankment and took quite a plunge down the side. There wasn't much left to clear away by the time the Flagstaff police got there. My man talked to them and helped with the clean-up."

"Did I tell you Grayson nearly ran me off the road when I went to see Eastman at that mountain resort he calls his house?

"No, you didn't. Was he driving the same car?"

"Yes, it was a beauty, too, the color of a Navaho jewel. He was swerving and braking like a NASCAR driver. The freaky part of this is the timing. Can you believe all these people dying in sequence, Brody murdered, Ramon a suicide, and now Simpson in a crash?"

"It's fairly unusual, all right," said Peters, "Unfortunately, I've been in this business long enough to have seen about everything. Too long I think sometimes."

"You sound like a man leaning toward a career change. I can give you some advice about that." Linda's voice had an easy, teasing quality that caught the man's attention in an instant. "What else did the officers up in Flagstaff have to say?"

"Just that Holly Brody launched into orbit when the

police went to the resort to inform the women of Grayson's accident. The license plates on the Lexus identified him right off, and it turns out the car was registered to the Eastman firm. When they called the company's offices, the secretary told them it had been assigned to Jay. The officer asked for Eastman and told him about the accident, and Eastman told him about Jay's journey to the Sedona area to fetch the women. He begged them to wait until he could get up there himself before telling them, but the officer needed verification, so he was forced to give them the bad news. He says they had to take the daughter to the hospital and that she's being sedated. Eastman's wife is staying with her while Mrs. Brody travels back here to Tucson. Sounds like a strange arrangement, doesn't it?"

"Yes, but my impression is they're a strange bunch. Anything else, or am I being too nosy?"

"You can be as nosy as you want, except I don't think it's going to solve your problem. I'm convinced your intruder is some crazy vagrant who probably won't try anything else now that he knows we're aware of him. As far as Grayson goes, there's not much else to tell." Peters stopped, then backtracked, "Oh, yes, his folks live in San Diego. His father's a doctor, a surgeon I believe, and his mother is a designer of some sort. They want the body, what pitiful charred remnants of it survived the fire, flown there when the police up north are done with it. That will probably be sometime tomorrow. Apparently, they and the Brodys either didn't know or didn't like each other, because no services or even acknowledgment of Grayson's demise will take place here, except for what might appear on the local news."

"Another bit of strangeness. With them being engaged, you'd think there would be some connection between the families," Linda was thinking out loud.

"I've about given up trying to figure out families, Linda," replied Peters wistfully, then his tone brightened, "but maybe not forever. What are you doing this weekend?"

"Matty's homecoming will keep us busy, I guess, but first I'll be meeting with Barron Kingley. I'll have to race downtown after school tomorrow, and then get back out here for the game."

"That's right, I'd forgotten about homecoming. I may mosey out to see the kid play. The way he loves the game, I imagine he's fun to watch. Maybe we can go for a drink or something after."

"I'd better not make any commitments. There might be parent things to do."

"Well, at least we can say hello." Peters sounded as though he would like to say a lot more. "Do you need an escort for your interview with 'the king?'"

"I really don't mean to sound disagreeable, but I don't think I'd get much out of him with the police in tow. I probably won't get much anyway, but we'd better give it a fighting chance."

"I understand that, should have thought of it myself. Linda, one last thing, you should keep that gun with or near you for another day or two, until we're sure that the stalker has gone away. Will you do that for me?"

"I'll give it some thought," said Linda with doubt in her voice. "I just hate what it symbolizes, the surrender to fear of living in my own place in my own way. I know that sounds silly."

"No, it doesn't," he responded quickly. "Get some rest now, and I'll see you tomorrow."

She spent a few minutes thinking about Peters, then she

pushed the idea into a tiny closet toward the back of her mind.
She had no room in her life for a man right now. She dialed
the rectory number at San Xavier and got Brian Flynn.

"Linda, I'm glad you called. Are you and Matty getting
over your scare from the other night?"

"Not exactly, Father." She filled him in on the mishap
with the coyote, Peter's theory about the perpetrator, and her
efforts to determine the facts surrounding Brody's murder.

He listened in grim silence, and then responded, "You
know the people here would never do something so
sacrilegious. Coyote-killing is an act common only to Anglo
ranchers and the mentally ill. I still think you should consider
moving into the village, at least temporarily."

"I just can't make myself abandon my own home, Father,
not yet. For one thing, I'd have to tell Matty about the
incident. I did inform Ron and Tom about the phone calls and
they're watching his back. I don't want him to live in terror if
I can avoid it.

"Have you heard anything from Brother Bart? I nearly
stopped by this evening to see if he'd returned. Tom told me
that Ramon had a girlfriend who came to the funeral with her
parents. I remember seeing the three of them talking to Bart
during the burial ceremony, and I wanted to ask him about
her."

"Linda, he hasn't shown up here since I confronted him.
I feel as though I've ruined our friendship, like I drove him out
of here and maybe out of his vocation. I wish he would
phone, or at least send some word about where he is. I know
he can take care of himself, but I'd like to straighten out things
between us, and find out what he's planning to do. "

"I can't believe he would abandon his work here," said
Linda, "He's been a lifeline to the community almost as much

as you have. I'm sure you'll hear from him soon. Do you know anything about this girl? She was attractive as I recall, about Ramon's age, and very upset. I'm kicking myself now that I didn't pay more attention at the time."

"I'm afraid I didn't notice much at all, except to observe that the family was not from the village. I'll ask around, but I doubt I'll have much luck. People were preoccupied with their own problems and sorrows that day."

"I was thinking the same thing," said Linda, with a disappointed sigh. "Please, let me know if you hear from Bart."

"Surely, but Linda, I haven't told anyone at the school or around the village about his leaving, much less why he went. I suppose it's partly because I'm ashamed of myself, and partly because I don't know what's happened. I'm hoping he'll show up soon and make an explanation unnecessary, but he'll definitely be missed if he doesn't make an appearance at the homecoming fete. I'll be forced to make some kind of announcement Sunday if he doesn't surface by then."

"Well, that gives you at least another day or two. One more thing, Father, do you know anything about Barron Kingley? I have an appointment with him tomorrow after school. As Eastman Inc.'s major adversary, I'm thinking he might have some information."

"The only contact I've had with Mr. Kingley was a few years ago when he set up a scholarship fund out here at the high school. Come to think of it, Matty might come up for one of those awards next year. The program provides tuition and books to the student's choice of public universities in Arizona. I believe there's enough money for two grants each year for the rest of the decade."

"Right, I've heard of that fund. Ron's mentioned it a time

or two as a way to get kids to UA, but I didn't realize that Kingley endowed it. It's not named for him, is it?"

"No, it's one of the few philanthropic efforts he hasn't yet marketed for publicity. Other than that, I only know him from the newspapers and television, although with his love of the camera, that's saying quite a lot. Sorry, I'm being unkind."

"No, just honest as usual, Father. Maybe he'll be as talkative with me as he is with the anchor woman on Channel 10. Let's keep each other posted."

"That's a deal, Linda. Goodnight."

But for Linda Bluenight, there was no rest. She had not slept well since the anonymous caller shattered her peace of mind. Now the coyote's ghost haunted her. Ominous statistics swam in her brain, three men down, one missing. She could not bring herself to admit that Bart Berdini may have come to harm as well, but she knew that death was stalking those connected with Eastman Inc.

Had he fled because he had committed the ultimate sin against humanity and his God, or was it because he possessed knowledge of the killer and did not want to expose him? That would place the murderer here on the reservation, and her other evidence, meager though it was, pointed in a different direction. Besides, she could not believe that Berdini would threaten Matty and herself, although whoever he might be protecting could be desperate enough to try to frighten them into silence.

She went cold with fear as she thought of Matty. Was he in danger because of her inquiries into Brody's murder, or because he had found the corpse and the murderer believed he saw more than just a dead body lying in a cold canyon? She tossed and turned and finally gave up. Stumbling into the kitchen, she tried a mug of warm milk, but ended up feeding half of it to Mouser. Tiptoeing into her son's room, she found a little comfort when she saw him sprawled across his bed, one pillow across his breast, the other cradling his head. She slumped in a chair across from his slumberous countenance and eventually dozed off, but her fitful rest was permeated with dreams of an animal's dying scream, shadows of leering men, and Matty complaining about his dirty laundry.

<>>>> Seventeen >>><>

Messages

The next day Mission San Xavier came alive with preparations for its high school's basketball fiesta. The O'odham converted many events into celebrations, especially when the events revolved around their children. Classes would dismiss an hour early for the pep rally, which would be followed by a parade around the village. Harking back to the ritual processions of another time, the march would be led by the school band, followed by carloads of team members, pickup trucks carrying homemade floats, and students on horseback. Contingents of younger students from the grade school would bring up the rear.

Parents who were not working spent the day cooking and decorating the school cafeteria. The loss of Ramon Morena had cast a pall over the community that needed exorcizing. Games and music and dance had forever been Tohono ways of cleansing the collective soul. All the teenagers participated, as players or cheerleaders or musicians or pep club members.

Throughout the day, Father Flynn scurried back and forth, assisting with details. Periodically, he checked the message machine in the rectory, hoping to hear Bart Berdini's voice announce his arrival at the village in time for tipoff, hoping for word from his friend. None came.

Matty was all over the place, feigning nervousness about the big game when he was really more worried about kissing Peg Grazia. He secretly fantasized about her solving the problem by throwing her arms around his neck and planting one when the team beat Gila Bend, if they beat Gila Bend. Hell, he could use consolation if they lost. He spent every break chatting up his teammates, overseeing the hanging of banners, or helping the mothers taste the red and green chili. He also organized a picnic for Sunday.

Such was the atmosphere as Linda walked her fourth graders over to the gym and installed them in their seats for the rally. Placing two of them in leadership positions as monitors, she wound her way to his locker to remind him of her trip to town. "You have to go this afternoon, Mom? You'll miss everything." He whined a little, trying to convince her to stick around.

"You want posies for this new woman in your life, don't you? I'd have to go in anyway, at least as far as Rena's Flower Shop on the south side. It's only the rally I'll miss. Your supper will be ready when you get home from the parade. Perhaps I can even get back in time to see some of the floats."

"Remember, Mom, just a light meal. I wouldn't want to barf in the middle of a lay-up."

"Right, how well you put it." Linda had to reach up to tweak him on the cheek. Then she made her exit before he could raise more objections or ask what could be important enough to drag her away at this crucial point in his athletic career. She felt a smack of disappointment herself as the village fell from sight in her rear view mirror. At present, however, the necessity of eliminating the threat to her little family and to the village community took priority over social pleasures.

Barron Kingley's office occupied the top floor of the building he owned in downtown Tucson. The new "mini-scraper" looked down on the Old Town Artisans complex and the scant surviving ruins of the Spanish Colonial Presidio. Old Town took up a square city block and was surrounded by a low adobe wall which enclosed art galleries, craft shops, and a courtyard restaurant complete with strolling mariachis. A pleasant and convenient place for lunch, it attracted office workers from nearby buildings and drew hordes of tourists, especially during the winter months. Its age and authenticity stood in contrast to Kingley's undistinguished ten-story brick and glass addition to the architectural chaos of late twentieth century urban America.

Linda encountered a minor delay in the first floor lobby while the receptionist phoned upstairs to get permission to let her use the private elevator. When she entered the cubicle to ascend to the top floor, she found the small space decked out like a brothel with red velvet padding and wall mirrors. The lift dumped her out on the building's north side. Looking around, she discovered that Kingley's headquarters looked more like a luxury condominium than a place of business. With no interior walls, Linda had a view of the entire floor, which contained a parlor-like section with a large stone fireplace, a kitchen, a spacious dining facility, and a game room. Glassed on all sides, it reminded Linda of an enormous gilded cage with brass fixtures and overstuffed chairs and sofas scattered through the spaces.

Then she spied Barron Kingley far across from her in the southwest corner of the place, where he sat behind an enormous mahogany desk. He had obviously chosen the spot for its symbolism as well as its view north toward the Catalinas and Ventana Canyon. Facing him was a pair of high-backed wing chairs in earth colors. On the desk before him were a tea service of sterling silver and a pitcher of margaritas with two large champagne bowls. The walls behind him were shelved with books about the history of the West and appeared to include collections from the pre-Anglo period.

He motioned her across the expanse separating them, and without rising called out a greeting, "You don't look like a bone-picker to me. I thought you were all supposed to resemble that 'Quincy' guy who used to ugly up prime time."

Linda had been the subject of that comparison before, and she had to confess that it served as a good icebreaker. Still, she was not at all sure she wanted to break any ice with this man.

"An ex-bone-picker as a matter of fact. I gave it up a long time ago in favor of live victims." Linda told this immensely tall and wealthy Arizona magnate a little of her background, about Matty's discovery of Benton Brody, and of how she came to perform the examination on the body. She revealed nothing about the recent threats to herself and Matty.

Kingley looked interested not so much in her biography as in her appearance, and his attention caused her to wonder if she had made a mistake choosing the rust-colored cotton jump suit with the Mexican leather belt. It fit her well, hugging a part here, suggesting a part there, but the last thing she intended was to make herself attractive or to create any distraction from her purpose. Besides, she often did not recall what clothes she had donned in the morning unless she happened to glance down at them later in the day.

"Sounds like you and your son have had an interesting time of it here in the Old Pueblo." He seemed amused by their single-parent situation.

Linda felt her temper rise proportionate to his amusement, and she decided to check both before either got out of hand. "I'd like to get your ideas about the murder and its potential impact on the Eastman company and on the direction of the real estate boom in Tucson."

"I don't have any ideas about the murder. Frankly, I don't care a damn about the repose of old Ben's soul, or that of his killer," he offered, referring back-handedly to Ramon. "I do care about this town and about what people like Eastman are doing to it."

She had heard that Kingley was the self-appointed protector of the Sonora, and now she detected that ring in his voice as he told her his concerns. He was backing, financially and politically, the University of Arizona's effort to re-excavate and restore the Presidio walls, some of which lay beneath his very own building. Of course, when his father built the structure, the business community was not as historically sensitive as it might have been.

"You know, back in 1885, when Clem Stephens returned to Tucson from the state legislature with the news that this town would be home to Arizona's first university, he came shoulder-high to a lynching for his pains. People here wanted him to snag the new insane asylum or the prison instead because they thought it would mean more profit. If it hadn't been for my grandfather, Stephens would have been run out of town on a rail and Old Main might never have been built." Kingley was also widely-known for his familial anecdotes. Next, he claimed that his animosity toward Eastman had intensified when the latter's completion of the Rincon retirement community had closed off the Hohokam ruins.

"Would you consider yourself an opponent of the cornucopia-based view of development?" asked Linda pointedly, trying out Matty's pedagogy for the first time.

"Cornu-what?" Kingley made a wondering face, and then laughed, "I know what you're talking about. I think the desert is big enough for both. Money can be made from new construction, open spaces can be retained, and scarce commodities like water can be conserved if the environmental, academic, and commercial establishments all work together. The job of the developer is to see that those interests come together to serve the land and the people.

"Look, Speedway Boulevard got its name because my great-uncle saw the first two automobiles in Tucson race each other down a dirt track out east of the campus. It was no man's land at the time. Only Mexicans and tubercular refugees lived out there. Now it's the busiest street in town. If we'd banned cars to prevent pollution, we'd still be pulling fire trucks with mules."

"Your company has built nearly as many new housing and resort facilities as Eastman's. Do you feel your projects are striking that balance between the profit-motive of cornucopia and the needs of preservation?" Linda understood that the size of Kingley's ego would not permit her to challenge him much further.

"Our profits aren't in jeopardy, and neither are the animals and plants in the areas we've developed. You certainly can't say that about Eastman's pricey dumps. I haven't made any secret of my contempt for that chowder-head, and I don't intend to start now, just because his brother-in-law caught a pile of lead, as we say down here. I'm just hoping it will motivate him to give empire-building a rest. He really should take all those women back East and get them out of their vale of tears."

Had this man just fingered himself, Linda wondered? Was he so brazen in his self-importance that he could sit around making pronouncements about how his enemies should live, and then go out and gun them down? Looking at him, stretched out in his giant leather chair, dressed head to toe in black Western shirt, vest, jeans, and heeled boots with silver spurs, she was tempted to answer her own questions. "I suppose you've read about the accident up north with Jay Grayson. Did you know him at all?"

"Sure," answered Kingley, sitting up and pouring himself a champagne glass full of green icy alcohol.

He lifted the other empty bowl to fill it, but Linda stopped him, "I'd rather have what's in that pot," she said.

"You women and your tea. My second wife drank the stuff morning, noon, and night. I always said that's what made her so hard to get along with."

"I only drink it in the afternoon," began Linda, then halted speaking abruptly when she saw that he was apt to take her casual remark as an overture. She changed the subject at once as she took the delicate porcelain cup and saucer from him. "Can you tell me anything about Jay Grayson's relationship with the family other than Holly? I know they were engaged."

"I'd use that term only as a loose description," Kingley corrected her, chuckling without humor. "He gave her a ring, but I think Eastman paid for it. The kid was a royal punk. He came over here from California, went to UA, graduated without distinction. His father was an alumnus of the med school back in the fifties. I'd bet that's how Jay got accepted, because he certainly wasn't medical school material. To prove it he dropped out after his second year. He took up with Brody's daughter and went to work for Eastman Inc. at about the same time, a year or so ago. She'd had a sporadic problem with drugs until then, now she's on something or other just about all the time. Her mother seems unaware of how much worse her condition has become. I think Grayson was supplying her, or at least making her crazy enough that she got to indulging on a regular basis. Nice guy, huh? She'll likely fall over the edge now. Her mother's certainly no help, running around, putting on weight and taking it off like another TV character I don't care for."

"How do you know all this?" Linda was amazed at his detailed knowledge of the Brody bunch. "You're not a regular guest at their table, I'll wager."

"Actually, I have been a time or two. They're no joy to break bread with, I can tell you. Eastman and his old lady can hardly stand to be in the same room with each other, except when they're on public exhibition. Brody never seemed to notice what size balloon his wife resembled on any given day, and the girl wandered about in a daze, drug-induced or natural.

"To answer your question," he was suddenly serious, "I have to know. Everything those boys did and do affects this town, my town." Leaning back and stretching a bit, he added, "Besides, the Tucson social circle is too small for secrets. I've been known to hire a private dick or two for information, but it's hardly necessary. The monied talk so loud in Tucson that money doesn't need to." He grinned, delighted with his pun.

Linda, on the other hand, felt a vague disgust at both the words and their author. "Father Flynn tells me you've created scholarships for the mission school students. That's very generous of you. Does Clay Eastman make many charitable contributions of that kind?"

"Are you kidding? I think he sends a pittance to his alma mater back East, but people around here don't see much benefit from the millions he's raked in at their expense. About the fund, I need to get hold of Flynn out there. I'd like to present the next pair of awards at the graduation in the spring. Would you have him call the office when he gets a chance?"

Brian was right, she thought ruefully, the guy was incapable of passing up an opportunity to pat himself on the back. "I'll try to remember."

"Thanks. You know, one thing that keeps Eastman from spreading his dollars around is the state of his overall finances. Not many people know this yet, although I'm sure it will come out before long, but the guy's little empire is a house of cards. His and Brody's very first projects were built on shaky ground, which isn't unusual, but it seems they got comfortable with the earth moving under their feet. They've not been above taking massive credit extensions from banks around the state and from as far away as New England over the past several years. The bank officers wring their hands about it, but they don't have much choice. They've tied up so much of their depositors' money in Eastman schemes that if his house collapses, so might theirs. I'm not saying it's sure to happen, he may be savvy enough to pull off a rescue. If not, the whole town will suffer and he'll have no place to hide, especially without 'Good Ole Boy' Benton to help him slide through."

Kingley would clean up if Eastman Inc. did fail, thought Linda. Any number of cheap properties would become available if the company went into receivership. The "Barron" would be able to pick them up for a song and the community would thank him for it. He would also be faced with one less obstacle to his own vision of how a Bonita Canyon resort should look. Killing Benton Brody might just be tantamount to placing Clay Eastman's other foot on a banana peel and giving him a push into the financial abyss. Competitors had put out contracts on their rivals for less, she knew, and this guy thought himself at least equal to the law if not above it.

Linda had to get a reaction from him and this seemed like a good time, "Do you think Ramon Morena killed Benton Brody?"

Kingley did a dramatic double take, "Of course, don't you?"

"I'm not sure." She told him about her and Matty's friendship with the family.

"But, lady, the suicide is its own confession. A kid young as that doesn't hang himself even before he's arraigned, much less tried and convicted, unless he's guilty as sin."

"Or unless he is driven to it by hopeless desperation and disgrace. Ramon's family is highly respected throughout the Tohono homeland. If Ramon felt he had ruined his family's name, justified or not, he might have thought suicide was the only way out."

Kingley's eyes roamed about the windows that overlooked Tucson from every direction, searching for answers in the mountain-ringed valley and its inhabitants. "Any suspicions?" he asked slowly.

Linda answered just as slowly, "Not a one. You?"

Kingley turned to her, leaned across the table, and made his announcement, "Clay Eastman, of course."

Linda felt as if she had just been shot with a stun gun. Barron Kingley sat silent, larger than life, but somehow smaller than human, proudly permitting the effect of his accusation to sweep the woman before him off her feet without benefit of an explanation. Linda tore her eyes from his and rose to her feet. Turning her back to him, she tried to come to terms with this new information. Was this man believable, was he attempting to draw attention away from his own guilt, or was he just so consumed by his hatred of Clay Eastman that he would say anything?

She walked with great deliberation to the wide west wall

of windows beside Kingley's monumental desk to gaze out at
Baboquivari Mountain. Was I'itoi listening to all this? Would
He, Earth's Elder Brother, send Eagle, the bearer of truth, to
help her?

"You sound sure of yourself, Mr. Kingley. Do you have
facts? Have you been to the police about this? How have you
arrived at such an unlikely conclusion?"

"To be perfectly honest with you, I'm still putting the
pieces together," he answered with a slight smile, as if he had
been working things out in his mind over these last few
minutes. "It might have been Morena, but Eastman had a
solid motive, and he's devoid of loyalty. A member of
Eastman's patsy board of directors told one of my people that
Ben Brody was getting nervous about Eastman's bumbling of
the Bonita Canyon project. The guy made even more enemies
than usual, and he stepped on toes until even his political
buddies began to howl. Brody was actually thinking of pulling
out. Too much risk was piling up and it grated on his Harvard
Business School sensitivities. Eastman apparently found out
about it and the two of them kicked up quite a scene at an
executive meeting last month. They got to accusing each
other of misbehavior the board would rather not have heard
about, and Brody shouted that he couldn't continue to put his
career in the hands of a loose cannon like Eastman. Then he
more than hinted that the sorry state of his wife and daughter
had something to do with the browbeating they suffered for
years at the hands of both Eastman and his mother. I'd like to
have been there to see the bastards carve each other up."
Kingley's eyes took on an evil, voyeurish look.

Linda ignored it. "I've heard that Brody was concerned
about the problems at home," she confirmed. "Do you have
any proof of his intention to leave the company? Fifteen
years and at least as many millions of dollars in net worth

would be a lot to turn his back on."

"At the moment I'm going mostly on rumors and hunches, but I've been right on both counts before."

At that statement, the wind began to go out of Linda's sails.

Barron Kingley finally admitted what she had feared, "If I did want to pin it on someone besides the Morena kid, Eastman would be my first choice, guilty or not. Evidence can always be found."

Or conjured up, thought Linda. Her hopes dashed, she concluded that the man was fantasizing. Looking over at him hunched in his chair, his face contorted with hate, she saw his powerlessness for the first time, especially when compared with the expanse of sky and horizon stretching out before them. He could not control or even fully comprehend the events that had taken the public spotlight off his own prominence and cast it onto someone like Eastman. He had succumbed to wishful thinking, taking advantage of their conversation to blow off steam, and Linda was back to square one. More depressing was the idea that this could all be a ruse designed to confuse her, with Kingley introducing suspicion and then erasing it in an effort to demonstrate his innocence.

As she said her goodbyes and made her exit, Linda Bluenight decided to think about this over a bouquet of flowers. Her situation was worsening by the hour, and she had neither the time nor the resources for the detailed inquiry the investigation seemed to require. For once she missed the privileges that accompanied her former position. How was she to fend off the stranger who had surfaced twice to terrorize them if she could not even sort out the cast of characters on Tucson's stage of economic players?

Concentrating on the pleasant business at hand, and

bypassing the more stylish boutiques downtown, she drove Sixth Street into South Tucson to Rena's Flower Pot, a small storefront shop. Each day, Mrs. Rena bought hanging plants, potted geraniums, and assorted hot house flowers from rural growers near the Mexican border and placed them on the sidewalk outside. The shabby street became a garden of roses, hibiscus, pansies, lilies, and carnations, and even boasted gardenias for the corsages Hispanic men were so fond of lavishing on the women they loved. Mrs. Rena sold them at bargain prices for the working class laborers in her barrio.

Linda spent a few minutes loitering about, pushing her nose into the baskets and arrangements and breathing deeply. She wished she could fill the Ranger with them and take them to her rancheria.   She chose a half-dozen baby roses, half white and half hot pink. Mrs. Rena gave an approving, "Ah, yes, Senora, son bonita, muy bonita," and created a wrist corsage with bits of baby's breath and lots of ribbon.

"Tu hace trabajo maravilloso, Mrs. Rena," said Linda, admiring the woman's handiwork. She hurried toward the old house on Los Reales, repeating to herself that whoever had been haunting the place had probably gone to Guaymas. After all, she and Matty had spent a quiet night, and it was important to resist the temptation to paranoia that her career in police work had always encouraged. She knew all was well when she entered the house because her son was head-first into the refrigerator. She pulled him out and showed him the flowers.

"Geez, they're gorgeous. You did real good." The boy could not distinguish daffodils from peonies, but he appreciated her effort.

"Go get your gym bag ready, Pancho, I'll handle the grub."

She fixed him a whopping hero with pastrami, salami,

provolone, and Italian bread with all the trimmings, and opened a can of minestrone soup to wash it down.

"Every time I think I've got our ancestry straight, you change ethnic groups on me," Matty quipped between enormous grinding bites.

Linda just shook her head and pushed the milk bottle his way, "The indigenous people of Sicily thank you for your understanding. Say, you don't have to get it all down in one swallow. There's plenty of time."

"Actually, Ma, I was gonna ask you to wrap it up for later, or I might have to reach for the stomach pump at half-time."

"Sorry, I forgot. I just don't want to see my skinny boy's bones sticking out of his uniform. I guess you're a little nervous besides. Don't be. I heard they kept that big center in Gila Bend for sassing his teachers."

"I wish," said Matty, slurping soup. "Any reason you've gone to town every day this week? I'm beginning to think you've got a new boyfriend."

"I don't have an old boyfriend," she chided, trying to think up an alibi. "I've just been making a few inquiries into the Brody case. I'd like to see Ramon's good name restored." She realized that she was about to open the proverbial can of worms, but she was also wily enough to realize that Matty had no time to waste.

"How do you go about doing that, not that I wouldn't be glad to see it?" asked Matty.

"I'm not sure, I'll let you know when I figure it out. You'd better get cracking."

The boy needed no reminders. He leaped out of his chair in a single bound, wiping his mouth and grabbing his bag all in one motion, "Wish me luck and give me five."

"You've got it," she said slapping his outstretched hand

with both of hers. "Here's two."

It was close but no cigar for the San Xavier High School Thunderheads on homecoming night. Matty had judged rightly about those Akimel boys being too tall and too fast for his teammates. The mission kids did sweat bullets trying, and when the final buzzer rang, they were only five points short of what would have been an upset. Matt was the hero with fifteen of the forty-five points scored by his team. He took stardom in stride, though he enjoyed shining for the Grazia girl and the largest crowd of the season.

Linda noticed that Rudy Morena was not at his usual post on the bench two spots down from Coach Orozco. She found Ron Verasca as people were filing out and asked him about the boy's absence.

"I'm about out of rope on this, Linda," he began, shaking his head in vexation. As he did so, Linda detected the first signs of grey in his dark hair. "The kid is in for big trouble if he doesn't straighten out. His parents have tried everything from prayer to threats. Father Flynn has been to see him at least twice this week, and I talked to him yesterday. He reminds me of a piece of that chert our people used to make arrows, hard and sharp and dangerous. I got a call from his brother, Steve, just before I came over here saying that Rudy wouldn't be at the game. Tom was sputtering mad when I told him. Steve was on his way into town right then to pick the boy up at the east side police station. They got a call from Lee Sims. It appears that Rudy has been prowling Tucson all day looking for Brody's killer, trying to clear his brother's name. He went to Sims' house, banged on the door, and confronted him. Sims talked him down but called the police afterward."

Linda thought for a moment and then started for Ron's

office, telling him as she went, "I'll call Sims now. It's not that I know him well, but we met the other day and he'll remember me. Let me see what I can do."

The phone rang through to Sims' answering machine, his crisp voice on the tape announcing the time and place for the next "Dump Eastman" meeting and throwing in a plug for membership in Santa Tierra. When the regulation beep sounded, Linda began her message requesting a call back. In the middle of it, she was interrupted by Sims' live voice. "Sorry," he apologized perfunctorily, "I'm screening my calls this evening. I had a problem out here earlier with Morena's brother, just thought I'd take the precaution."

Linda could hear a woman in the background talking to Sims. The voice did not sound happy. "Have I interrupted you?"

"No, but hold the line a second. Joanne, why don't you go now? Between you and that kid, I've had about all I can take. I'll send the rest of your things along tomorrow."

A female curse and the bang of a door signaled the end of that conversation, and Sims returned his attention to Linda as if he had just brushed off a door-to-door salesman. "Sorry again. Funny you should ring, I was thinking about you during my little altercation with the Morena boy. He looked awfully young, and I wouldn't have minded his hell-raising so much if I hadn't worried about his possibly being a gang member. I remember your saying you knew the family. What kind of kid is he?"

"A good one, Lee, just crazy with grief. I'm sure he wouldn't harm anyone. Besides, we don't have any gang activity here in the village, at least not yet." The very thought caused the hair on Linda's neck to rise.

"I'm glad to hear it," he replied. "What can I do for you? Is this about Rudy, by chance? The police asked me to come in tomorrow if I wanted to bring charges. They were planning to take him to the station, scare him a little, and have his family retrieve him. From one point of view, it's a pretty good joke, the cops being forced to protect me when what they'd really like to do is sling my ass in a cell."

"I called to ask you not to take action against the boy, Lee. I'm with the principal here at the high school right now. He and Rudy's coach are trying to keep a leash on him, and his family is very concerned. My son and I will help however we can. With all of us keeping an eye on him, we should be able to keep him out of your hair. The Morenas have had so much heartache, we'd like to spare them more if we can."

Ron Verasca was standing across from her nodding his head. His position midway between the door of his office and the front hall of the high school permitted him to call "Good nights" to some of the parents as they left and overhear her conversation at the same time.

"I understand the decent thing you're doing out there," began Sims in a moralistic whine that grated on Linda's ear. "I'd just like not to get caught in the middle of some misplaced vendetta. I remember reading Ruth Underhill's ethnography on Papago social organization in my college anthropology class. She said they weren't warlike people, but that their capacity for revenge was widely feared by neighboring tribes."

Linda corrected him, "I think you may be over-estimating cultural memory." The last thing she wanted was to get into an academic tete-a-tete with an alienated white man. "We give you our word we'll take every precaution to see that Rudy doesn't disturb you again."

"That's good enough for me. Now let me ask you something. Did you know that Eastman and Kingley are stirring up the city's political pot? They're going at it separately and doing it for entirely different reasons, but the fact remains that they're both trying to divert attention from the ecological and financial debacle the Bonita Canyon project is sure to generate by drawing attention to Brody's murder. They are going to insist on a law and order campaign to target the south side and your people out there. The first step will be a curfew on kids eighteen and under. They'll have to be home before ll P.M. or face a misdemeanor, a fine, or even a few days detention. They'll say they're enforcing it county-wide, but the squad cars and check points will be out your way."

Linda felt that one more surprise might send her synapses exploding through her skin. "How did you get wind of that? I haven't seen a thing about it in the papers, and I'm sure the village council would have issued a statement if it became aware of such a move."

"Eastman is going to request time at both the city council and county board of supervisors' meetings next week. Kingley, who's probably pissed that Eastman isn't on a slab like his brother-in-law, is planning to endorse whatever his arch rival recommends. The goal is to incite the Anglo population into an orgy of fear and scapegoating. By the time they come to their senses, that Frankenstein the developers call the ultimate resort will be a done deal. In the meanwhile, Kingley plans to wrestle Eastman for the zoning rights. We all know that murder makes better copy than corporate crime. While the public's not looking, they'll fight to the economic death, winner take all.

"Listen, I've got to run. The foul-mouthed lady you must have heard screeching in the background is my soon-to-be ex-wife, and she just absconded with my credit cards. I'll lay off your boy for now."

Linda sat with the phone glued to her ear. Sims' conspiratorial mind lent itself to such themes, but the story sounded feasible. She thanked him for his decision not to file charges against Rudy, rang off, and turned to Ron Verasca. She relayed the news and asked him if he had been aware of it any plans for a crackdown.

He shook his head vigorously and said, "We shouldn't be surprised, amiga. We've been on the kicking end of milgahn propaganda for hundreds of years. You had your Trail of Tears, the Apaches had the Camp Grant Massacre, we had our women and children stolen by the conquistadors. Things haven't changed all that much."

Linda saw a bitterness in her friend's face that pained her. She left him to lock up the school and walked to the Orozco house south of the church along San Xavier Road. Tom and his wife were having the team and their dates over for popover pizza and soda. To escape the din of heavy metal and giggling teenagers, they left the red brick house to their offspring and retreated to the backyard to sit in the crisp November air.

"Clouds coming in," Mrs. O. said, pointing to the south, "We could get showers tonight."

"I'd love it," answered Linda, peering through the dark. "Have you seen much of Mendina this week?" The two women were the same age, and had attended the mission schools together during "pre-enlightenment days" as they charitably called the period prior to the 1970s when Tohono children had been forbidden to speak their own language and suffered corporal punishment for failing to attend daily Mass.

"Only briefly," answered Rita. "I found her sobbing in her room one day when I stopped by, so I took the little ones home with me to give her some rest. Martha is coming in from Pitoikam with the twins tomorrow. She's always a big help to Mendina. Felipe seems like a broken man, and if Steve and Rudy don't stop fighting, I'm afraid for his heart. There just isn't much good news from that house." Rita's voice had that lilting quality that sang in Linda's ear.   She only wished its song tonight had a happier theme.

Rita turned her short round body to her husband and Linda and asked, "How about the boys?   Tommy makes a joke out of everything just like that one," shaking her finger at Tom, Sr.   "I can never tell what's in his mind, but the day after Ramon's funeral, his room smelled like a brewery. I worry that he's beginning to use alcohol the way my dad did, to escape the pain. My lovable old man died in a ditch outside Sells with his pickup truck on top of him."   She stopped, not trusting her lyric any further.

Tom went to her and hugged her like a pal. The two had known each other since childhood, and they had a partnership that Linda admired. "My Rosarita, you're such a sad flower this evening. Our boy has no stomach for the sauce. One beer turns his lights out. He told me he might sue Budweiser. 'Proud to be your bud, my ass' was the way he put it. Besides, Matty's a teetotaler, that's a good influence on him."   He tried to look as confident as he sounded.

Linda sat on a wooden chair and looked up at the stars playing hide and seek with the incoming clouds. "Ramon's death has been hard on all the children. Even my fourth graders are grieving."

"Have you had any more of those damn calls?" asked Rita. "Tom told me Matty was upset after they first happened. I worry about you out there by yourselves. Some men see women alone and think they can just do anything."

"Things have settled down around our place."   Linda still could not bring herself to talk publicly about the coyote. "In fact, I should get over there. It's been an endless day. Can I help with anything before I go? Don't let these party animals keep you up all night."

"Hey, my team has to get its beauty rest. Curfew during

the season is at 11:30, homecoming or what."

They walked Linda back to the Ranger and stood looking after her as she turned toward the set of dirt tracks on the shortcut to Los Reales and her casa.

She found Mouser snoring on the couch, a sign that no unwanted visitors had violated her threshold. She tousled his head to greet him and also to check for fleas. Matty had moved the living room phone back to its rightful place from under her pillow and reattached the answering machine. The thing was winking at her like a red-eyed flirt. She grabbed a pencil, held her breath, and pushed "Play."

She exhaled when she heard Morris Peters' voice. "Linda, I know you're probably at Matty's game. I wanted to tell you both I'm sorry I couldn't make it. This job is raising cane with my social life, what there is of it. Anyway, I'll ring you tomorrow, or maybe you could give me a call in the morning and let me know the score. We could also talk about dinner. I'm nothin' if not persistent. Goodnight."

She put the pencil behind her ear and was about to walk away when the second message clicked in, then the third, the fourth, the fifth, each one more obscene and vile than the last-- threats, sexual and physical, to both her and Matty, words about cutting and strangling, references to tortures so sadistic that she leaned on the small table for support and nearly tipped it over. The speaker's voice seemed to come from a distance as if he had held the receiver away from his mouth or perhaps put it inside a paper bag before making his savage pronouncements. The last one ended with "If not tonight, tomorrow. Gonna have some fun."

Linda Bluenight retrieved the gun from the kitchen drawer where she had stowed it after Peters left. She thanked him silently. Then she carried pillows, a blanket, and a book of poetry from her bedroom and propped herself up on the sofa. She was wide awake when Matty arrived home. She kissed him off to bed with some excuse about insomnia, and began her vigil. At 2 A.M. clouds roiled up and wrung out the rain they had carried north from the Gulf of Mexico. Yellow and gold streaks of lightening kept her company and stayed the darkness momentarily. She finally dozed off at dawn with the gun in her lap and the book open to Joy Harjo's "They Had Some Horses."

<>>>> **Eighteen** <<<<>

Where There's Smoke

When Linda Bluenight woke at mid-morning, the Sonora smelled like the orange tree in her yard. Small puddles dotted the sand, and finches, gnat-catchers, and English sparrows drenched themselves in the ready-made birdbaths left by the sudden rain. Hedge-hog cactus and teddy-bear cholla glistened with drops of moisture as translucent and precious as diamonds. The ocotillos, which had played possum since the summer monsoons, now turned green with new leaves that appeared as soon as the rain began to fall. Winged clouds feathered an azure blue sky and the air was crystal clear.

As she strained her sleepy eyes to gaze out the front window, Linda could nearly see the sloping entrance to Madera Canyon at the base of Mt. Wrightson, the highest peak in the Santa Rita Mountains. Minutes later, the sun began to shrink the pools and soak up the wet spots on the front porch. As she stepped out to retrieve the morning paper, she found herself already planning a siesta for the afternoon of this lovely cool day. Her eyelids were lead weights from too few hours of troubled slumber, and her neck and knees had stiffened from her semi-fetal position on the lumpy old couch. She intended to ask Matty to hang the hammock when he finally roused himself. Then she meant to monopolize it.

She needed time to devise a strategy for keeping this nightmare from him. She toyed with the idea of sending him to Kansas City. She could tell him his grandparents needed him which was true enough since both were in poor health. Matty was sure to revolt at the mere suggestion that he miss next week's game, but he would go if she insisted.

As she bent over to pick up the Saturday paper, she noticed the slumping Ranger. All four of its tires rested limply on the ground, causing it to list to the right like a sailboat with a bad rudder. The all-terrain heavy-duty radials had been ripped apart with what looked to be a small axe. She stumbled across the yard to see if the vehicle had been stripped and was relieved to see that it was otherwise intact, but someone had urinated on the driver's door. The smell was unmistakably human. Four obscene messages, four tires slashed, and four was the favored, nearly sacred number in Tohono O'odham mythology. It was being used to terrorize her, and the caller's final refrain had mentioned slashing her face.

Instinctively, she clutched her robe and peered around to see if she was being watched, feeling as she had when the coyote's glass eyes had stared up at her, as if she was caught in a cage with invisible walls. Then she remembered that she had left the gun on the sofa under her blanket. She hurried back to the house, entered, and locked the front door behind her. She found the weapon and placed it in the deep pocket of her robe.

Felipe Morena repaired his neighbors' vehicles in the shed he had built in the creosote grove behind his home. Linda recalled seeing him labor long into the night to earn extra income for the children's school wardrobes. He called himself a car shaman, and he had cured the aging Ranger's ailments many a time. For a moment she hesitated to call on him so soon after Ramon's death, but she guessed that the distraction and the extra money to allay Ramon's funeral expenses might appeal to him. If he was unable to bring fresh tires to her place, she could use Matty's pickup to collect them, but she hoped he would come himself before her son awoke to face this new fright.

She walked to the kitchen to place the SOS call and to make coffee. As she picked up the receiver, she saw the fire. Its smoke and flames were racing across the field behind her house, and it was headed directly toward her. The November breezes had shifted from summer southwesterlies to the northern gusts that characterized Sonoran weather at this time of year. They blew the flames along, obscuring the Catalinas behind and throwing up orange forks of heat, igniting weeds and brush like firecrackers, and giving off plumes of thick grey smoke.

She knew at once the blaze had been set. It was almost exactly the width of her house and as relentless as an army on the march. She dialed the Tucson City and Pima County fire departments. Both assured her they would answer the alarm, but in both cases it would take fifteen minutes for their trucks to reach her. They instructed her to turn on her garden hose and start soaking her backyard. As she did so, she also soaked her terry robe. She changed into her most tattered jeans and flannel shirt with lightening speed before she remembered the pistol. She wiped it clean with the ends of the robe and restored it to the kitchen drawer next to the knives, nearly laughing at her passion for order at such a time.

She returned to the phone to dial the Sax Xavier tribal office, although the fast-approaching inferno had started hundreds of yards from the reservation boundary. Looking closely, she now saw that its far edge straddled the line separating her land and some vacant county property. "Hello, I need to alert the volunteer firefighting unit." She had trouble keeping her voice level. "There's a grassfire behind my house. It will reach me within twenty minutes. The city and county are on their way, but they won't get here in time I'm afraid."

"We've already seen it, Ms. Bluenight," replied a female voice on the other end. "The truck is on its way and the men are coming in their own cars. Are you wetting down the place?"

"Yes, but I only have one hose, it seems like a trickle compared to what I need."

"It will help. Just hang on . . . maybe you'd better move some things out to your front yard if you can."

Linda banged down the receiver before the woman could complete her sentence. She ran to get Matty out of bed and had to shake him to get his attention, "Matt, boy, wake up for God's sake. We've got a fire out back. It may reach the house. We've got to get things out."

"Holy carrumba, vamos." He was alert in an instant, slipping into his pants and Nikes while he grabbed a laundry basket and commenced hurling things into it. Then he began to streak back and forth, piling possessions in his pickup. He was determined to save everything, but Linda made him help her first with the pictures, mementos, and important items that tied them to each other, to their family back in Kansas City, and to this place.

"Where's Mouser?" he shouted, searching frantically for

the cat.

"There he is, we scared him with our chasing around," said Linda, pointing to the animal's new hidey hole under the kitchen sink. She reached down, scooped up their pet, and carried him to the cab of the pickup where she placed him gently on the floor.

Matty was panting now, "We'll load the Ranger next. Are the doors open?"

"We can't use it, dear, someone slashed the tires." There was no avoiding the truth now, no way to protect this young life she had nurtured from the facts she knew would torment and terrify him. Unable to look at him, she raced back into the house for their clothes.

He was right behind her, cursing violently, "What the hell are you talking about? Did it happen last night while we were asleep? Or is that why you were camped on the sofa when I came home? Mom, was it the same guy? Tell me!"

"Matthew, honey, we can't go into it now. We've got to deal with one mess at a time. Get the rest of the things from your room. Please, hurry."

She remembered she had forgotten to call Felipe. Frantically, she punched in the numbers. Martha answered on the first ring, "Linda, are you all right, my daughter?"

"Yes, Martha, but I need Felipe's help. Is he there?"

"He and the family are on their way to your place now. The office called to tell us about your fire. I wanted to come myself, but Mendina needed me to stay with the babies. They should be in your road any minute now. Ahnih ho'ige'ithahun hekaj ahpim."

Linda looked into the face of the flames only a few hundred feet from her back door. "We're going to need your prayers, my mother." Just then she heard the sound of tires squealing in the driveway.

"Mom, they're here!"

The twenty-year-old fire engine from the village ground to a halt, followed by a giant flatbed truck carrying huge water tanks on its back. Behind it was a parade of cars and trucks full of Tohono families who had come to the rescue. Some of the men leaped out and began to connect hoses from the first truck to the tanks of the second. Others jumped on the bed of the second truck and prepared to turn the cranks which would initiate the flow of water as soon as the signal came. Still others, armed with rakes and shovels made for the blaze itself to dig trenches, clear brush, and set up a firebreak. Women carried blankets, buckets, and mats to douse hot spots as they arose. They had also brought water jugs and swaths of cloth to make wet masks. Rita Orozco approached Linda, lugging a first aid kit under her arm, "You and Matty all right, honey?"

"Yes, thanks," but Linda leaned on the other arm Rita offered her. "Thank God I woke up when I did or it might have been on us while we slept. I thought the rain we had last night might make the ground damp enough to keep the thing from spreading so fast."

Rita shook her head, "After three months with no moisture except those few showers last week, the brush out here is tinder dry. It would have taken more than last night's few sprinkles to protect it from someone playing with matches. The bastard probably started it in two or three places anyway." She looked at Linda protectively, "We'll fix him good when we find him." The primal vengeance shone in her eyes. Then she nodded towards the men and added, "Don't worry, these guys make Smokey the Bear look like a firefly. I've seen them put the Forest Service to shame fighting lightning strikes on Kitt Peak."

The calm, efficient organization of her friends and neighbors reassured Linda, although the smell of smoke was becoming stronger by the minute as the black seething carpet of charred earth inched ever nearer her backyard. A twin-engine truck from Tucson's west side station pulled up and its occupants sprang into action. This relieved some of the men from the village who entered the house and began to carry out furniture and heavy appliances. They loaded every pickup and car trunk available and drove the vehicles to the edge of Los Reales, just in case.

Matty and his friends formed their own crew and played Red Adair, helping the professional firefighters lug the heavy hoses from place to place across the plain in front of the blaze as the flames jumped and retreated unpredictably. Then the winds suddenly blew the fire forward. Standing next to the back wall of her beloved rancheria, Linda could feel it getting warm. The ground beneath her was too hot now to stand on comfortably. Then she heard one of the county firemen mutter that they would be lucky to save anything. She ran to a bucket, dampened a rag, and tied it around her hair. Then she grabbed a shovel and started toward the blaze.

"You ever fought one of these babies before?" asked Tom Orozco as she reached him at the fire line and began to shovel sand on it

"No, but it doesn't take an engineering degree, I'll bet," she answered grimly.

"Just keep your head turned aside, or the hot air will take the skin off your face. Spread the sand across the coals at the edge of the line, like this." He demonstrated his technique patiently, but without taking his eyes from the tongues of flame thrown up by the wind.

"Linda, why don't you come back to the house? I'll help Tom. You'll burn your feet in those tennis shoes." Brian Flynn had rushed over from the rectory, wearing heavy canvas boots and gloves.

"I've got to do something, Father, I can't just watch it all go up in smoke. My life is in that house."

"Your life is over there," Flynn admonished her, pointing to her son, "and over there," indicating the school which the heavy smoke drifting south had nearly hidden from their view. "Besides, people are about to hose down your walls and roof. You can make sure the windows are closed and help dig a trench around the foundation. Go on now, and have Rita bring us some drinking water." If the firmness in his voice was not sufficient to persuade her, the burning on the soles of her feet did the trick.

The Morenas worked as a unit around the perimeter of her house. Mendina soaked the outside, beginning with the wooden window frames and fanning out to the adobe walls. She took particular care to wet them down without dissolving the clay base, proceeding from the back to the sides and then turning the blast of water full on the roof. A shingle slid off here and there, crashing to the ground.

"Fore," shouted Rudy, laughing as his brother scurried from a falling missile. He and Steve shoveled dirt away from the base to create a sort of dry moat, their quarrels quiet as they stood shoulder to shoulder in the face of present crisis. Felipe and the twins cleared away any residue of brush that might carry a spark. They worked quickly and efficiently, the girls encouraged and instructed by their father who spoke to them gently and in low tones.

A few minutes later they and everyone else redoubled their efforts as the flames reached the backyard. The young people, complaining, were sent by their elders out to the road to await the outcome. Their parents and the firemen retreated slowly, giving only the inch of ground they simply could not save with water and sweat. Matty, his face streaked with soot and tears, refused to leave. He snatched up the garden hose and walked bravely and foolishly toward the highest flames. Linda went to him and wrapped her arms around his waist, "Come on boy, I couldn't stand to have you barbecued along with everything else."

"But your garden, Mom, you worked so hard on it." They were both sobbing now. The posies and vegetables she had lovingly cultivated through the hot summer evaporated in a paroxysm of light and heat.

"Lucky I got the tomatoes and peppers in last week," she began, meaning to make a joke. Then she remembered that the Mason jars she had used to can them were sitting in the pantry. She tried again, "At least we got rid of those awful oleander bushes. I've been trying to clear the place of those ugly, poisonous things for years." She steered him back toward the house as she talked.

Suddenly, in a hot desert minute, the wind shifted to the east in another seasonal mood swing, causing the fire to turn back on itself like a scorned lover. The Tucson firefighters pounced on it with a vengeance. The Tohono O'odham gave a collective yell and rushed to help douse the retreating flames, laughing and clapping each other on the back as they worked. Linda stood unbelieving, not knowing who to thank first. They labored for another hour to get the flames smothered. Then, while the firefighters patrolled the area checking for hot spots, the villagers joyfully moved the Bluenights' belongings back into their home. To reassure herself that the place was really safe, Linda took the opportunity to rearrange some of the living room furniture.

Martha called to congratulate them and promised to help Linda put in a new garden, assuring her that the charred remains of the burned plants would make wonderful fertilizer.

When she returned to the living room from the kitchen, Linda found the people gathered for an impromptu meeting.

The format was traditional. Felipe and Ron acted as moderators though anyone present was free to make a proposal or offer a suggestion. Len Rodriquez, who worked at the tribal office, requested volunteers to patrol Los Reales until the arsonist was caught. Hands stabbed the air from all parts of the room. Rita stood to say that since Linda was too courageous to move from her house, the other families should take turns spending nights with her and Matty for a while. A sheet of paper and a pencil were passed, and a member of virtually every household signed it.

"I need to say something," said Linda. "Because I've been trying to protect Matty, I haven't told you everything." She testified then about her discovery of the coyote and about the previous night's phone calls. "I worked for a police department for nearly eight years and never ran into anyone so vicious," she concluded.

Matty looked at her as if he had never seen her before. She had trouble meeting his eyes, but it all had to come out now that these people had risked so much for them.

An older woman complained that the police Linda had assisted during the Benton Brody incident should be doing more to assist her now. She promised to draw up a letter to the Tucson police chief and go door-to-door in the village for signatures. Brian Flynn added that he would make an announcement from the pulpit at Mass the next morning, asking for more volunteers. Copies of the letter could be placed in the church's tiny vestibule for people to sign. Another man reminded the crowd that no matter what the milgahn police might see as their duty, "We have to take care of our own."

Linda glanced around, moved beyond words at the unsolicited generosity and quiet heroism of these people. They sat without complaint after the ordeal of fighting the fire and formed a plan to help her which could put them in danger.

Now it was time for her to give back, time to find answers for the accusations against Ramon, time to give his family respite from the unacceptable circumstances of his death, time for her to take of her own. With a pounding heart, she looked over at Matty who wore the familiar grin that said, "Hell, I ain't mad."

<>>>> Nineteen <<<<>

Schemes and Dreams

Morris Peters walked through Linda's front door just as the head of the church altar society began to speak. Lining the room and spilling over into the kitchen and hallways stood sooty, tired, but animated Tohono O'odham villagers ranging in age from fourteen to seventy-five, men and women, old and young.

Peters' eyes quickly found Linda who sat on the edge of the sofa with her son at her side. She had seen him enter, but could manage only a weary smile. The edges of her dark hair were singed on the right side and black, streaky smudges were smeared generously through her clothes. He shook his head at her to convey his concern, but he succeeded only in giving off an air of futility.

"We should make a novena," the woman said. "Every night I will offer a candle to one of the santos on the altars in the santuario. I will begin with St. Matthew for the boy's sake. Before each I will say a decade of the rosary and the prayer for deliverance. Quien quieres venir con me?"

A dozen people raised their hands, including some of Matty's friends. They looked pleased that she did not propose to begin the vigil tonight, since the homecoming dance was still scheduled to commence at eight o'clock.

A man from the "Big Res," recently moved to San Xavier, announced that his brother-in-law out at Wawhia Chini was a healer who could perform a cleansing ceremony for the house now that it had been violated by an enemy. It had worked with the Apaches, why not on a milgahn scumbag? Linda's only expense would be to pay for the cost of the shaman's drive across the reservation. Linda nodded her ascent.

Then Rudy Morena rose to his feet. He was obviously shy about making himself the center of attention in front of his elders, and he was also a bit embarrassed, since everyone in the room had heard about his recent escapade. "I would like to say that the basketball team wants to help Matty out. We'll choose pairs and arrange to pick him up for school. Then someone will stay with him after practice and follow him home when he's ready to come so he'll never be by himself. That okay with you, bro?"

Matty was embarrassed, too. The last thing he wanted was an escort service, but he accepted the offer so as not to offend his buds. "Sure, " he said sheepishly, "but you guys aren't gettin' in the shower with me."

"Anything else?" asked Len, after the laughter subsided. "Preguntas? All right then, everyone knows who's in charge of patrols, stay-overs, church services, and petitions." He looked over at Peters and said this last word with amused emphasis. "Let's get to it. Oh, and don't forget the festivities tonight," he added as his teenage daughter nudged him from behind. "I'm told the band starts playing at eight-fifteen."

"Before we break up, I want to tell you how grateful we are," began Linda, getting a bit choked. " Tell you what, when we get past this, I'm going to throw a big cookout for everyone . . . and we'll do food this time."

As the meeting drew to a close, Peters walked across the room to Len Rodriguez and the cluster of tribal deputies who proudly served the San Xavier district. Their job had been made more dangerous in recent years by the drug trade from Mexico and the crush of illegal aliens from all over Central America. Smugglers used the vast expanses of the "Big Res" as a land conduit, but they also often passed through Wak Chekshani, the village's formal name, burgling and stealing cars as they went. In the case of illegal immigration, men who transported human life for a price and who had blasphemously nicknamed themselves "coyotes," often dumped their charges without food, water, or money in the desert. Each year dozens of Guatamalans, Hondurans, and Mexicans were discovered dead or dying across the Papagueria. This was the first time, however, that Len and his deputies had come face-to-fire with a milgahn arsonist and sex pervert. Standing together on one side of the room, they filled Peters in on their plans.

He concurred and added, "Let me coordinate between your office and the station downtown. We should be able to spare a patrol or two during the day. The county won't mind a little help from the city on this one. With the three agencies concentrating their resources, this area will be so thick with uniforms nobody will dare make another pass at these two."

Len was particularly furious at what he had just learned from Linda. A man worthy of his life did not spend his days tormenting women and children. "I'm going to put my hunting rifle in the car when it comes my turn to patrol. If I find his ass on the county side, I'll put one foot on reservation land and blow him away from there."

"No harm, no foul?" quipped Tom Orozco. "I think we ought to hang him up on one of the big saguaros out west and let the animals take their own revenge."

"I'm not hearing any of this," said Peters. He turned to where Linda and Matty were engaged in earnest conversation. "Will you be at the office so that I can call you when I get the chief's okay?"

"You bet," answered Len, "then I'll pass the word to the volunteers."

Ron added, "My wife and I will be over here with our sleeping bags tonight. The more of a presence people make here, the less likely the bastard is to leave any more 'gifts' at the door."

Linda rose from the sofa when she saw Peters approaching. Looking down at her son, she said, "You know I wouldn't have deceived you if I'd thought there was anything you could do to help."

"So you took all the crap the guy dished out. Mom, you're not giving me enough credit," Matty lectured, while also letting his mother know how much he admired her courage.

Peters interrupted gently, "If it's any comfort to you, Matty, your mother did confide in me. I'm afraid I haven't been much help, but that's going to change now."

"People are filing out. Let's be good hosts and say good-bye," Linda said, reaching down to pull Matty up and take his arm.

They stood beside the front door, shaking hands and hugging their neighbors, trying once more to express their gratitude for the hard work it took to save their little homestead. Matty walked the Morenas to their car, teasing the twins about their new look, "Those charcoal eyebrows will be all the rage at school on Monday." On either side of him, the girls punched him on the arms and laughed as he tried to escape their harmless blows.

Brian Flynn drew Linda aside with news of Bart Berdini. He looked both anxious and relieved. "There was a message on my recorder this morning when I returned to the rectory from saying Mass. Bart knew I wouldn't be there to answer when he called, and he also knows that Conchita normally does not work on Saturdays. He obviously didn't want any discussion or argument about what he is doing, although I'm still not sure what that is.

"At any rate, he said I shouldn't worry about him, that he is in New Mexico, somewhere up around Abiqui, north of Santa Fe. He drove up there with that family at Ramon's funeral to visit an Apache community where the girl's maternal relatives live. She was Ramon's novia and his death has devastated her. Her parents hope that a stay in the north will help her heal. He added that he has information about Ramon, and that when he gets back he'll tell us more about it. That was all, he didn't even mention my accusation. I feel even more stupid now. Still, I keep wondering why the man won't show that righteous anger in his own defense. Maybe he simply refuses to grace it with a denial, or perhaps he has some indirect connection to the crime. Now with these dreadful things happening to you, I'm completely confused."

"I know just how you feel, padre," Linda replied, "I wish I could wait until he gets back to see if what he knows will help end this parade of horrors, but I need answers now. He didn't say when he might return?"

"I'm afraid not. I just got the impression that it would be soon. As for answers, now that the village has stepped in to help, the police department should be free to step up its search. Peters looks competent enough."

"He is," Linda confirmed, looking over at her friend who had left the house and walked to the rear of the place, inspecting the ground for leftover sparks. "I'd better talk to him about all this. Please, let me know if you hear from Brother Bart again."

"I certainly will, but I have the feeling there won't be any more communication until he opens the rectory door. In the meantime, I'll help network the action groups as they get the "Bluenight Project" under way. Things will be easier for you now, dear. Try to rest and enjoy what's left of the weekend."

When the last guest was gone, Linda sent Matty to town with a list for groceries. She watched him drive away, and suddenly the adrenalin emptied out of her overcharged system. Her hands began to shake with fatigue and anxiety.

Peters had come back into the house. He made her sit in the kitchen, "I'd have come sooner, but I was away from my scanner for a while. I picked up word of the fire when I took the squad car to the diner by my house to get a late breakfast. I was afraid I'd find you burned out by the time I could get here. You've got good friends."

Linda nodded weakly. "I need to open all the windows,

the house smells like smoke," but she failed to part company with the chair.

"Let me." Peters moved quickly through the rooms, pulling back curtains and raising sashes. The breezes danced through the hallways and the air began to freshen as they continued to blow what remained of the smoke westward to dissipate as it approached the mountains near Kitt Peak.

He straightened and moved objects at her direction until the arrangements of the small pieces suited her and reassured her that she still had a home. Then he fixed tea and a sandwich and placed them in front of her on the kitchen table. He poured himself a cup of coffee and came to sit across from her. "We look like an old married couple," he joked.

She smiled wanly and took a bite of bread and smoked turkey. "You make a mean lunch," she answered, eating slowly, watching him, and letting herself relax for a moment.

"Should we tow the Ranger in for new tires?" he asked solicitously.

"No, Felipe is going to bring some this afternoon. Do you think my auto insurance policy will cover the cost?"

"I'm sure it will. Vandalism is usually included under the theft clause."

He took a deep breath. "Linda, I want you and Matty to come and stay with me. My place is a split-level and has four bedrooms. You and Matt can have the upper floor. It has its own bath. Jeanine's been gone four months now. A mutual friend of ours called last week and told me she's landed a job in Portland. She'll probably file divorce papers from there. Anyway, I'm alone and I'll be gone most of the time anyway. The shifts downtown are endless. You guys would have the run of the place, and it's not so far away from your job and

Matt's classes here at the school. I'm north of Grant Street on Copper Avenue. The boys in homicide love that one. I wouldn't try anything, Linda, unless you wanted me to, of course. These people mean well and I know they'll do their best, but they don't have law enforcement training. Will you think about it?"

She was already shaking her head, but she also reached for his hand to let him know how much she appreciated the gesture. "I am tempted, Mo, really. After this morning, I'm not sure there's safety anywhere. At any rate, Matty will never agree to an evacuation. You should have seen his face when I told him I'd been thinking of sending him to stay with his grandparents. You'd have thought I wanted to rent him a room on the moon." Her mind drifted toward a scenario that was only now beginning to take on form, a scenario in which Morris Peters could play no part.

"When there are no concrete leads in a criminal case like this, an investigator's options shrink, but sometimes that simplifies everything. When there is only one route left to take, traveling it becomes a lot easier."

"Riddles make me crazy, Linda, what's up?"

"You sound like Matty now." Her attention returned to him then and to his offer. "When this is all over, I'll let you buy me that dinner, and maybe a bottle of champagne to go with it. Right now though, I'm swamped. I've got to get Matty ready for the dance this evening. It will be a nice break from fighting fires. I'm also supposed to chaperone, though I think I might duck out a bit early and spend the evening preparing my classes for next week. Believe it or not, Matty and his bunch are going to Mt. Lemmon for a picnic tomorrow. I may be making sandwiches until dawn."

"Fine, fine, but I need to know more about this route business so I can take it with you," he coaxed, attempting to keep pace with her metaphor. "You cannot resolve this by yourself, babe, and I'm not going to let you take any more chances. Don't get me wrong, I admire your guts, but you just mustn't put yourself at risk."

"I want you to trust me, Mo. I haven't quite figured out what needs doing yet, but you'll be the first person I call when the smoke clears." Surprised that she was able to joke about such a near disaster, she wondered if her new found energy was the result of the food or the sudden surge of confidence that came with this decisive moment. "Thanks for feeding me, I feel a lot stronger."

Rising from the table, she cleared the table and placed the dishes in the sink. She felt Peters behind her. As she turned to face him, he put his arms around her for the first time. She began to shrink away, almost by instinct, but then, feeling the warmth of a man's physical nearness for the first time in years, she leaned into him. His cologne was fresh, his white shirt was soft, and his brown chest was hard under it. His strong hands encircling her back supported her. Even though she could not include Morris Peters in the actions she was about to take, she felt in that moment protected and cared for. She wished mightily that her tormentor would disappear from the face of the earth.

"You're holding a woman who has the aroma of over-baked bread," she said softly, resting her head against his shoulder. "I feel like I've used Liquid Smoke for deodorant."

"You can be my barbecue queen anytime," he answered, chuckling under his breath.

As she felt his rhythm beneath her, Linda Bluenight

realized that she had forgotten, perhaps by choice, the rewards of intimacy. Not now, she thought, not yet.

He bent down to kiss her.

She gave him her cheek.

He accepted it.

<>>>> Twenty <<<<>

The Whites of Their Eyes

When it opened its doors a decade before, Las Canyones Resort won every major architectural award in the United States. Its pueblo-style stair-step buildings nestled the Santa Catalina Mountains much as did the ancient cliff dwellings they were designed to imitate so that, from a distance, they were nearly indistinguishable from the mountains they embraced.

The first view for guests as they arrived via Sunrise Drive was the golf course with its xeriscaped fairways. The tee area at the first hole and the green at the eighteenth lay just beyond the hotel's wide glass and brass doors, and man-made ponds connected to overflow dams welcomed golfers to the final green from a series of holes where diamondbacks and horned lizards presented as many obstacles as sand traps. The Lingerer's Lounge beside the duck-laden pools provided a picturesque patio for tallying up a score card at the end of a round.

Inside the baked brick buildings, guest suites, each with its own hot tub, also sported sumptuous Southwest furnishings and private patios which bordered a desert stream to attract burrowing owls, cottontails, and Gambel quail. Advertisements in travel magazines boasted that the hotel offered 402 pools.

Two restaurants catering to Latin and Continental tastes were located on separate levels of the complex, and a central tower provided a view which at sunset compared to none in the Sonora. Visitors reserved standing places there to "ooh" and "ah" at the prism of color cast on mountain and valley many miles distant. They also looked down on a landscape which appeared so natural that the human constructions upon it seemed to have evolved of their own accord. Centuries-old saguaros forested the grounds and golf course. Varieties of cholla, prickly pear, barrel cactus, and cenita lined the walkways. Desert willow, mesquite, ironwood, and a dozen other native trees belied the northern stereotype of desert as barren waste. Las Canyones was the most sophisticated example to date of tourism's success in simultaneously attracting profits and quieting conservationist outcries.

The fact that it used precious groundwater by the megaton was unnoticeable to an eye insensitive to the delicate relationship between organism and moisture in an arid landscape. Small ground critters had reproduced so numerously on the protected property that they had to be trapped and transported to other areas. Their over-abundance testified to the fact that large predators like the coyote and mountain lion were disappearing from the scene. Meantime, car exhaust from the onslaught of traffic was beginning to "brown down" land near the increasing number of paved roads.

Now, in November, the tourist season was building steam, and the hotel was filled with affluent vacationers escaping the trials of winter in places like Milwaukee and Chicago. Business people had flocked to this desert oasis as well. A convention of Teflon representatives congested the massive lobby, and several ballrooms were filled with demonstrations of cooking utensils from microwave pans to food processor attachments.

The main exhibit hall had been reserved for several computer firms. State of the art PCs lined the walls, including one which eliminated the need for a keyboard. The user could now simply speak into the machine which in turn printed the words on the monitor.

Linda Bluenight chose the place that Sunday evening partly because of the crowd. It was unlikely that her culprit, should she find him, would turn violent in the midst of so many onlookers. The hotel was also proximate to the site of Benton Brody's demise, and she hoped that the guilty person might be suitably unnerved by the fact to reveal himself under her questioning.

During the past twenty-four hours, she had made dozens of telephone calls, running down information on her list of suspects, trying to determine their whereabouts on the day of Brody's murder. She had dashed back and forth to the library to bother the patient reference clerk for more old news accounts about the connections and relationships, personal and professional, between Benton Brody and her possible "perps". She had even made excuses to the other parents at Matty's dance so she could spend a sleepless night in painstaking reconstruction of the events surrounding Brody's last day while the Verascas camped out in her bedroom.

Morris Peters had helped at every turn, spending hours

with her on the phone, answering her questions and taming her speculations. He had filled in gaps from file reports on police interviews with business associates, family members, friends, and acquaintances.

Now she waited in the gigantic lounge just off the main lobby. The easy chair she had chosen sat near the grand piano next to the glass rear wall of the hotel. She wore a white long-sleeved shirt and a loose-fitting blue denim skirt. On the right arm of her chair lay a matching jacket. Inside its pocket a tiny tape recorder was loaded and ready to record. She had only to press a button which she could accomplish simply by placing her hand against the fabric.

A woman in a black velvet dress played show tunes for the crowd huddled around low tables, potted palms, and fireplaces. Linda looked for a moment in the opposite direction toward the immense glass panels at the front entrance. In the early evening, lights were beginning to appear in the city far beyond the ponds and the golf course. Her village and her home seemed very far away.

She turned back toward the piano player to catch the refrain from "Don't Cry for Me Argentina." Then her eyes wandered to the enormous swimming pool in the middle of a mammoth terrace outside. Beyond it were hot and cold hot tubs at the bottom of a hillside. Water poured into them from artificial openings at the top of the hill and gave them the appearance of spring-fed mountain pools. Far back from the rooms behind the main building, she could just make out the waterfall, enchanting in a man-made way as it cascaded down a steep gulch. A pair of golden eagles had built a nest at the top of the hundred foot elevation. From there they could watch the water careen down into a stone-lined pool to pass through various streams on the hotel property. The portion that did not evaporate along the way was finally recycled after use in the duck ponds.

Linda cradled a cup of tea in her lap and experienced a calm she had not felt in many days. She intended to resolve this crisis tonight, or prepare to leave Tucson with Matty tomorrow. She could not permit the people at San Xavier to wrap their lives around the needs of the Bluenight household indefinitely, and the two of them could not continue to live in fear and foreboding. Tonight she would finger the man who had made the hideous phone calls, the man who shot the coyote, the man who came within yards of them while they slept to vandalize her vehicle and set fire to her property, the man who either had murdered or was responsible for the murder of Benton Brody.

At six-twenty, late as usual, Lee Sims strode through the hotel entrance. Looking aggravated and uncomfortable, he ignored the ingratiating advances of the bellboy. He wore a grey felt Aussie hat at the top of his husky frame and heavy hiking boots at the bottom. Both were coated with dust as if he had taken pains to show his contempt for this immaculate setting. His knee-length khaki shorts were torn on one cuff, and he carried a six-foot walking stick that he swung carelessly as he crossed the room to where she sat.

"Hello, Lee, I'm glad you could make it." Last night she had requested a meeting with each man who answered her phone calls. She had lured them to this place with an offer of information concerning their specific interests in the Brody matter. Sims had agreed to the rendezvous with some reluctance, telling her that after the encounter with Rudy Morena, he was sick of the whole mess. From what Linda saw in this morning's *Tucson Tribune* however, his illness was not serious enough to keep him from pumping as much publicity out of the situation as he could. "I saw the piece in the paper. Did the reporter contact you or did you volunteer the story?" No reason to play diplomatic footsy with these guys anymore, she thought with some satisfaction.

"I called the editorial desk to inform its staff of the incident," he answered without embarrassment. "I also wanted to request space in next week's Sunday edition for a guest column, to give people the skinny on that coming crackdown I told you about. The bastards refused me the space, but at least they printed something. We can't pass up a chance to publicize the havoc Eastman is reeking in this community, can we?"

Since such an opinionated inquiry did not demand an answer, Linda wasted no time providing one, "Did you find your credit cards?"

"I canceled them," he said with a satisfied smile. "It was easier than chasing all over Tucson for the damn things. I shouldn't have them in the first place. Santa Tierra's image might take a hit if people saw its fearless leader filling his gas tank with poison and then paying for it with plastic."

"It does conjure up a contradiction or two," Linda agreed. She would have to be more direct and aggressive with her other interviewees, but this one was easy. That morning she had verified his alibi. He had appeared in municipal court the day Brody died. Afterward he celebrated the dismissal of the "Disturbing the Peace" charges which the police department and Eastman Inc. had filed against him some months ago following his outfit's civil disobedience in the Tucson Mountain incident. The court records showed his presence at the first event. Several S.T. members and Peters had confirmed his attendance at the second.

"I mentioned to you in our conversation last evening that

our little session would be crucial to your cause."

"It's the only reason I came," he responded with more than a hint of impatience.

"I'm about to crack this case," she said in a steady voice, without introductory remarks. Sims was fully aware of her intense interest in the Brody slaying. "When I do, it will change forever the relationship between your side and the other, between the interests of cornucopia and the needs of preservation. It will shake the foundations of some of Tucson's major institutions. People will suffer, a lot of people. Investors, small holders as well as fat cats, may lose their savings and their livelihoods. Environmental activists, especially high profile organizations like yours, could experience a backlash when the local economy crashes. Working people, especially in the minority communities, will get the shaft if jobs and resources dry up as a result. I wish I could change those outcomes. I can't unless I refuse to act, and for my son's sake, I can't stand by and do nothing. I'm telling you this so that you can prepare yourself and your organization. Comprende?"

Sims looked at her as if she was speaking the Tohono lingua franca she had been studying, then he sat silent in the face of such a dramatic statement.

Linda was a bit abashed by it herself, but because he was first on her appointment calendar, she could not be more specific. She did not admire the man, but the work he was doing had value, despite its dubious methodology. Many of those who stood with him had made substantial sacrifices to keep the Sonora from further despoliation.

"You're saying you know who wasted Brody, and that whoever it is has a name I would recognize?"

"I think so," Linda measured her words, "We'll know

manana."

"You thought it might have been me for a while, didn't you?" Sims asked the question with a slight show of malice.

"For more than a while, Lee."

The matter-of-fact tone in her voice stopped him cold, so he simply rose to his feet and left without a word.

The steely hardness in her voice came as a surprise to Linda, as if she was equally inured to them all, the guilty and the innocent, as if her anger at being forced into this situation needed a variety of outlets. She justified her actions with the thought that Sims was thick-skinned enough to handle a little sarcasm, and she remembered how many of her friends had said that she was not very skilled at it anyway.

Her mind shifted to Matty. She wondered what the boy was up to. He had risen early for a day on Mt. Lemmon with the Grazia girl and a half-dozen classmates. It relieved her to think of him in the protective arms of the Catalinas. The winter was still too young for much snow to have fallen on the 9000 foot peak, so he and his friends could scamper about on the slopes and cook lunch down by the lake in Rose Canyon. He had nearly refused to go when she told him she was working on the case. He had discovered her slumped over the kitchen table asleep, with the cold coffeepot beside her and a legal pad full of hand-written notes for a pillow. Together they had prepared a food basket, and she had coaxed him to his truck.

Looking up now, teacup raised half-way to her mouth, she saw Allen Linton, as prompt as his predecessor had been late. He made his entrance and stood by the massive front desk looking around with obvious displeasure. He had stated flatly during their phone conversation that he also disliked Las Canyones, but for different reasons than Lee Sims. He was simply not temperamentally fit for the artificial civility of such places.

Linda placed her cup and saucer on the spotless glass table beside her chair. Then she reached toward her jacket pocket and gently pressed the "Record" button on the taping device, feeling the vibrations begin in the tiny machine under her finger. Finally, she gave a small wave of her hand to attract Linton's attention. He walked over, filling up the room. At last, a man big enough to bring this place down to size, she thought, smiling to herself, trying mightily to stifle the thread of fear that began to unravel within her when she saw his huge frame come lumbering toward her. She had discovered no alibi for this man. Trying to knot the thread, she cut right to the chase, "Professor Linton, thank you for meeting me. I appreciate your conceding the place and time. I need to ask you a few questions, 'mano a mano' you might say, about where you spent your afternoon a week ago Friday."

Linton's face grew darker with Linda's every word. "That was the day Brody bought the farm, wasn't it? You've been dogging that one like a bounty hunter. I'll tell you once more that whoever did it committed a moral act. Brody and his family have killed everything they've touched in this desert, its legacy, its land, its future. Why can't you let him rot? Is it the dead kid, Morena, you're trying to protect? You can't help him now."

"I'm aware of your low opinion of Eastman Inc. That doesn't tell me what I need to know. Where were you at the time the man was shot, Dr. Linton? I've been able to determine that you were neither on campus nor at home."

The look of murderous rage which spread across the professor's face and the clenching of the enormous fists nearly convinced her that she had her man. Then she realized that the rage was directed not at her, but toward the memory she had evoked. He looked as if he might lift the Steinway and hurl it through the window into the swimming pool beyond. "I drove up to Florence to visit that graduate student I told you about. Her name is Karen Dugan. She has been confined to the psychiatric wing of the state hospital there for over a year, thanks to your victim and his boss."

Linda's ears caught the only softness she had ever heard in the man's voice as he uttered the woman's name. She asked her next question carefully, "Is she the woman you were involved with at the time of the controversy over the Rincon sites?"

"We were engaged."

"God, I'm sorry, I had no idea. I guess the hospital people saw you then?"

"Of course."

"And you were there all day?"

"I stayed until around five in the afternoon. Then I drove over to Casa Grande to visit the archaeologist who curates the museum and the ruins at the State Park there."

Eight hundred years ago, the Hohokam had constructed an astrological observatory on a flat stretch midway between what are now the cities of Phoenix and Tucson. It was the only "high-rise" structure prehistorians had ever found connected to this town-based society. As a popular stop on tourist maps, the structure was now in danger of collapse from the constant vibration of traffic from roads surrounding it and from the thousands of visitors the park received each year.

"We're trying to find a way to stabilize the walls before the damn thing comes crashing down on some Cub Scout troop," Linton continued. "At any rate, I didn't get back to

Tucson till after eight that evening. You think I killed Brody? Hell, I wish I had. The thing is, I'd have done them both and made a real job of it."

Linda realized with insight that releasing his anger was the only thing that seemed to give the man any comfort. His anguish permeated the room.

"Karen broke after we lost the Rincon excavations. She'd put years of work into the project. Her career revolved around preparing for both the dig and the long-range analysis afterward. It was as though she'd had a miscarriage. I'd asked her to marry me a long time ago. I met her when she enrolled in a seminar I was teaching. She was the brightest, most energetic student I ever had. She said she would consider it after she finished her dissertation, but when that came to a halt because of Eastman's bribes to the zoning board, so did our engagement. Then she tried suicide. She nearly succeeded the second time, the scars on her wrists and neck still haven't healed completely. Now she's an invalid. Heard enough?"

"Yes, I suppose I have." Linda's list was shrinking. "Eastman Inc. seems to have destroyed people and places all over this town. Do you have any idea who might have done this murder? I have a lot at stake in finding out."

"What happened to the case against the Morena kid?"

"It's still there, but as I told you, I can't buy it, and now that I've started asking questions, someone is threatening my family."

"The bastard." He stared at her a moment, assessing her acumen and deciding on his next words. "There's only one person in this town who hates the Eastman/Brody contingent as much as I do. That person could afford to have the job done by contract, or he could have paid one of the toughs on his construction crew. Do you know who I'm talking about?"

"Barron Kingley."

"That's right, Barron Kingley." Linton spat out the name as if it were sour milk. "He's no better than the others, just louder. Wouldn't that would be rich, if you could bring down one robber baron by proving he killed another."

In fact, the man was due at Las Canyones Resort within the hour.

<>>>> **Twenty-One** <<<<>

Dinner and Danger

The rancheria lights were glowing when Matty returned from his excursion to Mt. Lemmon. He parked his pickup in its usual spot and sat a moment listening to it wheeze. Its sixteen-year-old engine was exhausted from the journey up and down the narrow winding highway. He gave the dashboard an affectionate pat and lingered a minute more, remembering the day. At sundown he had led a motley caravan down the twisting two-lane that connected the desert floor with the tallest peak in the Catalinas. As he had descended the several ecological zones along its route, he had longed to spend the night high up in the alpine forest. Peg had been sitting close to him, her head resting on his arm while they listened to rock music by a Navaho group called Thunderhead. Now, having just left her at her parents doorstep, the memory of her lightly scented hair spread across his shirt made him warm all over.

As he climbed out of the cab of the truck, the sky above him turned an indigo blue, another early night in a state which refused to acknowledge Daylight Savings Time. He disliked the early onset of darkness, but Linda said an hour was a small price to pay for not having to adjust one's clocks and one's body twice a year. The note on the kitchen table informed him that she had gone to town for one more meeting, but that this would be the last. The absence of detail in the message concerned him some, but it read casually enough. He also learned from it that if he opened the right doors, he would find one course of his dinner in the oven and another in the refrigerator. He should heat one and dress the other.

The mother wrote that she was looking forward to hearing about his day, and there was the obligatory question about his homework. The Verascas would be returning around 9 o'clock to spend another night. They could use her room, she would bunk on the sofa. She signed her message, "Love, M."

Not tonight, Mom, thought the son.

Going to his room to survey the damage, the boy began to hurl clothes and books and tapes into his chest of drawers and onto shelves along the wall of his closet. He searched out clean sheets from the cedar cabinet in the hallway, stripped his bed with two jerks of his long arms, and made it up fresh, neatly tucking the corners of white percale for a change. Taking a shoe box from the littered closet floor, he scooped in the coins, torn movie tickets, gum wrappers, and assorted litter from the top of the chest, slapped on the lid, and shoved the box under the bed. Finally, he gathered up the remnants of dirty laundry scattered in small heaps around the floor and deposited them in the "mystery hamper" as his mother called it, this in reference to the fact that she could never be sure of its contents on wash day. Examples from past excavations included a bicycle pump, a chameleon alive and kicking, several rounds of ammunition left in Matty's pants pocket after his one and only hunting trip, and a girlie calendar given to him by the one and only Tommy Orozco.

Satisfied that the room was no longer lethal to the sensitivities of adult visitors, he fetched the "Welcome" mat from the front porch and placed it in front of his door. Then he grabbed some bedding, piled it on the sofa, and marked it "Matty's" with a sheet of paper from the notepad near the message machine beside the telephone. Only then did he notice that the red light was blinking. He decided to ignore it and walked into the kitchen to see what dinner surprises awaited him. Thirty seconds later, curiosity overtook good sense and he returned to the phone table. He stared at the instrument as if it were an enemy, but its incessant glow was too much of a challenge, an evil invitation he could not refuse. With a trembling finger, he pushed the appropriate button and waited for the singing cellophane to begin the playback. He wondered if his mother had changed that silly outgoing she had recorded a while back. As he recalled, it went something like, "Matt and Linda are out punching a few doggies. Leave a message and they'll get back to you. Until then, vaya con Dios." His friends were all over him about it.

Ron Verasca's voice interrupted his train of thought. He was just phoning to confirm their arrival time. Not to worry, he said, the security team of Verasca and Verasca was up to the job. Matty smiled at the notion of a slumber party with his high school principal. As the tape clicked off, he heard himself sigh with relief. After all, there was no one around to notice how jumpy he was under his cool-guy exterior.

The girl thing reared its pretty head again. Peg and her

folks had gone to town on a family shopping trip when his
house terrors were taking place. She had been understanding
when he told her the whole story at the dance, but she had
been careful not to seem worried that he might not be able to
take care of himself. Showing that she respected his manhood
made her even more attractive. In fact, he was due at the
Grazia house for desert at eight. Peg's mom had invited
people over for flan, and her version was the most famous in
the village. People often asked her to make the dish for their
baptism and birthday fiestas and paid her for her efforts. Her
custard as light as air, and its caramel sauce blanket went
down like liquid silk.

The modest get-together would wrap up the weekend
festivities. His basketball ascendancy, a new girlfriend, and a
near holocaust, all in less than forty-eight hours, made for a
full life. He looked around his little domicile with the eye of
a proud property owner, and it occurred to him quite suddenly
how much a part of his life this old place had become. His
mood became fierce as he contemplated what might be
required to protect it. He thought to borrow one of Tommy's
shotguns. His experience with firearms was limited to that
single hunting adventure with Tom, and he had missed his deer
by a mile, but he also knew that accuracy was not as important
as the sound and fury such a weapon would make. Besides,
if he had to nail the dirty A-hole he would. The thought of his
mother or any woman having to listen to those obscene
messages made him rigid with rage.

He returned to the kitchen and checked for groceries.
Peg Grazia might fill his heart but his stomach was empty and
it would be nine o'clock or later before they sat down to the
sweets. As promised, a pan of lasagna and a loaf of garlic
bread were waiting for him in the oven and a huge wooden

bowl filled with salad sat chilling in the fridge. He lit the oven to warm the pasta and chose the bottle of vinegar and oil dressing for the greens. Then he set the table with two plates just in case his house partner showed. He wondered what had turned his mother on to the Italians lately, thinking with a smile of his mother's ethnic eccentricities. She tended to stick with one culture until she exhausted its food supply. Last year, he had given her a wok for Christmas and they ate stir-fry every night for a month. When they first moved here, she had learned Southwestern cooking. Now she could make masa and roll fry bread balls with the best of them.

He showered and used two kinds of soap, a deodorant for his "pits" as he referred to them, and an astringent for his face. He shampooed vigorously and splashed a musk-smelling conditioner through his dark hair. Hopping out, he gave his body a swipe with the towel, wrapped it around his waist, and inspected his stubble in the mirror. Not much there but he decided to scrape it off anyway. He wanted his chin to be baby-bottom smooth for the big good-bye. The moment of kissing was definitely at hand. He was determined to make a statement about the weekend, and he also intended to make a date for the next one. They could drive to Nogales and go to the bullfights, although Peg might find the sport a bit macho. She had indicated that the world revolved too much around boys and ignored the "rest of us." Her little declaration had made him a might uncomfortable. He wondered if heterosexual matters had been easier in his grandparents time. He had always been hesitant to ask his mother about hers. Fatherless before birth, he had no knowledge of his parents' love life, and he had yet to see her involved with a man. The world of love and sex was just now beginning to puzzle him.

He caught a whiff of tomato sauce and hurried to the

kitchen, clutching the towel as he ran, to switch the oven off before the lasagna turned to toast. Then, since he seemed destined to dine alone, he decided to do so au natural. Sitting at the table with a fork in one hand and a large serving spoon in the other, he rearranged the plates, putting them both directly in front of him. He ladled half the lasagna into one and most of the salad into the other, broke the loaf of bread into two parts, and placed a piece on each plate. Then he poured Romano cheese over the pasta and the better part of a bottle of "Little Italy" over the tossed vegies. Finally he proceeded to consume the entire meal in five minutes flat. Silently, he congratulated his mother on a job well done and promised to return the favor.

He dressed carefully in light blue denims, matching shirt and sockless white Nikes, and opened the bottle of expensive after shave he had received for his birthday last August. With nose puckered, he dotted a little on his neck. Then he rubbed some into the twelve hairs on his chest before buttoning his shirt.

It had been a bad hair day since they had hit the peak at Mt. Lemmon. The wind had played havoc with the thick black manes of all the kids. Later they had taken turns combing each other out after they got to Rose Canyon to spread their lunch baskets and blankets by the lake. Peg had untangled his locks first and then handed him her hairbrush. His hand had shaken and he nearly plunked her on the head with it trying to pull through her long shiny tresses. The night before at the dance, she had worn it piled on top of her head with a vivid pink ribbon wound through it. Combined with her matching dress and its capped sleeves which showed just a touch of shoulder, Matty had trouble keeping his eyes off her for even a minute. Now he slapped his cowlick and prepared to surrender to the fate of his pate when it occurred to him that if aftershave was good for chest hair, it might work wonders on his head. "You're a genius, Bluenight."

Remembering that company was due, and that his supper dishes still occupied the table, he hurried back to the kitchen to clean up. He took a spoonful of lasagna and put it in Mouser's bowl. The beast gazed at his dinner and at Matty with a "Say what?" expression. "Ingrate," chastised his master. The boy added a note to the note on the table, addressing it to both Linda and the Verascas. "To who/whom ever gets here first. Gone to Grazias for flan. Back by l0:30. See yas soon. Matt." He turned on more lights, but knowing that the Verascas would follow minutes after his departure, he left the front door unlocked for them.

The boy stroked the pickup on its bumper. His mother had surprised him with it last summer on his sixteenth birthday and paid its owner $500. The man had bought it new the year her son was born, and that had sold her on it. Matty liked to say that he and his wheels were growing up together. Felipe Morena had rebuilt the engine and Steve did cosmetic surgery on the interior. Matty continued to be ecstatic about having his own transportation and cared for the vehicle as if it were a child.

Just before he lost sight of the house proximate to the turn off to Indian Agency Road, he glimpsed a late model Bronco behind him. When it reached his place, it suddenly veered into his driveway. Unless the Verascas traded in their sedan yesterday, he knew it could not belong to them. Curious and fearful, he turned back, realizing his mistake in leaving the front door vulnerable. Though he possessed the teenaged tendency to think of himself as immortal, fires and murdered coyotes had altered that impression. There was no

Bronco like this one on the reservation or among his friends. Even from a distance, he could see that it was expensively detailed, its black and chrome exterior gleamed under the clear night sky. Why hadn't he borrowed the damn shotgun from Tommy earlier? He could have kept it under the dash out of Linda's sight. They had nearly argued about the gun Peters loaned them. Now it sat in the kitchen drawer, useless.

The boy turned his headlights off, slowed the pickup to a crawl, and drove past his house, keeping his head low to the steering wheel. He turned around at the dirt track they used as a shortcut to the mission and made another pass. The Bronco was parked in a dark spot beside the house. Apparently, the driver had entered through the front door which was now slightly ajar. Who was this poser, a burglar? The creep was doing awfully well at his trade, thought Matty, unless he had stolen that fancy four-wheel before he paid this little visit. Then the boy realized that his thoughts of burglary were wishful thinking. This was the slimy cucaracha who had been stalking them. He tried not to lose his head. He could drive to tribal headquarters, but by the time he got there, the slime-ball might be long gone. He turned the truck around once more and drove back. At least he could keep the guy in his sights, maybe get a license number as he drove away, if he drove away. With sudden fear, Matty remembered that the Verascas were due any minute, and that his mother could return at any time. Maybe the intruder was waiting for his victims. True, his interest did not lie in Ron and Verona, but if they should get in his way...

Before he reached the house again, he switched off the truck's engine. Then he wheeled the vehicle just off the road into a shallow drainage ditch behind a clump of tall creosote bushes and let it roll to a stop. From this vantage point, he could see the front of his house, yet if luck was with him and the moon did not rise too quickly, he could stay out of sight of the stranger who had invaded their home. He decided that if the man did not come out within the next few minutes, he would go straight to the San Xavier headquarters and report the break-in.

As Matty sat in the dark, fearing and hating and planning, a lone figure made his exit through the front entrance, closing the door behind him carefully. He carried no loot, and he wore a hooded grey sweatshirt that covered his features, including his face. The garment was so bulky and loose-fitting that, obscured by darkness, it was difficult for Matty to discern how the man was built, whether he was heavy or slim, wide or narrow. He appeared to be about Matty's height, maybe an inch taller. He walked rapidly to the Bronco, his hands shoved in the pockets of the sweatshirt, and it was the walk that Matty recognized. Its familiarity jarred him, though its step was not particularly distinguished. It was simply imprinted in a general way in the boy's mind. He knew this man somehow and the knowledge increased his fear.

Matty felt some relief that the villain was leaving his house, that no harm would come to the people he loved. The Bronco backed into the front yard, turned around, and proceeded down the driveway toward the road. Instead of turning right toward Indian Agency Road, the vehicle wheeled left toward Matty who prayed feverishly that the small grove of greasewood would provide enough cover to camouflage the pickup from the driver's view. Apparently it did because the stranger continued beyond Matty's hiding place and did not hesitate. The dark hood pulled around his face shrouded the man's profile, but Matty caught a sense of his general appearance as the Bronco, going at modest speed, passed directly before him, giving him a clear, upward, momentary glimpse. The feeling of familiarity ran through him again, and caused the hair on his arms to stand straight up.

The Bronco turned down the dirt track and headed for San Xavier Road and the village. Matty turned his key in the ignition when he became certain that the man was far enough ahead not to notice.

<>>>> Twenty-Two <<<<>

Reckoning

Clay Eastman moved through the ornate lobby of Las Canyones Resort with the brazen assurance of a man about to become its master. As he entered, close upon the heels of Allen Linton's departure, he greeted the doorman cordially and approached the front desk to chat with a clerk.

Eastman appeared to be in familiar surroundings, hobnobbing with the help, checking out the competition. Dressed in white slacks, matching blazer, and royal blue Polo shirt, he looked like any hotel guest out for a drink and a good time. He spotted Linda in the crowd, nodded in her direction and went about his rounds, passing the time of day with the chatty woman at the information desk, and leaning around to peek at the event schedule on her computer screen. Scrutinizing the customers, the bar trade, and the decor, he wound his way to Linda's chair. "Hello, again," he said, "You look comfy."

"I was just about to ask for a refill," Linda answered, showing him her empty cup. "Join me?"

"Sure, but not with that stuff." He motioned to an attractive female server, tastefully dressed in a tan skirt and western-style white blouse. "Bring us a pair of tequila sunrises, please, and go easy on the grenadine."

Linda was no in mood for fashionable drinking, but she decided to indulge Eastman for the moment. "Quite a place, isn't it?" she offered.

"It will look like a bed and breakfast when we open the Bonita Canyon resort," Eastman replied, ungraciously.

"You're continuing with the plans then? I thought you might delay construction for a while. As you said, your family has been through a difficult time, especially your niece."

"Oh, yes," Eastman's eyes narrowed, "Jay was a good kid, worked for me, too. We'll all miss him. Matter of fact, I'm thinking of sending the women back East for a while. If it weren't for my mother, I'd have them on a plane right now. She's in a coma, the doctors don't expect her to live through the week. Once she's gone, my wife will accompany Ben's people to our place in Bridgeport. Is that why you asked me here, to talk about the family?" The facetiousness in this remark was unmistakable. Clay Eastman sounded not so much like a man grieving as an executive working out his business itinerary.

"Not really," Linda answered. She paused to let the young woman serve their drinks while Eastman pulled a twenty dollar bill from a soft calf-skin wallet.

"I'm still unclear about the circumstances surrounding your brother-in-law's death. I know you were at your offices when it happened, holding staff meetings, but can you tell me what Jay was doing that afternoon? I understand that his job was to assist you with errands and courier duties and such?"

Eastman took a long, level look at her and then nodded toward the piano player, "That woman has nice hands. They stretch an octave across her keyboard. Maybe I'll make her an offer she can't refuse and steal her away for our supper club. I'm not sure where Jay was that day. I don't think I had any special assignment for him. He might have been gadding about somewhere, or with Holly for that matter. Did you check with her?"

"I didn't want to bother her at a time like this, but I did review the police report. It said she was playing golf with some friends. Jay was not one of them. That checked out. Any other ideas?"

"You suspect Jay of foul play in my brother-in-law's death? It's unlikely as hell. The two of them were close. Jay had helped Holly, and Ben was grateful. That's why we gave him the job. You're on a fishing expedition. You won't catch much out here in the desert." His tone was not as casual now. He picked up the large goblet, removed the straw from its contents, and dropped it with a clink onto the table. Then he took a long drink and frowned at the glass, complaining, "Premixed, not a good idea at $5 a crack. Speaking of jobs, yours doesn't pay much I imagine."

"I do all right," replied Linda, surprised by the sudden shift in subject.

"I'm sure. It's just that I have an associate who's recently built a resort complex on Kauai. Much of it is in year-round condominiums, and he's thinking about starting a small private school for the children of his buyers. He'll need a headmistress, and he'll pay at least double the salary the mission school can offer you. I could put in a word. I should think your son would like the idea. Hawaii would be a nice place for him to finish growing up."

"Mr. Eastman, what in the world are you talking about? Matty and I aren't interested in leis and luaus. Could we get back to the topic?"

"We're on the topic, lady. I'm offering you a chance to get out of your predicament here before it's too late. I heard about your close call yesterday. Jay's ghost didn't set that fire. Whoever did is a desperate and dangerous man. The two of you might not be so lucky next time. I'm just trying to help."

"Or to bribe." The words came out before she could stop them. No choice now but to follow them up, she thought, her pulse quickening. "Until this minute, I wasn't sure, but now I'm finally beginning to put it together. I believe you know exactly where Grayson was the day your brother-in-law was killed, because I think you sent him to do the job."

"For your sake, I'm going to ignore that little speech. I'll call Mr. Ho and have him contact you. Accept the position, and I'll pay your moving expenses and find you a place on the island to live, a beach house maybe. I might even manage a stipend for Matty when it comes time for college. That is the boy's name, isn't it? Do yourself a favor Ms. Bluenight, take the money and run."

His mention of her son made Linda's skin crawl. Now that she knew the truth, it both outraged and terrified her. "You miserable cretin," she began as the color in her face heightened to a high crimson. "You sent that sick, inept young man to kill your own kinsman. You didn't like the idea of hiring a professional because you wanted full control over the assassin. You probably gave Jay your pledge that he would always have a position with your company and plenty of money to go with it, and you let him believe you would actually let him marry Holly Brody. You might even have told him how and where to purchase the murder weapon. Then you ordered him to take Benton Brody for the proverbial ride.

"Brody had gone home that day to lunch, maybe to get away from you. Jay was probably staked out at your place waiting for Brody to leave on his return trip to town. When he came out, Jay must have run down the hill and asked him for a lift. He might have said that you had phoned, asking them to meet you here to discuss how to improve this setting when construction began at Bonita. Once they were in the car, Jay somehow convinced Brody to drive to the Ventana Canyon trail. He might have had to show Brody the gun to get him to do that. His first and last murder was quite an accomplishment, considering that he wasn't very bright and was a big time drug user, but that is just what made you nervous enough to eliminate him.

"He was also making Holly's addiction worse, and the poor girl is like the daughter you never had. You came to despise your brother-in-law for more than just his misgivings about the direction of Eastman Inc. He hadn't been a very loving husband to your sister, or a very devoted father to Holly. You might have even thought you were doing them a favor.

"As to the details of Jay's demise, it's hard to envision you dirtying your hands on a car engine, but you probably know enough to loosen a brake lining or cut through a clutch cord. There were many ways to transport "the women" as you call them back from Flagstaff, but you sent Jay because you knew he'd never get there. How am I doing so far?"

"Too well, my snooping friend, but before you go on, understand this. First, you have no proof. Your little scenario is nothing but hearsay and fantasy. Assuming it's correct, remember that a man as ruthless as the one you describe wouldn't hesitate to take out someone else who got in his way.

"Ben had become a spineless wonder. He was a hindrance to my business and a burden to my family. In fact, he was threatening to tear them both apart by pulling out of the company. He also planned to take Evelyn and Holly back to Connecticut. Once they were there, he planned to divorce one and put the other in a sanitarium. So you see, he was preying on my interests. As for Jay Grayson? He was a social cannibal, nibbling his way into Holly's heart and my bank account.

"A man capable of killing his own brother-in-law and a whining failure like Grayson would have no compunction about doing the same to you. In fact, he could do worse, he could kill your son, and he could tear that grimy Indian town of yours apart. Hints of sexual molestation by that high school coach of Matty's or by the good padres would lead to the kind of scandal that might just result in suicide among a people who have a knack for it anyway. You can't lay a finger on me, but I can do worse than take your life. I can make you end up taking your own, like old Ramon did." Clay Eastman finished his confession with an ugly, low-throated laugh.

Linda was shocked at how easily he admitted his guilt, as if murder and merger were part of the same vocabulary. The man was more evil than she suspected, and she realized that for all his cunning, he was as much an amateur at committing violent crimes as she was at solving them. He had made enough mistakes to permit her to sit there and work out his pattern, though he was nearly right about her not having any concrete evidence. The tiny tape recorder containing a single thread of verbal testimony was her only claim on the truth, all that she would have to show Peters and the police to verify a story that now seemed too fantastic to be credible, and the only shred of material worth an indictment of this monster. Too late, she began to doubt the wisdom of her strategy. She was far from the nearest police station, and there were few patrol cars in the affluent foothills. She needed to grab her jacket with its precious cargo and get to a phone. "If you're trying to frighten me, you're succeeding," she said to keep him talking while she thought of how to get out of her chair and passed him.

A bank of telephones lined the wall opposite the front desk near the doors, about fifty feet from where they sat. A bevy of bellboys loitered beside it. Beyond the phones, a long hallway ran along the lounge and extended back to the ballrooms. Eastman was positioned directly between her and her objective. She silently cursed herself for her seating arrangement.

"I wish that were enough, for both our sakes." Eastman's jaw was clenched.

Linda looked at him sharply. This murderer was also a megalomaniac willing to take other people down with him, an economic zealot whose sense of prophetic self-importance surpassed concern for any form of life. She thought of the goings on at her place over the last few days. "Who did you hire to terrorize us, another weakling like Grayson?"

He ignored her as he looked toward the pool and the rear gardens, then turned to survey the front entrance.

Linda glanced at her watch. Barron Kingley was overdue for their rendezvous. She had intended for their meetings to overlap, hoping that a confrontation might reveal the truth. Such a face-off was unnecessary now, but she needed a distraction, and she felt semi-confident that she could locate a phone in a different area of the hotel.

"Let's go," Eastman said suddenly, making her jump.

"Where?" She clutched the arm of the chair as if he might be about to snatch her out of it.

"We're leaving," he answered, nodding toward the front doors. "My car is in the lot just across from the Lingering Lounge. I need some air, and you need to stay where I can deal with you."

"I don't think so." Linda answered as she came carefully

to her feet.   She picked up the hip-length denim jacket and slipped into it, pulling her arms through the sleeves slowly. Then she took a step away from him, turned quickly on her heel, and walked toward the telephone nearest the bellboys who were chattering away about their plans for an after work beer bash.

She felt him behind her, since he had taken two strides for every one of hers. Placing his right hand on her shoulder, he came close against her so that his breath weighed heavily on her neck, and she sensed something hard against her back. He had put his left hand inside the pocket of his sport coat to grip the handle of a small caliber pistol. He nudged her with it again and turned her toward the glass doors.

"Don't make me shoot you, lady. I really don't want to, at least not here." His voice had an almost sensuous quality as he guided her past the semiconscious young doorman, who grinned at Eastman in recognition and nodded at Linda. "He thinks we're lovers," Eastman said with wishful amusement.

Linda shivered with revulsion.

They stood for a moment in the massive driveway. Directly beyond them lay the duck pools where mallards and shovellers slept peacefully beside the artificial dam. "I hit a ball into that water the last time I played here. That's too frustrating a way to end a round for most out-of-town visitors. We'll make our Bonita course more subtle." He spoke as if he were out for an afternoon of light-hearted corporate spying.

Below them to the south, the twinkling lights of Tucson were coming up fast, like the tails on a million fireflies at mating time. The view of it in the soft light of dusk was beyond lovely, and it suddenly occurred to Linda that it might be her last. She decided not to go quietly. "I'm not getting into a car with you, mister."

"Here's the point, lovely Linda," he broke in, ramming the

nose of the gun painfully into her side, "If I have to shoot you here, I'm out of business anyway, so you'll have to die while you watch me knock over a few other people. You'll know you're responsible for their deaths as well as your own. I'll start with the help." He indicated the doorman who was not much older than Matty. "The management will have to put an ad in the classifieds tomorrow. Now, be a little cooperative, can't you?" But Clay Eastman was sweating profusely though the air was cool and clear. Suddenly, he changed his mind again and forced her back into the lobby, through it, and out the rear entrance toward the vast pool area.

Linda began to understand that he was half-frantic. She also knew that she had to stay one thought ahead of him. He might have tampered with Grayson's Lexus, but other people had done his face-to-face killing for him. He might lose his nerve and try to buy her off again or attempt to intimidate her into silence, but he had too much at stake to simply let her walk away.

They watched as the pool party roared into full swing. The sound of laughter and clinking glasses rose in pitch with each endless moment. Then he began to talk in her ear, trying out his still evolving plan while she silently questioned his sanity.

"After you called this morning, I drove to Tombstone where I didn't have to worry about being recognized. I found a pawnshop named for the OK Corral where the owner only takes cash and doesn't mind winking at the waiting period. I love this country. We're going to walk toward the hill behind this badly designed water hole. Up the path where it's darker, I'm going to put a bullet through your pretty head and get the gun into your hand to make it look like a suicide. I even bought a pearl-handled beauty a woman like you might carry in her purse for protection. The police will think you purchased it recently and decided to use it on yourself when the going got tough. What do you think, sound plausible?"

Linda could not decide whether the voice she was hearing belonged to a man going mad before her or just a sadist enjoying his work.

"I guessed from your phone call that I was on some kind of suspect list. I had to come and see how near the top you put me, and whether or not you had already contacted the police."

The police, that was it. "Of course I've contacted the police. You don't take me for a complete fool, do you? Morris Peters knows everything. I asked him to meet me here and I also asked Barron Kingley to show up," she lied. "I wanted them both to see you squirm when I confronted you with the truth. Too bad they missed that part of the show, but they should be arriving any time."

"I don't think so," he responded, doing a poor and somewhat grotesque imitation of her earlier remark. Eastman curled his free hand around her waist, pulled her to him, and pushed them both through the scores of revelers by the pool. Some were dancing precariously by the water's edge. Others clustered round the bar across the way. A drunk New York computer salesman dropped his porta phone into the deep end, cursed, then laughed and jumped in after it, splashing them as they hurried by.

"Excuse him," laughed his wife from her chaise lounge, "Too much stress and Scotch, I'm afraid."

A flight of shallow stairs rose away from the twin hot tubs which looked even more like mountain pools with their underwater lights glowing in the darkness. Linda stumbled as Eastman pushed her up and away from the affluent array of guests. They climbed a hill where wings of rooms blended with the desert to another path which led to the waterfall at the northeast corner of the property.

Eastman shoved her in that direction with only the light of the waning moon, risen moments before, to guide their way. If she walked any farther, all hope of attracting help would be lost.

Linda whirled to face him and took a mighty swing at his arm to loosen the revolver from his hand and give her time to duck into the brush. In response, he fired a single round. She felt as if someone had poured scalding water on her left side at the waist.

Then she heard another shot.

<>>>> **Twenty-Three** <<<<>

The Pain

Shocked by the impact of the first bullet, Linda searched her body with her hands to discover where the second had hit her. She found no wound, because her assailant had not fired the shot. Incredulous, she peered into the eyes of Clay Eastman who stared back at her in amazement, and in death. He fell toward her, and she stepped aside, letting him hit the ground face down. A bullet had penetrated the back of his neck, neatly severing his spinal cord from his brain. Finding such a target in the darkness took a crack shot.

Now she was surprisingly alert. In a nanosecond, she had looked her own death in the face and then had watched as the second of Eastman Inc.'s executive officers passed from this world. The sight of the man who had been about to murder her crumpled dead at her feet and the searing pain of her injury combined to clear her head. Straining to look down the path beyond Eastman's lifeless body, she spotted an angular figure

holding a revolver. A voice called to her. It belonged to
Morris Peters. She reeled with relief until he came close
enough for her to see the mixture of sorrow, fear, and panic in
his eyes as the moonlight flickered across his face, until she
realized that the gun he held was pointed directly at her.

"You should have stopped, Linda. Why couldn't you just
stop?" As he walked slowly toward her, Linda Bluenight
turned cold and empty, as though the blood oozing from her
side and down the length of her skirt carried with it the hope
that had so far filled her life.

"You're part of this?" she asked, breathless, not really
wanting an answer.

"As much as you are, unfortunately. I tried to spare you.
I did everything I could to stop you from pursuing your
ridiculous investigation into the Morena kid's death, but you
wouldn't let it go. Now it's too late, and that's too damn bad,
because I really do care for you. Are you badly hurt?"

Linda groped for the recorder in her pocket and felt it
pulsating against her hand. "Please, Mo, tell me what's
happening here. You were involved with Eastman?"

"Yeah, the bastard sucked me in good," said Peters with
an astonishing lack of anger, "but I didn't mean for it to end
this way. I originally intended to turn this guy in for killing
Brody or to make sure he paid me well to keep quiet. You
see, I followed a few hunches about Jay Grayson, and I was
able to piece together a probable picture of his whereabouts at
the time Brody was being shot. I also found out about his role
as Eastman's combination valet and toady boy. Did Eastman
tell you that part of Grayson's job description called for him to
serve as a mole in Brody's household?"

"No, but he did admit to paying Jay for Brody's murder,
so it makes sense to think that he'd been using the kid as an
informer."

Stay calm, Linda counseled herself, keep him talking, as her eyes suddenly clouded over with pain.

"The night after the killing, right about the time poor Ramon was getting arrested for it, Jay got ripped out of his skull and went to Eastman's place. He demanded a bundle and said he was going to Fiji to spend it. If Eastman didn't fork over, Jay swore he'd spill his guts. First, he would tell Eastman's wife and then the cops that Ramon was innocent. In his confession, he would claim that Eastman drugged him and forced him to commit the crime. With his father's influence, he would probably get off with a few months in drug rehab. Eastman would get life, if not lethal injection. You can imagine what effect that little announcement had on our man here. He was pretty well freaked out by the time I arrived, which was not long after you and I talked out at the school. I missed Jay by just a few minutes, but I could tell Eastman had decided to dispose of him, either by making him the fall guy or by using more direct methods."

"Yes, all right," replied Linda, wondering how heavily she was bleeding and how she was ever going to get away from this murderous charlatan who had posed as her would-be lover. "And then you blackmailed Eastman, or was it the other way around? I can't tell the difference between the two of you anymore."

"Really, Linda, I didn't decide what to do until I scoped the man out. I hadn't asked for a warrant or even reported to the chief about what I suspected. I wanted to get the lay of the land first. I thought Eastman might trip himself up or that Jay might bolt and run and give himself away. I could always turn them in if a better opportunity didn't present itself."

Looking down at the prone figure before him, Peters continued, "He certainly was a clever bastard. His talent for conspiracy was demonic, especially when it came to defending his interests and saving his skin. He'd have gotten the proverbial book thrown at him if I'd fingered him, but as it turns out, I didn't. His offer was too tempting. All I had to do was play with Grayson's car and a little automobile accident would take care of the rest. That left just poor Ramon. I knew he'd be held in the county jail so I could pop in to see him any time I liked. The personnel situation there is deplorable, and I have passing acquaintance with the guards, a few of them are actually drinking buddies. Paying him a visit the next morning was no problem."

Whether from loss of blood or the numbness produced by these new revelations, Linda's mind was began to whirl like a run-away Ferris wheel. She struggled to concentrate, "But why kill Ramon, Mo? He hadn't even given the police an alibi for his whereabouts. That and the credit cards were enough evidence for an indictment. You might have gotten a conviction. Even if it were for second-degree murder, you'd have been rid of him."

"You were responsible for it, partly," Peters announced to her with some satisfaction. "You were the one who insisted that the killing wasn't part of a robbery attempt. Your report incorporated those comments about premeditation, remember? That might have caused enough doubt in the mind of a judge or a jury to let Ramon off and leave the file on the case wide open. Eastman couldn't risk it. Besides, young Ramon gave altogether too honest and earnest an appearance for us to take the chance."

Linda staggered a bit, but there was nothing on which to lean apart from the stands of cactus beside the path, so she tried to breath evenly until she could regain her balance. The idea that she had unwittingly contributed to Ramon's death made her nauseous.

"The kid was sleeping when I went to his cell. He'd taken

off his trousers and slung them over the bed. He was a small guy, too, though he was stronger than he looked. Anyway, he was groggy and off-guard so it was easy to take the pants and strangle him with them. Then I strung him up and let him fall. I remember one of the inmates down the hall calling out and asking what had happened when he heard the thud Morena's body made on the concrete. I told him I'd slipped. Some of those guys are smarter than they look."

Linda's pain and fatigue now dissipated again in the face of the unrelenting hatred she felt for this man so proud of his horrendous crimes. "I let you touch me," she hissed at him. "How many pieces of silver did Eastman throw at you?"

"He was going to see that I got a silent partnership in the company. Naturally I wouldn't be a part of the firm's overt business dealings, but I'd get a cash cut of Eastman's own profit shares. I planned to leave that bottom-sucking homicide department next year, buy a ranch in Mexico, and live like a regular human being."

Linda's jaw dropped as she tried to reconcile multiple murders with the normality in Peters' perverted vision of his future.

"Don't look so astonished, sweetheart. Killing is an event, not a process. It happens in a flash of time, then it's over and life goes on. The sad part is that I had to go after you when you wouldn't take Ramon's guilt for granted. When you started asking questions, people were bound to at least consider your doubts. Hell, I fought Eastman tooth and nail over you. He wanted me to erase you on day one, but I persuaded him to let me try some scare tactics first. Unfortunately, you didn't budge.

"When you went to see Eastman, he began to crack. I got worried that he would find a way to make me the fall guy. Bribing a few law enforcement officials wouldn't have proved much of a problem. You understand the guy was raving crazy. Come hell or high water, he was going to remain a free man and get that Bonita Canyon Resort under way. He would have arranged to kill half the people in Tucson to see that place looming above it."

Raising her eyes wearily to his, Linda asked slowly, "What now, Mo?"

"If you would promise to clear out tonight, I might consider not killing you."

"It will never happen."

"I know. I hoped the same thing before I bashed that monk's head in an hour ago. He wouldn't keep his mouth shut either."

"God, no. You didn't harm Father Flynn?" She could not bear much more.

"No, it was the other one. I was on my way to your place to retrieve this." Peters motioned with his gun hand. "I took the route passed the church and I saw Berdini outside the rectory, so I stopped to see what he was up to. I heard he'd left town with the Morena's girlfriend, and I suspected he was trying to find an alibi for the kid. Jesus, I hate zealots. He's been downtown raising hell about their rights a dozen times.

"He recognized me from one of those meetings, and he told me the girl was with Ramon the afternoon of the murder, that they had a doctor's appointment to see if she was expecting. Turns out she wasn't. Morena would not even mention her name to the police, much less tell them about her possible pregnancy. Berdini was planning to check with the physician tomorrow to verify the girl's story, but he was personally sure it was true. Then he was going to take it to the chief and have Morena's case reopened.

"It was no use arguing with him about it. When he offered me a cup of coffee, we walked around to the back door of the priests' house. There was a heavy spade in the rose garden there, so I just did what the moment called for."

Linda was breathing hard now and growing stronger as the rage within her took root.

"When they find him, it will look like someone was trying to break into the place and bumped into Brother Berdini along the way. You've got to believe me, Linda, I'd give a lot to avoid shooting you. When I invited you and Matty to stay with me, I wanted to convince you to drop your senseless snooping and marry me."

Linda staggered as if he had just fired another shot at her. If she had not been in fear for her life, the irony of this suggestion would have made it comic.

"Surprised? You shouldn't be. I am as in love with you as I've ever been with any woman. Now it's too late. I've got to have cover for doing Eastman, and you're it. That's why I went to your house for this gun. He told me about your appointment this evening.

"My fellow officers will conclude that you asked Eastman here to blackmail him. When he refused, you forced him to this secluded spot and shot him from behind. Before he fell, he managed to turn around and shoot you, twice. I'll just get that little pistol from him, finish you with it, and return it to his hand. Then, with you dead beside him, I'll put this weapon into yours. Lucky for me, the rushing water will cover the sound of the shots. I'm sorry, Linda, really," he said as he approached Eastman's prone body.

Like a dreamer out of time, Linda watched as Morris Peters, almost in slow motion, stooped to retrieve Eastman's weapon from the walkway near his still hand. She stood quietly and felt her strength returning now that the moment was upon her. A large Engelman prickly pear half-straddled the pathway beside her. It stood over three feet high and branched off in several directions. Its dozens of pale green protrusions resembled ping pong paddles glued together in strings. Many of them were still crowned with the remnants of the large red fruits they had produced last June, and the entire plant was covered with thick yellow thorns sharp as sewing needles.

Linda took as deep a breath she could through pain which had by now reached exquisite proportions. Then she spat on her hand and grasped a large paddle at its base, wincing as the spikes dug deep into her palm. It snapped off at the stem, and with one smooth motion, she hurled it as hard as she could at Morris Peters.

It struck him flush on the side of his face and stuck like cement to his right cheek and jaw. The shriek that came from his contorted mouth was a blend of infuriated howl and excruciating groan. He dropped his weapon in surprise and torment and put both hands to his face to pry the thing from his skin, cursing in a way that made her think only of escape. The pistols were now too far away for her to retrieve without Peters grabbing her, nor could she hope to reach the rowdy throng of revelers since Peters stood directly between her and the pool area. To further seal her off, the small streams on either side would drown out any call for help. All that remained to her was flight, and the only route open to her led to the waterfall.

# <>>>> Twenty-Four <<<<>

The Battle

The torrent from the top of the waterfall glimmered and flashed in the moonlight. Its cascade was the crowning jewel of the Las Canyones Resort, and now its mirror-like image drew Linda Bluenight like a magnet. She knew with certainty that if she remained on her present course along the path taken by the hotel guests, she would be little more than a moving target for her pursuer, a slow moving target at that.

She searched for a side trail and found none. In his haste to put distance between her and the party at the pool, Eastman had pushed her past the outermost wing of suites, so there were no small walkways she might use to dodge Morris Peters who would be on her trail as soon as he dislodged the cactus from his face. Linda hoped his skin and flesh came away with it. That would be partial revenge for the screaming in her side which in its turn had caused her ears to pound with a drumbeat that intensified with every step she took.

She crossed one of the small stone bridges that covered the flowing streams which wound through the property. Beside it a family of pocket mice played beside the water. Her movement frightened them, and they ran across her path. Then they scampered up the steep incline toward the top of the fall as if they were beckoning her to follow them. She had little choice, because the walkway ahead of her ended below the fall beside the holding pond and provided no shelter.

She looked briefly down at the left side of her waist and saw a mass of blood. Gingerly she placed her right hand on the center of the red stain, but could find no hole going into her body. Instead, the surface of her skin was torn and oozing, as if someone had taken a serrated knife and carved out a fleshy section. Not a good way to lose a skirt size, she thought wanly. She understood her increasing weakness, though the adrenalin surge caused by her sudden and decisive attack against Peters had provided temporary energy. She checked again for the tape recorder and pushed the tiny "off" button when she felt it tucked safely in a corner of her jacket pocket. Then she removed the garment, wincing with every stretch of her arms, and tied it securely around her waist below the gash. It gave the wound a bit of protection and support, and she hoped it would slow the bleeding.

Linda thought of Matty with a spasm of nostalgia. She wanted her life because she wanted to see him again, to hear him laugh and watch him chase the cat around the house as he had done since the thing's arrival. She longed to hear about his adventures on Mt. Lemmon with this pretty girl he had found. She wished she had been able to stay through the dance the night before so that she could have seen them together. He had cut a charming pose for her before he left that evening, though the two of them had wrestled with his necktie before they succeeded in securing a proper knot.

She pictured the mission and its White Dove, symbol of peace and center of her little world, beloved of the Tohono O'odham, sentinel of the Sonora. Her future, if she had one, was out there among the desert dwellers and their children. Once they had opened their doors to her and Matty and helped them create a decent life. She owed them more than she had so far been able to repay. She had to survive this night so they could all share the morning together.

Looking skyward toward the top of the nearly vertical rise above her, she left the path to climb its length. At the apex were a few small caves and crevices, havens for bats and places for raptors to nest and raise their fledglings. Perhaps she could find one to share with them and hide from Morris Peters. Perhaps he would not see her, not imagine that she would try such an acrobatic stunt in her condition.

Unfortunately, the moon glowed like a street lamp, her white blouse luminous in its light. Too late, she realized the mistake she had made in removing her jacket. She climbed on, but she could not be quiet about it. Rocks and shale particles bounced down the hill as she kicked at the ground, trying to keep a foothold. Her hands began to bruise and burn as she used them to help pull herself along, clawing at the sharp edges of the hill's rocky surface. Her legs felt heavy under her and they trembled as she struggled to find foot holds. She feared that she might be going into shock. Now she could hear Peters coming, behind and below her, and she knew she must be within his line of vision.

"Linda!" His voice froze the blood in her veins. "Please, stop. Let's try to work something out. This is crazy. I love you too much to go through with it. We'll go to the police together and I'll turn myself in. Anything is better than ending it this way. I know you're hurting from that damn bullet wound. There's blood all over the trail here. Let me get you to a doctor before it's too late. Answer me, please." The words were tender, but they were bordered by submerged rage and murderous determination.

If she had hoped Peters might retreat from his intent to take her life, either from fear or some sick brand of affection, that hope was dashed against the boulders around her as she heard the streak of lies coming from his mouth while he panted and scrambled up the hill in pursuit of her. Trying not to panic, she began to hurl whatever she could lay to hand down the hillside. The fist-sized iron pyrite pieces scattered by the landscapers to look like huge gold nuggets were just large and hurtful enough to distract him for a moment and cause him to slide back a step or two. Then he cursed and came forward. She could hear the gun clatter against the ground as he, too, used his hands to help his ascent. They struggled upward, one behind the other, both on all fours, she from fatigue, he to gain a position from which to overtake her. Looking behind her to see how much progress he had made, she sympathized with every living creature ever stalked by men with weapons. She would tell Matty, no more hunting.

Peters was only a few yards behind when she saw that she had climbed further than she thought. Her head spun with a minor case of vertigo as she watched the water falling and swirling in a torrent beside her. Its deafening sound drowned out Peters' pleas. She grabbed another fistful of debris, this time dirt and small pebbles, taking aim at his battered face. He was so close to her now that she could see the thorns sticking out of his jaw. The rubble she hurled at him hit him in the nose and he flinched and rubbed his stinging eyes as they filled with dust and tears. "Goddamn it, Linda, this has got to stop! Now!"

She reached the large opening at the uppermost crag where the water emerged to plunge one hundred feet to the pool at the bottom. With great difficulty she rose to her feet, trying to steady herself, high above the city of Tucson which shone like a diamond in the desert below. Jewel of the Sonora, she recalled from a poem, dreaming again for a moment.

Harm arrived as Peters scrambled up to join her. Linda Bluenight turned to face him, a rock in each clenched fist. She flung the first one at him, but he ducked it and nearly lost his balance. He rose upright again, looking at her with red and troubled eyes. Dozens of tiny black bats swirled above their heads. The Seri, the Tohono people's southern neighbors in Mexican Sonora, believed that these nocturnal creatures harbored the souls of their dead ancestors who returned at night to circle the earth and protect their descendants from evil. "Protect me now, Grandmother," Linda prayed.

In the distance, a coyote cried out for vengeance. Peters shuddered and glanced around him, as if he expected an attack from an invisible enemy. Linda drew strength from the animal's high-pitched yelp and took a precarious step toward him.

The water roared by in a recycled frenzy.

Morris Peters released the safety catch on the weapon he had taken from Eastman's lifeless grasp, and wearily took aim at the woman standing before him. She spat on his gun hand.

Then a human voice rose above all the noise and silence around them.

"Mom!"

<>>> **Twenty-Five** <<<<>

The Final Round

As Morris Peters prepared to commit yet another murder, Matty Bluenight's cry of alarm caught him off guard for a split second. Tense and incredulous, he stared at the base of the waterfall. "That kid is as stubborn as you are, Linda. Now I'll have to take care of you both."

Linda was stunned as well. There stood Matty beside the rushing water, his anxious face upturned, his hands cupped around his mouth.

In an explosion of rage and fury, Linda lunged at the man who would harm him. With both hands, she clutched his gun arm, clawing at it, and at the same time, throwing her weight against his side, trying to trip him or somehow force him to again drop his weapon. The ground was wet and slippery with spray, and their footing was precarious among the rocks and razor sharp cacti. They fought for balance as well as against each other.

Normally, Peters would have been able to simply shove her aside with a sweep of an arm twice the circumference of her own, but at sky level and on treacherous terrain, he was forced to move cautiously, twisting her first to one side, then the other, planting his feet firmly in one spot as she pounded at his body with hers. His shirt began to absorb some of the blood from her bullet wound, and he knew that her ability to endure this kind of physical punishment was fading.

Matty began to scramble up the incline shouting, "Hold on, Mom, I'm coming. Hold on to the bastard!"

"Get back!" she screamed, "For God's sake, get back!" For an instant, none of them was sure who she was shouting at.

Matty climbed on. He started a mini-landslide behind him as he pulled himself up with great strides toward the place where the two figures were silhouetted in their life and death struggle. His own struggle was equally desperate as he tried to reach them before his mother succumbed to Peters whose identity had shocked him almost as much as the sight of his mother engaging in hand-to-hand combat.

For the last hour, he had followed Peters' hooded figure north to Las Canyones Hotel from the reservation. Along the way, he had been forced to fall back in a hurry when the dark-colored Bronco suddenly stopped as it passed the rectory at San Xavier. After a few minutes, the vehicle had resumed its journey with him tailing it at a safe distance. At the time, Matty could not have guessed that Brother Bartolemew Berdini lay grievously wounded and bleeding beside the kitchen door. He only knew that the driver of the Bronco was responsible for the terror that had shadowed them during the past week, and that the terrorist was not a stranger.

It had quickly become clear that the man was headed for town, and it was then that he began to fear for his mother's safety. He had kept the vehicle in his sights during the long drive on I-l0 through downtown Tucson and into the foothills, but when they turned east off the highway for the final five-mile journey to Las Canyones, the Bronco was going so fast through the suburban traffic that Matty's old pickup could barely keep pace.

Finally they had arrived at the resort where he parked across the lot from where Peters put the Bronco, but before he could catch up with it, the grey sweatshirt had disappeared into the crowd inside the lobby. Minutes later, Matty had been astonished when he caught a glimpse of Morris Peters, hood thrown back on his shoulders, through the windowed rear wall against the backdrop of the monstrous swimming pool. Assimilating this revelation and what it meant in an instant of time, he had pursued Peters, but came up empty-handed again as one of the revelers offered him a drink, slapped him on the back, and nearly pushed him into the water.

After asking a few frantic questions of the people around him, the wife of the drunken businessman who had taken a dive to retrieve his cell phone had told him that she noticed two or three people headed for the waterfall and that she thought one of them was a woman.

Praying that he was on the right track, he had followed and found Clay Eastman's body sprawled headlong on the pathway before him. The corpse was already growing cold. Panicked by the sight of another murdered man and now knowing that his mother was in mortal danger, he had sped on toward the waterfall. He could scarcely believe his eyes when he caught sight of her and Morris Peters locked in battle so far above where he was standing.

He thought for a moment of racing back to the lobby to alert the hotel security, but he realized that by the time they returned, his mother would be dead either from the gun in her attacker's hand or from being thrown one hundred feet into a shallow tub with a concrete surface.

Meanwhile, Linda was losing the battle for Morris Peters' pistol. She was bent down on one knee, and he was stooped over her, ready to pull her from him and cast her over the precipice. Still, she attempted to drape herself over his arm to keep him from aiming the weapon at Matty. In a valiant last effort, she tried to bite his wrist but he shook loose, and they both nearly lost their tenuous hold on terra firma.

"Give it up, Linda, it's over," he growled fiercely.

She tried to get to her feet, but he held her down and at bay with his free hand. "You're not going to do this," she spat at him.

At that moment, a red scorpion, a dubious miracle of nature, appeared from under a rock beside Peters' right foot. Native peoples of the Southwest wove legends and other morality plays around the animals with whom they shared their lives and habitats, but the scorpion played no part in their oral literature. Blind and venomous, it spent its life groping in the dark for its victims like a vampire, sucking the life force from any animal unlucky enough to satisfy its need for blood and flesh.

This one was the size of a grown man's thumb, with a tail twice as long as its body. Its first cousin had nearly nipped Matty's bare toe the week before. Angry at being disturbed and ready for its nocturnal constitutional, it too lunged at Morris Peters, and with more success than Linda, wrapped its pincers around the outer part of his ankle just above the shoe line and clamped them together.

Tiny scarlet drops oozed through his sock as the parasite made the engagement permanent. Its deserving victim shrieked and staggered as he looked down in horror to see the thing hanging from his body, "Christ Almighty, what now?!" Then Peters grimaced in fear and pain, knowing that the poison the scorpion was at that moment depositing under his skin would begin to infect his circulatory system within the hour.

He pushed Linda away and she nearly slid over the edge of the cliff-face. Then, unsuccessfully, he reached down to try to pry the animal from his ankle. The tail would need to be surgically removed, but the way things were going, he concluded grimly that he might have to cut it out with his pocket knife as he headed for Mexico and then hope he could find an anecdote after completing his getaway. He might be able to lose himself in Hermosillo, or maybe even further south in Alamos.

Linda struggled to her feet and stood looking with a kind of rapt amazement at the two predators, one perfectly content with its position, the other hobbling around on the slick surface in agony. As Matty had discovered, scorpions were harmless when given a wide berth. The same could not be said of men like Morris Peters. He came after her for the final time, limping now from this latest insult. Aiming for his left side to take advantage of the newly inflicted weakness on his right, Linda gave him a mighty shove, trying to make him put painful weight on the crippled foot.

Surprised first by the animal attack and now by her desperate assault, Peters lost his hold on gravity. He staggered and tried to catch her arm to reestablish his balance. She drew away, then reached out to shove him again. He nearly grabbed her but stumbled backward instead. Morris Peters looked at her for just a moment through a haze of misting spray and helpless wonder and then went tumbling over and into the waterfall. With his bloodthirsty companion still attached and screaming at a pitch that quieted the coyote, he dropped the entire 100 feet into the shallow pool. Nothing broke his fall and the screaming stopped when he reached the bottom.

Linda approached the water's edge, weaving dangerously back and forth. She peered down at Peters and took grim satisfaction in the fact that he would never again hurt another human being. Soon she became dizzy, and she tore her eyes from Peters' seemingly lifeless form to search the area for Matty. She could hear him nearby, but her vision was beginning to double. Realizing she was about to pass out, she called his name as she slumped to the ground and began to slide backwards down the hill. The last sounds to reach her were the singing waters and Matty's "Geez, Mom, I think you killed the son-of-a-bitch."

<>>>> Twenty-Six <<<<>

Winners and Losers

Linda Bluenight awoke to the sound of a soft knock and called a "Come in," from her pallet on the old sofa. As she opened her eyes, she saw Mrs. Segundo and her two young sons at the front door. Linda was rarely sedentary, but the cat naps she had been taking over the past few days had healed many of her wounds.

The Segundos were the most recent arrivals in a stream of villagers who flowed into the house with get-well goodies. The Bluenight cupboards were stocked with empanadas, pickled pigs' feet, smoked venison, and fried chicken. Matty's kitchen detail was light, though he'd decided to make his green chile burros "especiale" this evening. He had even suggested that Linda continue her rest for another few days in hopes of acquiring a greater stash of his favorite dishes.

"How is our heroine today?" Flora Segundo asked as she sent Tony and Sammy to the kitchen with a sack of fresh tamales.

"Just fine, except I'm getting spoiled with all these presents." Truth be told, Linda was getting bored with the sick role, and she was eager to get back to her kids and her classroom. She gently interrogated nine-year-old Tony about the woman from Tucson School District who had come to substitute for her. When she was satisfied that things were running smoothly in her absence, she changed the subject to soccer. The grammar school team was doing well in its first year of organized play.

"Our guys can kick the culata of those milgahn," the little boy bragged, leaping and gyrating to show her his moves.

"Tony! Shush!" his mother admonished, embarrassed at this ethnic slip from her son.

"That's all right," laughed Linda, "they can call me anything but 'Hey, you.'"

"The village is planning a dinner for you when you return to the school," confided Mrs. Segundo. "Did the mahkai say how long it would be before you are strong enough to corral these burros again?"

"I'd like to come back manana," said Linda, with a frown of impatience, "but Ron says he's going to stand in the schoolhouse door to keep me from entering until Monday. He called Dr. Felix to check on my so-called injuries because he said he knew I'd try to come back before I should. Some father hen he is."

Mrs. Segundo chuckled at this piece of zoological gender confusion and rose to leave. "We'll be on our way now. I'm glad our principal is looking out for you, that's what we're all going to do from now on." Linda started to accompany them to the door, but the woman waved her down, corralled her sons, and bid her good-bye. She watched them walk the shortcut across the fields. Mrs. Segundo stopped along the way to gather some sage to dry for use as medical remedy and cooking spice. Linda leaned back and considered her good fortune. The bullet had torn through her left side and grazed her hip, but had failed to shatter or even penetrate the bone. She would carry a small scar, but otherwise her recovery would be complete. The tumble she had taken down the hill after she sent Peters to the showers did almost as much damage as the shot Eastman fired at her. Her fall had been broken about half-way first by the remnants of a fallen barrel cactus and then by Matty in his rush up the slope to catch her. They were both still picking thorns out of various parts of their anatomies. Kino Hospital on the south side had kept her overnight for observation and had insisted on these few days of bed rest at home, since she was weak from the loss of blood.

Now the the village was conspiring to make sure she took enough time to get her strength back. She worried if she spent many more days on the couch eating donated entres, her recuperation might have to be followed by a diet.

Mouser slept beside her, and she stroked him absently. Then she reached for the teapot on the table beside her and poured a cup of the aromatic Red Zinger that Matty brewed for her before he left. Against her wishes, he had insisted on driving into town to witness the arraignment of Morris Peters. Through a kind of perverse miracle, Peters had survived his involuntary dive down the waterfall at Las Canyones with only a fractured tail bone, a broken leg and clavicle, and a concussion. Matty said that the man should be forced to face at least one of his accusers, since so many others were either dead or injured.

As she sipped her tea, she saw her exuberant son come barreling up Los Reales in the ancient pickup he loved so well. She fretted that it would not survive the year unless he gave it more TLC. He twirled the truck into the yard and parked it

facing the front window so that he could make his most
dramatic entrance.   Then he jumped out, leaped over the
porch railing, and sailed through the front door, talking a blue
streak before she could even inquire about the proceedings.

"I wish you could have been in that courtroom with me,
Mom. We'll turn on the tube in a few minutes so you can see
for yourself. All the local television crews were filming. The
five o'clock news will probably have the pictures. It should be
the lead story."

In fact, the whole sordid mess, including the hair-raising
events of last Sunday night, had consumed the local media all
week.   The publicity had prompted Linda to change their
phone number when the constant ringing began to tweak her
last good nerve.

"I've seen all the courtrooms I care to," she replied,
reminding him of her former work. "Tell me, though, was the
place crowded and how went the hearing?"

"Judge Departo and the grand jury hit old Peters with
everything but a baseball bat," Matty answered with grim glee.
"The formal charges amount to three first-degree murder
counts in the deaths of Clay Eastman, Ramon Morena, and Jay
Grayson, conspiracy in the fact of murder in the death of
Benton Brody, and assault and attempted murder on the lives
of Bartolemew Berdini and Linda Bluenight. That should put
the bastard away for about five lifetimes, if they don't fry him
first. Sorry, Mom." Matty added this back-hand apology
when he saw the pucker around his mother's mouth.

Silent gratitude replaced it when she heard Brother Bart's
name. "We need to call the med center again to check on his
condition," she said, reminding herself more than Matty.

On that fateful Sunday evening, Brian Flynn had returned
to the rectory after a dinner engagement with the parish priests
at Holy Family Church on the south side. After he parked his

car in the garages beside the house, Flynn used the nearest entrance which turned out to be the kitchen door, where he found and followed a trail of blood and discovered his friend trying to crawl toward the phone on the counter. Berdini had returned from New Mexico only a short time before, and they had just missed each other's comings and goings. As Flynn's colleague and companion of many years lay close to death, he had phoned for an ambulance, administered the last rites, and listened as Bart told him what he had learned from Ramon's novia. It proved Ramon's innocence, and he made Flynn promise to go to the police, but not to speak to anyone except the chief since a member of the homicide unit named Peters had just tried to silence him.

The Franciscan monk had undergone five hours of surgery to repair a skull fracture and halt a subdural hematoma. He remained in a coma for two days. Now he was under a twenty-four-hour watch in the intensive care unit and plagued with partial paralysis down his right side, but the specialists believed that with time and plenty of physical therapy, he would eventually recover. Bart insisted that he would be coaching the boys' soccer team next year to show them how the Romanis played the game.

Brian Flynn had rushed from the hospital to the police station that night only to learn that Peters was nearly dead from a fall he had taken at the hands of Linda Bluenight, and that she was on her way to the hospital with a gunshot wound. He had relayed to the police chief what Bart Berdini had told him, and Matty contributed the contents of the tape recorder he retrieved from his mother's jacket pocket. The two pieces of evidence had ensured that the case against Morris Peters was "open and shut."

"You'd have enjoyed the look on old Mo's face as the judge read that list of offenses," continued Matty. "The creep

turned about three shades of green. Of course, he almost got
lynched when they rolled him into the courtroom. He was in
this wheelchair, see, and one of his wrists was hand-cuffed to
it in case he decided to try to leave the party. You could hear
people all over the room hiss and boo when the bailiff put him
in his place at the defense table. The judge had to warn the
crowd to behave itself. Those officers he worked with in
homicide would like to string him up themselves. I've never
seen cops as mad as those guys, especially that Sergeant
Griffin, makes you think maybe they really are underpaid.
Get this, when it came time for Peters to enter his plea, not a
soul offered to help him stand up. He pled 'not guilty,' if you
can believe it. You and Brother Bart were stars in absentia,
Mom. People actually cheered when your names were
mentioned. It was quite a show. Tommy went along with me.
He says we oughta make a movie."

"You oughta make dinner. Mrs. Segundo brought
tamales if you've changed your mind about cooking."

"No, I'm doing burros, remember? I invited Peg to join
us, that all right?"

He disappeared into the kitchen, and Linda sat thinking
about his description of the day's legal doings. Matty was
accurate in his crude but graphic account of Morris Peters'
likely fate at the hands of law and order. He was without the
wealth he had so desperately sought and killed for, and unable
to hire the high-priced lawyer he needed to keep him out of
the cubicle where needles had replaced nooses, gas, and
electricity. As much as she despised him, Linda could not
reconcile the state taking his life. Far from being a deterrent,
she believed that capital punishment was an abandonment by
the community of its own commitment to the value of human
life. When Bart got back on his feet, perhaps the two of them
could appeal to the judge on Peters' behalf. It would not be a

popular move, and it would certainly stop the applause. Even in her own house, she would have difficulty explaining herself.

On the economic front, the current picture in the Old Pueblo was a portrait of confusion. The Eastman empire had collapsed with staggering speed, and the Sonora was feeling the consequences. The company truly had been a house of cards. The deaths of its senior officers, one by the other's hand, had amounted to instant bankruptcy. A number of other top officers, managers, and corporate board members had been indicted for their roles in the company's attempts to bribe zoning commission members. Apparently, much dinero had changed hands to obtain recommendations for the Bonita Canyon project. Two high-level assistants to the Pima County Board of Supervisors had also admitted to receiving expensive perks for their efforts to hurry the resort from drawing board to construction without proper attention to building codes or environmental impact.

Word had been leaked to the news media concerning the planned, bogus law and order campaign which would have poisoned the social well. This sinister attempt to distract the public from the development's obvious problems had come under intense public scrutiny. In addition to Eastman, Kingley and his company had been named in the ugly little conspiracy, and the man was being mightily criticized by the home town to which he claimed such devotion. Reporters were having a field day publicizing the skinny on the "Robber Barron" as he was now universally known.

Several local banks were on the verge of a panic and were threatening to close their doors. Their simplistic over-reliance on Eastman for their economic well-being, their penchant for land speculation, and their willingness to sign off on soft loans for the Eastman Inc. expansion fund had cost them and their customers dearly. Every one of the numerous residential editions and commercial properties that bore the Eastman name had defaulted. As a result they had been turned over to a government agency which would try to recapture a portion of the financial loss suffered by the real estate establishment and its clientele, the taxpayers of the United States. This would compound the already burdensome task left to it by the last downturn in the housing market in the mid-1980s. If Eastman had gone unchecked for another year, he would have made Charlie Keating's escapade look like a choirboy picnic. Tucson's local brokers were being forced to close branch offices and terminate workers. Land development all over the county had come to a grinding halt.

Evelyn Eastman Brody and Clay Eastman's wife had escaped the criminal arm of the law. Their names did not appear on any of the company's legal entities. Nonetheless, their personal lives had been shattered and they were no longer residents of the state of Arizona. Evelyn had taken Holly to their home in the East to escape the scandal and to try another round of treatment for the girl's addiction. Eastman's widow was reported to be somewhere in the vicinity of Buenos Aires. In a final and tragic irony, the elder Mrs. Eastman had died on the same night as her son. The cornucopia was bursting with rotten fruit, decayed by the worm of greed.

On the other hand, environmental groups including Santa Tierra were breathing a collective sigh of relief. Bonita Canyon had been saved from the bulldozer and the chain saw, for now. Building proposals in that area of the Santa Catalinas had been put on the back burner indefinitely. Lee Sims had issued a statement saying that he intended to turn off the stove once and for all.

Using their new found solidarity, conservationists in the upper Sonora were preparing for a historic push toward new zoning regulations. They also wanted to place restrictions on land leases, urban and rural, throughout the county, and they were lobbying local and state governments to increase public purchases of private holdings around riparian areas and wilderness lands. Allen Linton had lined up an impressive array of academics from the university to join forces with the "civies" as he called the movement's members. The "no tax, no rules" contingent within the Chamber of Commerce conceded that preservation and its adherents had the upper hand. Even the Arizona Eighty had been put on notice that the Sonora was no longer for sale to the highest bidder.

Linda was gratified at the results, but the new smugness of nature's defenders made her a bit nervous. Their victories had come at high cost: loss of life, community humiliation, financial hardship, and political polarization. She could only hope that the coming environmental consciousness would be a compassionate one, but she also realized that hard asses like Linton and Sims had their place. Just this morning, the newspaper carried an article entitled, "New Nukes in the Neighborhood," and it described an area north of the Mogollon Rim as a possible site for a future nuclear waste dump.

The sound of the phone ringing a few minutes later was no longer identified with fear and apprehension. The voice on the other end belonged to Len Rodriquez, " 'A:ni hoin 'a:pi, Linda. How are you feeling?"

"And greetings to you, nawoj. I'm getting ready to bust out of this sickbed. How about you? Things settling down at tribal headquarters?"

"You bet, I'm looking forward to chasing the petters out of the parking lot for a while. I wanted to tell you that Jacob Zepeda has been chosen by Tucson P.D. to replace Peters on the homicide squad. He's a former tribal officer on the Big

Res. Do you know him by chance?"

"I've heard of him," replied Linda. As a matter of fact, Verona Verasca had tried to fix her up with him last year. Besides being an eligible bachelor, he was also the first cop from the Tohono nation to be named to the city's homicide unit.

"The guys at the tribal headquarters are going to sponsor a welcome dinner for him when he moves here next week. Will you come?"

"Sure, I'd love to. Say, you haven't been talking to Verona, have you?"

"Do I look like the matchmaking type?" Len's throaty laugh belied the innocence of his question. "Listen, though, he has already recommended you to the department. They should be calling you about a position in the pathology lab."

"They'll get my refusal. When the choice is kids or cadavers, you can guess what mine will be. I might agree to consult occasionally, but that would be the extent of it."

"I don't blame you a bit, nawoj. See you next week."

She leaned back, listening to her son banging around the kitchen, rattling those pots and pans. This was her favorite time of day. She watched the sun as it hovered lovingly over her Sonora, embracing it, a guardian of light. It caressed Iitoi's penthouse to the south, gave wing to the White Dove across the way, and wrapped its arms around the gentle desert winds of November. As always, she was looking forward to their holidays, Christmas Eve Mass with the children's choir at San Xavier, a brief ski trip to the Apache resort in the White Mountains with the Orozcos, no cops, no corpses.

Matty stuck his head through the door to the dining room. "Hey, baby, que paso," he sang in his best Texicana. "Cuantos quieres, Mamacita? These rellenos son muy caliente."

"Dos, I guess. You need help?"

"No, I've got a handle on this comida, but there is something I forgot to tell you."

"What's that, hijo?"

"Before I left for town, during one of your many naps, you got a call from a Lieutenant Jake Zepeda. He'd like you to phone him when you're feeling up to it, something about a case."

———••┅••———

About the Author

Rebecca Cramer is a career cultural anthropologist at Johnson County Community College in Overland Park, Kansas. She has lived and worked in the Southwest for long periods of time over the last ten years, and currently divides her time between the two areas. Born in Kansas City, Missouri, Cramer has also done field research on the Caribbean island of St. Lucia and has traveled extensively through the American West and in Mexico.

Cramer's second book in the Bluenight Mystery Series, *The View from Frog Mountain*, will be available soon. She is currently working on her third book.

About the Author

Me 'n God in the Coffee Shop   10.95
René Donovan
A spiritual journey, a lullaby, an awakening. A remarkable book!

The Best Kept Secrets, Wright   12.95
Mystical stories that bridge the gap between realism and fantasy.

From the Hearts of Angels, Dezra*   12.95
365 angels to guide you through any situation that may
arise.

Little Book of Angels, Dezra*   6.95
Little Book of Angels Reflections Journal, Dezra*   5.95
365 angels to provide a daily inspirational thought.

The Antilles Incident, Donald Todd   6.95
A true face-to-face confrontation at sea with a submerged UFO.

365 Days of Prosperity, Telesco   5.95
365 Days of Luck, Telesco   5.95
365 Days of Health, Telesco   5.95
Each of these little books contain daily ways to attract
prosperity, luck, and health into your life!

Cataclysms?? A <u>New</u> Look at Earth Changes, Hickox   12.95
A controversial approach to what some say are the coming
'end times.' Highly recommended.

The Ascent: Doorway to Eternity, Cross   6. 95
A channeled book regarding the true story of Jesus and his life
as it was meant to be written. Truly enlightening!

Check your local bookstore or send check or money order, plus $3 s/h for
one book, .50 for each additional book to: Book World, Inc., 9666 E
Riggs Rd #194, Sun Lakes, AZ 85248.

Prices reflect U.S. only; foreign orders, add $7.00 per book
Allow 4-6 weeks for delivery